The Hidden Voice

Chandraish Sinha

Legal Notes

Published by Books District Publication

Dublin, OH, USA

www.booksdistrict.com

About the Author

Chandraish Sinha is a software engineer by profession. Born and brought up in Jhansi, India, he currently lives in Columbus, OH. Writing short stories and novels is his passion. He wishes to share his love for writing with you. 'The Hidden Voice' is the author's debut novel.

Visit http://chandraishsinha.com/ for more details on his work.

Jhansi is a small town in the Northern part of India. It gains importance in the history of India because of Rani LakshmiBai, Queen of Jhansi. She was also called 'Veerangana', for the courage and bravery she displayed in fighting the British forces in 1857. She became the symbol of woman power in the whole country. Though she perished in the battle, her legacy continues to inspire generations.

She fought centuries earlier, but the war has not ceased yet...

People are still fighting for their pride and honor.

"Things happen because we let them happen to us"
Ian

Prologue

Jhansi, UP. India.

There were hundreds of people facing her. She tried hard to recognize the faces but couldn't see clearly. The crowd was chanting her name – it was a deafening sound.

Suddenly, she heard a loud thud, someone had thrown an object at her; she tried desperately to speak but choked, her voice failed her.

Devki heard the sound again, she opened her eyes but stayed still in bed, holding her breath. Beads of sweat formed on her temples and dripped from the corner of her ears. A faint light from the streetlamp escaped through the bolted windows and challenged the darkness in the room. Devki moved forward and covered the twins with her body. She waited for the unexpected. The sound ceased momentarily...

Squinting at her surroundings, she saw nothing except a few idle utensils stacked against the wall. She heard the sound again at the door. She clutched her daughters closely. There was the sound again and again. This time she got out of her bed and looked nervously in the direction of the door.

Rubbing the floor, Devki moved her bare feet in the direction of the sound. Old broken furniture and cardboard boxes restricted her movement. Lack of ventilation made the room damp and a mild stench emanated owing to the humidity and clutter. For fear of waking her little babies, she carefully navigated herself between the littered items and reached the door.

Devki pushed the door gingerly, expecting it to be locked. The door opened instantly, and fresh breeze gushed in. To prevent any noise from the door, she grabbed the knob and cautiously stepped in the open space outside. She shivered – the touch of the fresh air and a glimpse of the sky after many months soothed her body and eyes. It was still dark, yet she was able to see in the dim flickering streetlight.

Saira was about to throw another stone toward the door, when Devki spotted her neighbor. Saira's swollen lip and black eye conveyed a recent incident. The two women hardly spoke to each other, and whenever they did, they used gestures and signals. They had many such muted conversations in the past.

Saira made deliberate lip movements for Devki to understand; Devki peered at Saira's lips and panicked as they read "RUN!"

Devki signaled her hands and moved her lips, "Why? When?"

Saira showed her right fist and opened her thumb to run across her neck like a knife. She then pointed her index finger down, "Now, right away," and moved her arms sideways furiously as if she was running, "Run! Run!"

Devki froze for a moment. *How on earth? With people downstairs! Moreover, the main door would be locked.* She had attempted to escape earlier and the consequences gave her chills even today.

Saira had the answer for Devki's confusion. Over the months, she had visualized the escape, hundreds of times in her mind. The higher floor of the two houses was connected by a small strip of concrete. In olden times, there was a shed between the houses, but it was long broken. The concrete strip was weak and damaged, nevertheless, one could still walk on it, especially, when facing a life-or-death situation.

Saira pointed toward the stretch of concrete and directed Devki to walk over and come to her side of the house. The wall was slightly lower on Saira's side, from where she could jump onto the street below.

Devki's eyes widened in horror. With two babies, how will I manage all this? She looked at Saira for affirmation. Saira threw her hands up in the air – *that's the only option you have!*

The unexpected information clouded Devki's mind. She hastily looked around for the best possible way to escape. On her left, there were steps leading to the terrace, but the door in front of it was locked. There was another staircase going down, which ended in the center of the house, but it posed a risk of being caught. There seemed to be no other option.

Devki returned to her room and opened a cupboard. She pulled two white bedsheets and tied a knot at the end of each. She hung the bedsheets crisscrossing over her head, on both her shoulders. She checked the knot again, and satisfied with the strength, she placed her babies inside each of the bedsheets. She stuffed two milk bottles and a water bottle in a blue handbag. She flung the bag across her shoulders and walked toward the door.

As she approached the door, she paused, and hurried back. She lifted the mattress and pulled a wrapped object hidden away under the bed. She checked on the twins again, they were fast asleep. She came outside and slowly closed the door behind her. Saira waved at Devki, gesturing her to move on and slowly jump on the street below.

Devki pressed her lips together and stepped over the concrete patch. Her legs quaked but she balanced her weight and walked a few steps to reach the adjacent house. Saira was already on the alley below. Devki took the bedsheets carrying the kids and lowered them one-by-one to Saira. Once the kids were safe in Saira's arms, she jumped. There was a little thud; the women held their breath for a few seconds and then started running.

Soon, they were on a deserted street. Devki whiffed fresh air after several months, and felt hungry. She was accustomed to hunger; her meager meal was hardly enough to feed her babies.

"Run fast," Saira pulled Devki's hand.

Tears filled Devki's eyes, making her vision blurred. "Yaya you…you uu also cacca come with mm me." She pressed her teeth hard, her face flustered; bursting veins on her face showed her despair, a few words stumbled out with much difficulty.

"No, I have some time."

They reached the main road. A huge community water-storage tank by the side of the road witnessed Devki's liberty. An abandoned Tonga-stand, reminiscing the past, was silent in the darkness. The atmosphere was still, except for an occasional neigh of a horse.

The women darted in all the directions looking for some transport. There were none at that hour. The ladies turned right and ran past the railway-colony intersection. There was no sign of anyone on the road.

Devki squeezed Saira's forearm as she spotted a vehicle-for-hire. The young ladies ran toward the auto rickshaw, but the driver was drunk. Devki pushed him gently at first, and later vigorously. The driver stirred a bit, looked at them and slumped again on the rear seat. Devki panted hard in panic.

Saira turned to Devki, "Now you have to rush, your train to Kanpur leaves in 20 minutes." She unfolded the corner of her dupatta and took out a few crumpled currency notes.

"This is all I have," she thrusted the money into Devki's trembling hands.

"Youu you aa al so ssss so come, caca cannot lee leave you alone."

"No, I can't, I am not yet as lucky as you."

Saira looked at Devki's bare feet, she slipped out of her sandals and motioned Devki to wear them. "Now Devki …run, run!" she pushed Devki.

Devki held Saira's hand, "I will nnnn never fff forget this Saira. Ththth thank …"

Saira wiped the tears on her cheek, "Don't worry. Now leave and don't waste time."

Saira turned back and started to run – she couldn't be away from home for long.

Saira looked over her shoulders, "Devki, run! Run! As fast as you can and as far as you can. Once your daughters grow up, tell them about me. If you survive, tell people about me, about us."

"Wawa waa iitt wait!" yelled Devki.

Saira stopped in her tracks and stared as Devki pulled out something from underneath her dress.

*****

Exactly 30 minutes later, in the same house…

He climbed stealthily toward the bedroom. It was a familiar space to him, yet he hesitated; with a canister of inflammable liquid in one hand and an iron rod in the other, he had to be careful. He looked behind and nodded toward the older couple who were guarding the bottom of the stairs. They had similar iron rods – in case she tried to escape. They had devised a perfect plan for the night.

He pulled the door slowly – he had unlocked it a few hours earlier. He peeped in and stepped inside without making any sound. He listened holding his breath but heard nothing. He waited for some time and then placed the canister cautiously on the floor, took out a small lighter from his pocket and lit it.

The bed was empty. She was gone. The babies were gone. The room was deserted.

He came outside disappointed but relieved. Killing was not his thing, he was more into torture. He looked down the stairs,

"She's gone."

"Gone in the sense?" came the icy voice of the old female.

"Means she ran away!"

They gaped at each other for a moment. "File a missing person report!"

The old man cleared his throat, "Call the Police."

Chapter 1

The afternoon sun warmed the city of Atlanta, Georgia, announcing the arrival of summer. Some days were still cold, although the temperature was rising. The sunlight escaped through the windows and sprayed across the wooden floor. Devki liked the sun and its brilliance; she hated winters.

She checked her scar again in the mirror. It was a bite mark above her left breast. The other day, she showed it to Renu on a video chat. Renu had remarked, "Aww! My brother loves you like crazy!"

The music system played a song, beautifully rendered by a male singer. The environment in the house was noisy due to the cleaning and dusting by Martha.

Martha approached Devki, who was standing between her and the dust on the dressing table. Martha frowned, "Can you please move aside and let me finish my work?"

Devki turned back. Her face flushed, and forehead strained. She wanted to belt out the perfect sentence, but words hardly surfaced. Her tongue deceived her again. She managed to mumble something; it strained her throat.

The cleaning lady smirked, "I've been working here for the past 6 months but haven't understood a single word of yours."

Devki tried again but could only manage to let out a few inaudible words from her lips.

Martha rolled her eyes, "If it's important, can you please write it?"

Martha squinted at her employer. Devki wore a blue high-neck button-down top. It covered up to her chin. A beautiful, above-the-knee skirt hung neatly on her tiny waist, and her hair fell carelessly on her shoulders. The use of blush highlighted her cheeks pink. Her eye make-up was impeccable. She was over-dressed for any occasion, but Martha knew she was not going out; Devki was at home on a regular afternoon.

Martha scratched her head. *Weird! Why would anyone dress like this every day for no reason?* "You look beautiful today," Martha called out. "Are you going out to a party?"

Devki looked at her with dry eyes, "Nnnn no, wa waiting for the kids."

"Oh yea, four kids are a handful, they will keep you busy," said Martha. *Yet, you get time to dress like this every day.* "Please move and let me finish my work!" Martha shrugged her thoughts.

Devki looked at Martha's cell phone which lay face-down on the table.

"Now, do you want anything?" Martha raised her eyes, halting her hands on the dressing table.

"Yeye yes Yess pho phone call."

"Whom do you want to call?"

"Sa Saira."

"Saira, your daughter. You want to call your daughter's school?"

"Nnn No," Devki dropped her head, embarrassed at her mistake. "India ...wan want to caca call Indi India."

"My phone cannot call India – it's only good for local calls. You should be able to call from your phone. Ask your husband, if you don't know how to make a call."

"Yeye Yess. I shou should," Devki's eyelids drooped.

Devki checked the clock, it was four in the evening. She promptly removed the music CD and placed it in the cabinet and switched on the TV. The image of a famous psychologist addressing his viewers, flickered on the large LED screen.

Martha peered at Devki. "Why did you stop the music? It was beautiful. What language is that? You are from India, is that an Indian language?"

Devki turned pale. She mumbled, "Nn n...No. I haa v ee have ttt to improve my engg English so eng English channel."

"It looks like you were hiding the music," said Martha. "Is it some secret?" She laughed.

Devki's terrified expression told Martha that she spoke too much. She tried her best to comfort Devki, "I know you weren't hiding anything and even if you were, this is your own house and I am not going to say anything to anyone."

Devki's lips twitched but couldn't produce any sound. Her expressions hardened as she used her index finger to point Martha toward the door, which meant – 'It's time to leave.'

Martha's face turned red. *This arrogant, ill-mannered lady. I shouldn't have spoken to her. I will never talk to her again.*

*****

The psychologist on the TV was briefing, "Abuse occurs because the aggressor is convinced that the victim has no way out, and is totally dependent on him." He continued, "Abuse is also the responsibility of the victim, since the victim fears to take any action against the abuse she is facing."

Devki flipped the channel as the squeaky and crackling sound of the garage door filled the room. Two teenage girls barged into the living room.

Kajal untied her shoes and flung it across the hallway, "Devki, I'm starving, can you make me a sandwich?"

Esha dropped her backpack on the floor, "Me too. I am famished. Devki make it fast!"

Devki hurried to the kitchen, which was spacious with numerous wooden cabinets and a gas stove in the middle. A large refrigerator hummed in the corner. Devki climbed a small stepper and grabbed a loaf of bread.

The entrance door of the house opened again and two small girls came running inside, screaming with joy, "Mommy!"
The house brimmed with laughter and noise. Devki served sandwiches at the dining table – the kids were already seated and banged on the table playfully.

A look at her plate made Kajal scream, "You burnt my sandwich again!"

Devki fumbled with words, "oo oh Esha lala like mmm more toasted so o gg got confused. I... I will make agaa again."

The teenage girl frowned, "You better hurry Devki!"

Devki tied her hair and ran to the kitchen. She picked fresh vegetables and got back to chopping them.

The knock on the door gained everyone's focus. A male voice spoke gibberish from outside. The girls' eyes widened and flashed a smile, *Dad!*
A middle-aged man of medium height and build walked in with a briefcase in his hand. The baldness in the center started when he had turned 40 a couple of years ago. The exhaustion of his day faded away upon seeing the girls.

The little ones screamed, "Daddy!" and rushed toward him. They hugged, kissed and clung to his arms, while the elder ones watched in amusement. He extended his arms to embrace them all.

13

Gagan soon freed himself from the pampering showered by his daughters and looked around. Shoes and socks on the floor...books scattered all over...a streak of mud ran across the floor. Blood rushed to his face in rage, "Devki! Devki!" Gagan's voice echoed across the entire room.

"What the hell! Why is my house in such a mess? What were you doing the whole day?" His anger spiked, "Tell me what you were doing the entire day!"

Devki shivered, "I...I... cle cleaning...ing lala lady..."

"Don't tell me about the cleaning lady...you are the cleaning lady of this house. Keep the place clean!"

Kajal interjected, "And Dad, she burnt my sandwich again today."

Gagan caught Devki by the elbow and ushered her into the kitchen. Her eyes widened in horror as Gagan caught her by the hair behind her neck and spoke right into her face,
"You woman!" he glowered at her. "You have just a few things to take care of...Take care of my kids and my house. You cannot do even this!" He looked at Devki's legs. "Where are your heels? You cannot keep your man happy too." Gagan's nostrils flared, "You, godforsaken woman, keep things in order or pack your bags and go back to India."

Gagan returned fuming into the living room but softened upon seeing the kids.

Devki followed him, "I ... I...ll trrry...I ..." Her face flustered, with words failing to come out. She banged her hands helplessly against her hips.

Gagan jerked around and howled, "What the hell are you saying? Can you, for heaven's sake, for once, talk clearly? I can never understand what you say!"

Esha, the chubby teen, commented coldly, "Forget it, dad, don't spoil your mood, she'd take the whole evening to complete one sentence. Let's not miss the game on TV." She gestured Devki to go into the kitchen.

Devki managed to say, "I will trr try my best," but no one cared to listen. *It was my fault. I should have cleaned the room; kids will be kids and they will throw things around.*

As Gagan watched TV surrounded by his daughters, Devki washed, cleaned and cooked dinner. She double checked to be sure nothing was burnt and everything was in order. She usually served dinner at the table, but since the game was on, she served them on the couch. Later, when they were done, she collected their plates and did the dishes.

At night, Devki was still in the kitchen, when she heard two, "Good night Devki!" and two, "Good night mom!" with hugs. *Kids,* her eyes crinkled at the corners.

Gagan hugged her from behind and whispered in her ear, "Come on dear, it's show-time now!"

Devki stopped her work and proceeded meekly upstairs toward the bedroom. The large room with a smaller bed smelled strongly of perfumes and colognes. It was dark with heavy curtains and a thick carpet.

The dressing table on the left was crowded with assorted bottles. Doors on the right lead to his and her closets.

Devki walked to her closet. Dresses of different colors and sizes hung neatly. Earlier, Devki was fond of clothes, but they no longer made any difference to her. Clothes were used to cover or sometimes just to expose her body.

Half a dozen shoes were neatly organized on a small shoe rack. Devki slowly unbuttoned her top and dropped it on the floor. She picked a red low-neck and backless top. Her eyes scanned the hangers and narrowed on a small thigh-length black skirt. She slipped into boots. She was probably the only girl who wore shoes to bed. Gagan liked the way she walked in the boots and removed them just before sliding into bed. She walked over to the dressing table and redid her makeup. Devki did all that she was instructed earlier. She knew all her effort would be short-lived – the deer's color never bothers a lion; he is just after the meat. Gagan looked at her greedily.

When she was done with her routine, Devki walked deliberately toward the bed as a model walking on a ramp. She looked at Gagan. She remembered the scar on her chest and all the other scars under her dress came alive. She recalled a TV program, which showed how the meat industry reared and slaughtered animals. After watching the episode, she stopped eating meat.

Gagan enjoyed what he saw, he grinned, "You are the most beautiful woman I've ever seen."

She mumbled, "gaga give me a min n wawa wan ttt talk."

Gagan pulled her closer, "Aww! Come on! You can talk later!"

As Gagan sunk his teeth into her waist, she squeezed her eyes shut. Devki wanted to scream, but she could not. Her life had become a silent scream. Gagan had commented earlier, "It's better that you cannot speak, otherwise our lovemaking would have lost its glamour by your sounds."

When the pain became unbearable in body and soul, Devki let out a little cry.

Gagan pressed her neck hard choking her, "Are you crazy? My daughters are sleeping in the next room. I will kill you if they hear a thing!"

After he was done with creating new scars and poking the existing ones, Gagan's head was cleared. He cuddled Devki, paused for a moment and spoke, "Devki, you are nice and I like you. I married you because I took pity on you and your daughters."

Devki wanted to turn her back on him but couldn't.

Gagan continued, "I'm a guy who supports people in need. Having undergone much trauma myself, and on seeing your situation, I knew that you'll not be able to survive without me. My life is dedicated to the needy and the destitute."

Gagan's legs were crossed on Devki's, holding her down. Devki squirmed under his weight. He continued, "When I met you, I wondered, 'Where will this poor girl go with her kids?' You were in an awful state!" Gagan kicked the comforter off with his legs, "But, sometimes, you make me feel that you're using me. I gave you and your daughters a home. I provided you with a luxurious lifestyle."

Devki turned her face away from him.

"And you seem to be self-centered," said Gagan. "You don't take care of the house; you don't look after the kids. You don't dress well." Gagan caught Devki by her chin and turned her face forcefully toward him, "I would strongly suggest you improve your ways. Otherwise, as you know, your visa is temporary right now. I can send you back anytime."

Devki couldn't recall how many hours she cried and slept

through the night. She woke up with a heavy head the next morning and noticed a text message waiting for her on the cell phone. She instinctively knew it had to be from Renu. The text read, "Call me Bhabhi."

Devki called from the other room. Renu was chirpy as usual, and her topic was the same. Devki had heard her sister-in-law's chatter several times.

"Bhabhi, brother loves you a lot!" Renu paused for a second to check on Devki's reaction and continued, "He called me yesterday from work and was telling me how much you mean to him. He cannot live without you."

Devki breathed heavily.

Renu continued without waiting for a reply, "I know my brother can go crazy when he's angry but he has a heart of gold. Just make him happy, do whatever he says. He loves you but fails to express his feelings. I'm so lucky to have a loving brother like him and a sweet sister-in-law like you."

When Renu's call was over, Devki slumped on the chair and gazed out of the window.

He was supposed to be my savior.

Chapter 2

The previous interaction with Devki was still fresh in Martha's mind. She detested visiting Devki's house, yet the need for money left her with no choice.

I should finish my work as soon as possible Martha resolved to herself before entering the house.

Gagan hired Martha a few months earlier, when a colleague recommended her. She spoke excellent English for a non-native speaker. She worked as an English teacher in her country, but once in the USA, finding a teaching job proved difficult for her, with all the visa hassles, mandatory exams, and her increasing age. The cleaning profession was an easier choice.

Martha worked at many houses, her clients ranging from attorneys, doctors to business owners; her good manners and professional behavior gained her respect. Gagan's house was the last place she wanted to work at. Interacting with Devki posed a challenge, but with less alternatives, she decided to bear with Devki for a few hours each month.

Martha worked fast for her age, especially at Devki's house. *I should get out of this place before this insane woman comes up with something.* As Martha entered the living room, she found Devki standing before the mirror again.

"Crazy lady," muttered Martha under her breath.

As she hastened to leave after completing her chores, "wa ww Wait!" Devki's voice stopped her.

What does she want now?

Devki scribbled something on a piece of paper and handed it over to Martha. *God, this will take time!* Martha placed the note on the table, crossed her arms and sat. She squinted her eyes to read the note, *it's getting hard to read without glasses.*

The note read, 'Our home gets messy more often. Can you please increase your frequency of visits? Maybe you can come for another two hours on a different day. Please don't tell my husband. It will be between us.'

Martha held the note at a distance and re-read it. "Okay, but you have to pay me more for cleaning, plus some money to keep this secret," she said with a frown.

Devki leaned forward. Martha grasped the opportunity to

fill her pocket, "You will pay me fifty dollars for cleaning and another fifty for keeping the secret."

Devki drummed her fingers on the table for a few seconds, and then scrawled again on the paper and pushed it across, "For your regular work, we pay you $100 for 5 hours, so for 2 hours it should be $40. And as far as the secret goes, $50 is too much. I'm asking you to clean the house and not to sell drugs. $20 should be enough."

Huh! She's not as dumb as she looks!

"Ok fair enough," Martha nodded. "I will take $60 for each additional visit." Martha grinned and held out her hand, palm up, "Now can I get some advance?"

Devki stared blankly at her.

"What's that supposed to mean... you don't have money now or you won't give an advance?"

Devki kept staring at her.

Martha lost her patience, "Say something or write it down!"

Devki had no response again.

Feeling suspicious, Martha spoke softly, "Okay, okay, not today, but you will pay me for additional visits...right?" Martha found herself questioning and answering all by herself. "You have money to pay me, don't you?" Her voice grew louder. "Do you have any money at all!"

Devki turned her face away, hiding her sight.

The old woman heaved herself out of the chair, "You are telling me that you don't have a single penny to give me!"

Devki's eyes dimmed – neither accepting nor refuting the allegation.

"What a bitch!" Martha cursed silently and sank on her chair again. She tried to control her voice, but it got difficult with her bursting anger, "Look here! ...whatever your name is. You are an ignorant, arrogant bitch. Yea that's right! I said it aloud today. You have this look – Hey! I'm all dressed, I'm rich, I'm gorgeous, look at me!" Martha spoke in one breath, "You hardly speak to me; on more than one occasion you have rudely asked me to get out of your house... But today..." Martha tapped on the table with her index finger, "You have the nerve to ask me to work for free." Martha threw her hands in the air, "Ha what boldness!".

Devki closed her eyes. Martha lifted herself from the chair

and walked around the room, shaking her head. The wooden floor creaked under her weight. She peered at Devki across the room and spoke again, "But guess what," Martha could not believe her own words, "I will accept it."

Devki clapped with gleaming eyes.

Martha paused and narrowed her eyes on Devki, "Tell me, when I come here, will there be anything to clean?"

Devki moved her head left-to-right in "No."

"Okay, in that case, I will follow my usual cleaning schedule, and will stop by whenever I have time."

Martha ran her fingers through her hair still unable to believe what she had committed to. She leaned forward, lowering her voice, "For your information, I have kicked many butts in my life and if needed I can kick some more…just let me know."

Startled, Devki pointed Martha toward the door, which meant 'Stop speaking and leave.'

"What a bitch!" Martha cursed again and left.

It was ten past four when Martha left, and Devki turned off the music and switched on the TV. A yoga guru was lecturing his viewers, "Yoga gives you freedom from mind and body. Yoga will provide you eternal bliss."

Devki kept the remote on the table and attempted some of the yoga postures shown by the Swami. Unable to control her balance, she fell to the ground, but soon picked herself up and ran toward the window. She peeped outside; *I can just run away from everything. No one can stop me.* She opened the door and ran outside. The lawn grass felt like a carpet under her barefoot. She panted in excitement. *I can run away, no one can stop me!*
Her father's voice from the past echoed in her ears, "Never call us. Never come back to India! They are still searching for you. Save yourself, save your daughters!"
Devki froze.

Yellow colored school buses bustling with children, started arriving in the neighborhood. Devki turned back and trudged toward the house. Her legs trembled as she climbed the steps to the entrance. She pushed the unwelcoming red colored front door and stepped inside.

A school bus stopped in front of her lawn. Her two little

angels raced each other to the house. A few minutes later, Esha and Kajal pushed each other and made their way. "My daughters," Devki wiped a tear from her cheek with a hint of a smile.

*****

Martha visited Devki whenever her schedule permitted. She started understanding Devki better as their interaction increased. They spoke about different things. Devki learned much about Martha and her work, although she herself spoke less and gave brief responses to Martha's questions.

"Martha, do you know about th this ppp place Jhansi?" asked Devki in one of their usual afternoon chats.

"Jhansi, what's that?"

Devki's eyes opened wide in surprise. "You have never heard about rrr Rani Lakshmibai, the brave Queen?"

"I don't know about Jhansi or any Rani, but I observed one thing, if you don't mind me saying it."

Devki looked puzzled. Martha continued, "Looks like either your speech or my hearing has improved, I can understand you much better now." Martha raised her collars proudly, "Perhaps the effect of my company!"

Devki laughed at Martha's humor.

"Why don't you accompany me to work?" asked Martha.

Devki hesitated, "Me? Can I go out on my own?"

"Yes, why not?"

"Bbb mm my family, they will not aaa allow, I mean they will need me."

"Come on, they'd never know, I'll drop you back on time, say, around three thirty, before your family returns." Martha continued, "Why don't you drive on your own? You can go around at your will."

"I don't have a driving license."

"We'll get you one. Perhaps you should take some lessons. I can let you borrow the money you pay me for these extra visits." The two ladies laughed. "But please do something about the way you dress. If you overdress like this, all my clients will fire me and hire you." They laughed again for long.

Devki turned out to be an exceptional assistant to Martha in her cleaning job. When Martha paid her the first time, Devki was surprised, "II was jjj jus just assisting you."

"You worked too, so you deserve it. I cannot keep your money."

Devki was happy with the small amount she received. It made her feel confident and important. She accompanied Martha on most of the days, but returned on time for her family.

Chapter 3

A cry of anger and frustration startled Martha and Devki as they entered Desai's house. Devki first noticed Saurabh, sitting amidst books and papers, looking upset. The mother appeared disheveled and frustrated. Saurabh's little sister stood next, pulling her mom's dress.

"What happened?" Martha inquired.

"My brother is confused," chirped the 5-year-old girl.

"Saurabh is having an elocution contest in a few weeks," Mrs. Desai answered. "But he's having a tough time preparing for it."

Martha and Devki settled their cleaning tools on the ground. Martha ruffled the hair of the 9-year-old boy, "Did you ask your teacher?"

Mom replied, "We did inquire; however, speaking on the stage is a totally different ball game. He did get some advice, but it isn't an academic subject for teachers to handle."

Devki wiped the microwave glass, with all ears on the conversation. She had accompanied Martha to Desai's often for cleaning. In her past visits, she observed and found Saurabh to be a bright kid. She noticed him practicing for speeches and debates. He seemed to be passionate about speeches but couldn't get his grip on them.

Devki remained a silent spectator on previous occasions, but today as Martha and Desai discussed, she could not contain herself. She stepped forward, "I cacaca can help," surprising herself with such an interjection.

All eyes turned to Devki when Martha responded, "Yes. You are indeed dear, and I appreciate it. Please continue your cleaning."

"Nnn no nott clean cleaning but in spea speaking ....in the boy's speech." Devki managed to complete the sentence. She was out of breath and took quick deep breaths.

Both Martha and the boy's mom were surprised. Mrs. Desai had noticed this shy, timid girl accompanying Martha for the past few months, but had hardly heard her speak.

Devki spoke again, "Leh leh me see the ttt topics."

Martha's eyes widened, "Are you sure you want to assist in

speech?"

"Ye Yes!"

Saurabh's eyes lit up. "I have to speak about myself in the next speech!" He jumped and reached Devki with a bunch of papers in his hand. "I prepare a lot, but forget at the time of speaking," he spoke in haste. "I can choose some other topics too."

Martha picked up the cleaning liquid. "Devki, we should focus on cleaning. We have less time." *Why on earth does she want to get involved in a speech?*

Devki scanned Saurabh's notes and smiled to herself. It felt like yesterday when she was seven and was struggling to narrate a story.

"Papa," little Devki called.

"Yes, my dear."

"I need to recite a story in front of my class, but no matter how hard I try, I keep forgetting it. I will look dumb if I don't recite it properly!"

Papa looked at his upset little daughter who was ready to cry, "Because love, the stories should not only be on the papers, they should also reside in your heart."

"In my heart," Devki raised her eyebrows. "You mean here." She pointed at her heart.

Papa's eyes softened as he pointed toward his temples, "Yes, first here and then here," he pointed at his heart. "Live your story and speak from your heart. You can never forget the things you take to your heart."

Devki tried to remember the lesson for her whole life. Today when Saurabh showed her the list of topics and some notes written on himself, Devki couldn't restrain her smile.

She read the topics intently and set them aside on the table. Devki gazed at the boy – she saw herself in him. "Which gaga grade are you in and wawa what are your interests?"

Her eyes were fixed on Saurabh as he narrated all about his school, friends, and sports. When he finished, Devki stroked his hair affectionately, "Youu are sa such a smart boy. You rrr are only nine and you are inlv involved in so many things. Dddd did you notice whatever you just tol told me, you spoke without looking at any of your papers?"

Saurabh listened attentively with a twinkle in his eyes.

Devki continued, "You don't have to lala look at the notes for the things which are close to your hhh heart. You uuu have to speak with passion, from your heart, and the listeners will connect with you."

Saurabh's eyes glinted, "Can you please show me how?"

"Mmm me?"

"Please, please!" Saurabh jumped on his feet.

Now starts the embarrassment! Martha shook her head. To save Devki from any humility, she promptly intervened, "Probably next time." But Devki's expression told her it was too late.

Devki's composure showed Martha that she was about to speak. Devki surveyed the room. It was a large square room, a combination of a living area and a kitchen. A kitchen table was in a corner and a microwave was on the far wall. They were all standing near the kitchen table which was also used for the kids to study.

Devki started, "AA AII SSs."

Martha turned her face away. *God! Save her from mockery.*

Devki paused. She took a few steps backward allowing some distance between herself and the others. She closed her eyes momentarily and took a deep breath. She opened her eyes and sized her audience – Saurabh, his little sister, Mrs. Desai, and Martha. Their faces became blurred for a second and then came back crystal clear.

Devki 's posture was tall and still – chin up, elbows stuck at her waist with palms open in front. Her shoulders opened up and she looked straight. "My name is Saurabh Desai." Devki's voice echoed all over the house. "And today I want to tell you about the real Saurabh."

The unexpected power in the voice jolted everyone once, and then its sweetness along with sincerity pulled them in.

Devki paced around the room as if it was a stage and she owned it. Martha was amazed to see this new avatar. Devki looked different, her voice sounded different too. She was completely transformed, there was a distinctive air of confidence in her movements. When she walked, her flowing hair swayed across the shoulders. Her long skirt followed her, sweeping the floor. She was like an actor who changes her persona once on stage.

Devki finished her first speech, "And that's why friends, I

want to become a soldier!"

After finishing one speech, Devki started on another topic and then another. She selected them from Saurabh's list and delivered one after another, spontaneously, eloquently, without any notes, without any preparation, without any hesitation. She articulated each word with precision. Her strong voice pierced through the silence in the room. There was no other sound; nothing prevailed except Devki's captivating voice.

Martha was awestruck, she had never heard anything like that before. *Who is she?* If sound had a soul and body, Martha was sure, it would look like Devki.

When Devki stopped, the group was in front of her, mesmerized. The sound of clapping and cheering broke her trance. Devki had failed to notice the kids' father who had joined them too. They were all jubilant.

Martha remembered her daughter. She ran across the room and threw her arms around Devki.

Jayesh Desai, the kid's father who was a mute spectator till then, spoke, "That was beautiful! Your voice has such power, such connection, you enthralled us! You were...as if..." Unable to draw any comparison, Jayesh stopped and looked down smiling, "Sorry! I'm unable to describe the experience, you were just magical!"

Devki's eyes shone as she looked around to see all the happy faces. Jayesh continued, "I haven't seen you before. What's your name?"

Devki and Martha exchanged quick glances. Devki had hardly given a thought to her identity in the outside world. She looked sideways, fidgeted with her dress, and her eyes brightened, "My na name, Ian... Ian Scovich."

Jayesh chuckled, "Hmm... strange name for someone from India. Sounds Russian – in fact, sounds like a Russian boy name!"

"My ancestors were Russian."

Everyone laughed at the joke.

"Jokes apart, you seem to be a talented speaker." Jayesh looked directly at Devki, "What we just witnessed was absolute magic. The way you spoke these small speeches, I can see you have so much to offer." Everyone smiled in approval.

Jayesh continued, "Will you please coach Saurabh for his speeches? He likes to take part in elocution contests. He will benefit from a mentor like you."

"Me! My eng…English not good. Ala also I cannot sss speak pro properly."

"No way! The way you just spoke – we were enchanted!" the kid's mom joined the conversation. "Your voice has a great deal of love and warmth. It's a treat for the soul."

Saurabh held Devki's hand fondly.

Sensing the opportunity, Martha moved forward, "That's alright, but you know she's busy, and it'd cost you more to get her time."

"We don't mind paying a reasonable fee," came the quick reply from the mom and her husband agreed.

All eyes moved toward Devki. Feeling the burden of decision on her, she replied, "Nnn no fee for a kid like Saurabh. It will be my privilege if I can gg guide him."

"As you wish. We will refer you to our friends too," said the mother. "And you will charge if our daughter wants to join."

"Nnnn no one else, just your kids."

"And your name is?" Jayesh wanted to confirm once again.

Devki paused awhile, trying to recall, "Ian Scovich."

*****

Martha controlled the steering wheel, "So, who the hell is this Ian Scovich? From where did that name come?" They were in the car returning from Desai's house after the surprising performance by Devki.

Devki giggled, "Sh she is aa Rushh Russian mafia in a fictional novel."

"And what about the Russian ancestry, do you think they bought that?"

Devki voice grew bubbly, "No, they did not, but they are kkk kind people. They ddd don't ask intriguing questions like you! Moreover, they should ff focus on my work, not on my name or country."

Martha's eyes were on the road, though her mind was trying to grasp this newfound person. "So, you say you've won many awards in speech contests?"

"Ye yes s, difficult to believe? Nnn now I find it ha hard to believe too!"

"And what about that voice? You sounded different when

you were delivering the speech!"

"I don't know. I all al alwways sound different when I deliver a speech." Devki continued, "So, ddd did you enjoy my sss speeches?"

"No way! They ruined my mascara!"

Loud laughter escaped from Devki's mouth as she banged on the dashboard.

Martha wanted to know more now. They have been friends for months, but she was still learning new things about Devki. "Tell me what's wrong with you? Why do you behave so weird in your own house? Does your husband hate you or beat you up?"

"He doesn't hhh hate me, he loves me, he la la la loves me crazily!"

"Then why you are so scared?" Martha was still unable to comprehend.

"I am used to hhh hate, but I am scared of this crazy love. Hate is not new to me... love is."

"Love!" Martha chuckled. "What kind of love is this? Many men loved me in my life," Martha winked, "though never like this." Martha's eyes squinted on the road, "One man tried to love my daughter like this." She glanced sideways at Devki, "They are still searching for him in my hometown in Mexico." Thinking of something...Martha sighed and suppressed her thoughts, "You are like my daughter too. Let me know if you want someone to become a past."

Devki's face stiffened.

"Why don't you leave him?"

"Ww who?"

"You know who...your husband!"

Devki looked outside the car window. Trees passed faster than her thoughts. "He's my husband. I mmm safe with him and mmm my daughters have a good future with him."

"Hmmm."

Devki gazed at Martha with raised eyebrows.

"What now?" asked Martha.

Devki shook her head left to right rapidly in hesitation.

"Tell me what you want me to do." Martha persuaded.

"Ca call Sss Sai Saira."

"You mean that India call?" asked Martha. A big smile

played on Devki's lips. "Who is she? Your friend, relative?"

"Yes s mmm ma frr friend!"

"You have her phone number?"

"Nnn no phone number of Saira."

"How do we contact her then? Do you have any information, neighbor's phone or address?"

Devki's eyes twinkled. She remembered the address.

"Ok give me the address. I have found people in Mexico. Will try to track one in India too."

"Thh Thanks."

"No thanks. You are a Russian mafia and I will do any job for you," said Martha dryly.

Devki pushed Martha on her arm in affection.

As they approached the street leading to Devki's house, Devki spotted a silver Honda car in the driveway. She froze. Her palms became cold and sweaty.

"We e la late today!"

Martha was the second one to see the car. *How is that possible?* She checked the watch; the time was hardly 3:30pm. "Damn! He returned early today!"

"Hhhh he will kill me now!"

Martha could not bear to see Devki's panic-stricken face. "Be strong Devki. Remember you are Ian Scovich, the Russian mafia and your husband loves you." The ill-timed joke did not bring any humor to Devki. She shivered.

Martha patted Devki's hand, "You have to face this situation someday, why not today? I am with you!"

As their car pulled in the driveway, Gagan's figure emerged at the door, fuming.

Before he could say anything, Devki rolled down her windows, "Ddd did doctor's assistant call you u? How come you got home early?"

"Doctor?" Gagan raised his eyebrows.

"Yes s…in the mo morning when Martha came, I felt dizzy and sick to my stomach. Martha took me to the doctor!"

Gagan squinted at Martha, who quickly caught-up with Devki's story, "She was throwing up. I rushed her to the doctor, we thought she was pregnant."

It was Gagan's turn to panic. Martha made the story

convincing, "After some tests, it was declared that she's not pregnant, possibly some viral infection. The doctor has advised complete bed rest."

"Thanks!"

"You can thank me later Mr. Mishra, take care of your wife for now. She was so sick when I came in the morning."

"Which doctor? Which hospital?" Gagan was not ready to give in easily.

"Dr. Ian. Our kind of doctor – doctor of the poor people. Not any fancy doctor whom you guys visit but knows his job."

Gagan gritted his teeth in embarrassment. "Any prescription from the doctor?"

"Nothing. He mentioned a little rest will do good but still I had to pay him one hundred and fifty dollars. These doctors don't take insurance," Martha added.

"Thanks for your timely help," Gagan fumbled through his wallet and handed her the money.

Devki tried hard not to smile. *Thank God!* Martha collected the money and waved at the couple.

Devki turned toward the house and walked slowly... not sure how to act out her sickness. Gagan walked beside her.

"I'm am sss sorry...I'm lll late... need to cook for the kids."

Gagan briefly thought about the kids and her infection, "Don't worry. You take rest and I'll cook today."

"Youu u sure will be able to coo cook?"

"Yes, sweetheart, don't worry, but I will make sure to stop by for some dessert later," Gagan winked.

Devki walked slowly, it was difficult to guess if she had a limp or a viral infection.

Late at night, Devki was in a deep sleep when rude hands removed her cover. Devki was startled as if woken up in the past.

"Leave me. I Isii sick."

"I am not."

"I got inf infection."

"Hold this pillow over your face, that will take care of your infection. Anyway, I don't have to see your face every time."

Devki sweated hard and struggled for breath under the

pillow. Soon Gagan pushed her aside and the sound of his snoring filled the room.

Devki breathed hard as she gasped for some air. Her whole body shook with outrage. She lost her balance at the edge of the bed and fell on the carpeted floor below.

She could feel the smell of the intruder's body all over her. With a deliberate effort, pressing the floor beneath with her arms, she lifted herself and looked outside the window. The moon shone across the sky. She heard the howling of an animal in the lawn below – it resembled the sound of the beast which scratched her soul years ago in Jhansi.

Chapter 4

A chance to coach Saurabh in speeches thrilled Devki, and it brought back her childhood memories.

She grew up in a railway colony close to the railway tracks. The train station was at a walkable distance. Her father worked in the Indian Railways and her mother was a housewife. The kids in the neighborhood played near the tracks, which had no safety walls or gates. People walked on them casually to reach the other side of the town.

Devki recalled the fun days with her friends, when she was about seven or eight, how they placed coins on the hard iron track and waited for a train to pass over it. They would stand at a distance, closing their ears with their palms, and once the train passed, they would collect and treasure the flattened coins.

Her life revolved around trains. She was fascinated by the sight of the train emerging from the horizon and approaching her. Even as a child, the endless tracks made her philosophical.

Devki went for evening walks by the side of the tracks holding her father's hand. "Papa, aren't you scared of trains and the tracks?" asked Devki. She had recently heard about a few mishaps on unguarded railway tracks.

Papa chuckled, "Trains and tracks are my life dear, my grandfather worked in the railways and after him, my dad. Actually, you aren't supposed to walk on the tracks – it's quite dangerous." He continued, "But if unavoidable, you must follow certain rules for your safety."

"What rules?"

Papa took Devki closer to the railway tracks and explained, "Always look to your right and then to your left before crossing the tracks. Don't step on the track, as you may trip – keep your foot by the side of the line on the gravel."

"What else?"

"You see the points where two railway lines are joined," Papa pointed his fingers at a spot on the tracks, "Never keep your foot between them, because they shift to change the direction of the upcoming train. Always cross the tracks straight, stepping over one line at a time." He paused for a moment and continued, "And the last and most important rule is…"

"What Papa?"

"Under no circumstances should you cross the tracks at night, because you may not be able to judge on which track the train is approaching."

Little Devki nodded. She had no idea that she will be forced to use this knowledge in a few years, except that she will break the most important rule.

Chapter 5

The speech contest was an annual event where all schools in the city participated. Students had to first compete at their school level and the winner was invited to participate in the inter-school contest. The contest had been introduced a few years earlier and had gained popularity as parents understood the importance of public speaking.

A panel judged the participants by various criteria such as speech content, confidence in speech delivery, body language and voice quality.

Saurabh won the contest first time ever, scoring the highest in his group. He was also the first student from his school to win any such competitions. The judges were surprised with his ease and flow. He seemed to be an excellent orator for his age; he barely referred to any notes and spoke with great passion and enthusiasm. He received accolades for the content, body language, and delivery. Devki was unable to attend the event which was held in the evening. Martha joined the Desai family to cheer Saurabh.

Later in the week, the Desai family hosted a small party to celebrate Saurabh's achievement. They invited Ian and Martha, to which Ian responded jokingly, "Please check with my manager." Martha pretended to check her diary and announced that Ian was unavailable during evenings or weekends. Ian later explained that she had to take care of her kids, therefore evenings were impossible for her. The Desais, though disappointed, accepted her privacy.

Soon Ian had another student, Saurabh's younger sister, who was also fond of Ian.

Within no time, Jayesh received inquiries from more parents. Communication was the need of the hour and everyone wanted their kids to be successful in it.

*****

"I caca ca nn cannot do th this," said Ian as she dusted the windows. Devki consciously stuck to her pseudo name 'Ian' whenever she ventured out with Martha.

She was at Desai's with Martha during a regular cleaning day. On a normal day, it took Martha and Ian around four hours to clean. After Saurabh's win, Ian became their close friend. The

34

family respected their company. They were familiar with Martha's English knowledge and now Ian's talent won their hearts.

"Why not? This is a great opportunity," Jayesh sipped his juice. He was discussing the inquiries he had received for Ian.

Ian looked at Martha who obliged to help. "As you know, Ian prefers privacy. Your family is fine, but not others."

Jayesh spoke to Ian again, "This is a golden opportunity; you can make a lot of money. You don't have to do this cleaning ever again. God has given you this unique talent of communicating your thoughts beautifully." He took another sip from the glass and continued, "You can teach the kids and who knows… Someday you can undertake corporate training too. You have such potential!"

"Bbb but I I ii like to do ca cleaning!" protested Devki, dusting the windows vigorously.

Jayesh looked at Ian, a woman who can easily be passed as beautiful – medium height, medium length hair, wearing a blue high neck top and a long skirt; holding a duster in one hand and washing liquid in the other. He laughed out aloud.

"There must be some personal reason, and I respect it," said Jayesh. "But you will be depriving the world of your talent." He scratched his chin, "How about this? If you don't want to be in front of others, you can make audio copies and sell."

Martha found it agreeable, while Ian was still apprehensive, "Ba ba but I cannot speak pro properly, who would buy my CDs?"

"You speak fine when you give a speech. However, if you have problems, you can hire a speech therapist," suggested Jayesh. "See, I don't have any financial interest in this. My concern is that your specialized skill shouldn't go a waste." He kept the empty glass in the kitchen sink, "I honestly feel you have a great flair which you should utilize."

Martha turned toward Devki, "And your voice sounds different when you deliver a speech!"

Jayesh clasped his hands together, "See, this world needs hope and communication. You can be highly successful. You can have your own company too."

"Yes!" Martha's eyes gleamed, "You can name it Ian & Daughters!" Martha used her hands to make an imaginary billboard.

Ian's scornful look silenced Martha. She winced, "I I wann to ga g go home."

It had started to rain by the time Devki and Martha walked out. Jayesh offered an umbrella but Devki refused, she wanted to walk in the rain.

As soon as they were outside and alone, Martha caught Devki by her wrist, "Why do you refuse to record audio tapes? No one will recognize your voice, and no one will see you. What are you scared of?"

Devki had been fighting back her emotions all this time. She busted out loud; thick tears rolled out, she held Martha by her shoulders and jolted her, "Why I am scared..., you want to know why I am scared, Martha?"

Martha gazed at her. *Now what? Every day brings new information about this girl!*

Devki's body shuddered with emotions, "Do you even understand how it feels to be chased by cops? Do you even know what it takes to keep your kids safe?" Devki's words were hardly audible between sobs, "Do you even know how hard it is to hide when the police in a different country are looking for you? Do you know how it feels not being able to go to your country or call your own family?"

Martha stared at Devki. They were drenched. Water dripped from their hair onto their face and shoulders. Martha pushed Devki's hands off her shoulders and spoke in a deep voice, "Yes, I know and understand exactly what you mean. Been like that, lived like that."

Devki's eyes widened.

Martha stared for long at Devki and then spoke, "You've never told me anything about yourself." She paused and shrugged. "Well, you don't know much about me either, but this is your calling. I have heard your voice, your speech. It is enchanting. I have never heard anything like that before. You should speak for others. You can help through your voice. You need to speak for yourself Devki. You need to speak for women like you, so stop being Devki and become Ian."

The heavy downpour pricked their skin like needles. Devki's mouth fell open in disbelief. "What did you just say? What do you mean I should speak for women like me? What kind of women? Tell me what you mean!" Devki's shrieks momentarily diminished the sound of the rain.

"Abused women!" Martha's words slapped Devki across the face. "No matter how much you hide Devki, it's as clear as it can be. You've never told me anything about yourself but look at you …abuse is written all over you!"

Devki showed mixed expressions of shock and anger. It was hard for Martha to tell if it were her tears or the incessant rain washing her face. Devki's heart sank. She felt insulted and cheated. The truth she was trying to hide was out in the open.

She looked at Martha with hate and distaste, "I tho thought you wawa were my friend," her rage brought hiccups. She clenched her jaws, "How ddd dare you say such things to me! I will nene never talk to you again. You are nothing to me now. I hate you, Martha! I will never see you again."

Devki walked fast.

"Wait Devki! I'm sorry," Martha tried to catch Devki's hand, but Devki snubbed her.

Devki raised her index finger in front of Martha, "Never again!" and continued to walk in the rain.

Flashes of Tijuana appeared before Martha. *I cannot let go of my baby this time.*

Martha jumped into her car and turned the ignition on. Devki failed to notice the car beside her. "Lady!" the voice called. Devki kept walking.

"Devki!"

Devki stopped, startled by Martha's voice.

"Get into the car right now!" ordered Martha. Devki still in tears, yanked open the car door and followed the instruction, not having the strength to refuse. "Now put on your seat belt young lady!" commanded Martha. "And from now on you will do as I tell you!"

Devki wailed. Both the women cried holding each other. Devki bit her lips to stop the sound of her crying. She took Martha's hand, hugged and kissed.

She looked at Martha with dreary eyes, "Fffff find Saira. You are with me bbb but Saira alo alone!"

"I will find Saira for you. I have already made some calls." Martha lifted Devki's face by her chin, "So will you perform the recordings, for others, if not for me? Trust me, you can make a change."

"I ddd don't know, I caca cannot, ppp please Martha understand me."

The stuff Devki blurted out in her emotional state, generated a whirl of questions in Martha's mind but she restrained herself. There was time for everything, she might get her answers later. But the question which troubled Martha the most was – *Why are cops looking for Devki? There must be a hideous past.* Martha snickered at herself ironically, *there is always a reason for everything.*

Chapter 6

Gagan was reading a financial report from a newspaper, when little Saira nudged him, "Daddy!"

"Yes, sweetie."

"Did you forget your promise?"

The family was lazing around in front of the TV after dinner. Saira's question made the other kids curious.

"What promise?"

"Remember you said the other day that if I behave well, I will get an ice cream!" She fluttered her eyelids with a broad smile. The eyes of all the kids sparkled on hearing the word 'ice cream'.

Gagan closed his newspaper and leaned forward, "So, you're being good. Are there any witnesses?" He looked around and noticed the other kids nodding in unison. Gagan laughed at their unanimity. "But dear, it's too late now!"

Esha jumped, "No dad! It's never late for an ice-cream. Plus, a ride in the late evening will be quite refreshing." All the four young ones surrounded their dad.

"Okay, okay, let's go. Ask your mom to get ready."

Devki overheard their conversation, "You gaga guys go ahead, I hhhh have some waa work."

Gagan gave her a stern look, "Come along! At least for the sake of the kids!"

"I I caca can't!"

Esha tied her hair at the back, "I think she's avoiding going out at night because she's scared of lights!"

"Moving lights!" Kajal added and laughed.

"It's not like that but..." Devki was unable to answer.

"We will take care of you, mommy. You can sit with us," said Mini.

Esha strapped her sandals, "Yea, you can sit at the back in between so that you don't see the lights. But please no drama this time."

Gagan picked the car keys, "Now cut it out. You're not a kid, have some shame, even kids are better than you."

Devki had no choice, she agreed.

Gagan drove a seven-seater SUV. Esha took the passenger

seat in the front and Kajal took her seat in the last row. Devki sat in the middle row with Saira and Mini on either side.

The night was darker than usual. As Gagan rolled out from the garage, a car passed with its headlights on. It made Devki uneasy, she yelped.

"She already started her drama!" Esha slammed her forehead.

Gagan looked back at Devki, "I don't want to hear any sound."

Devki nodded without any expression.

They came on to the main road, there were no cars on the street, Devki felt relaxed. Further ahead, Gagan slowed down at the traffic signal. Since it was night, the signal was blinking yellow. Devki edged on her seat. Mini squeezed her hand. "It's alright mommy, the light is not moving!"

Devki's eyes scanned the roads dreading a mishap. The twenty-minute journey was uneventful; there were not many cars on the roads. The kids ordered their favorite ice creams while Devki ordered none, she was anxious to return home.

On the way back, Devki's heart raced as Gagan approached a traffic signal. Devki noticed cars on either side of the road waiting for their turn. Their lights were on, Devki's eyes widened in horror. The cars looked ready to charge onto her. She looked in both directions. There were numerous cars at the intersection. Gagan had a green but by the time he reached the signal, it turned red. He came to an abrupt halt while traffic flowed in the other directions.

The intersection was curved; terrified with the lights coming from all the directions as if to crush her, Devki panicked and screamed. "Ahhh....ohhhh God..stop it!."
She clutched the twins closer to her, their ice creams smudged onto her dress. The twins squealed.

"Can you stop it!" shouted Esha.

A faint voice echoed in Devki's ears, 'Devki Run! Run! Your train leaves in 20 minutes.' Devki struggled with the car door, trying to open it. She felt trapped.

Gagan immediately put the child lock and Kajal on the back seat pushed on Devki's shoulders to hold her down. Devki was in a trance. Her hair disheveled, she jolted the doors looking for some means to escape.

She looked like a maniac. With her hands covering her ears, she screamed on the top of her voice. "God! save me… help! help!"

Gagan changed the gear to parking and turned back at Devki. "Shut up!" He growled.

Devki stared at him as if she didn't recognize his face. She shrieked again, "My… my… babies!"

"They are with you!" howled Gagan. He caught Devki by her shoulders and shook her back and forth intensely. In a few moments, she came back to her senses, looked around trying to recognize the surroundings.

She clutched her daughters tightly and whimpered. "I want to go home!"

Gagan's face strained. *This woman spoilt the kids' evening.*

Once back home, Esha jerked open the car door and stomped. "I am not going out with this crazy lady ever again. People are afraid of the dark and here she is – scared of lights."

Chapter 7

"Hello," Martha answered the unknown call.

"They are digging up the old dirt," said the caller. His voice was old and sounded soaked in alcohol and tobacco for years. The call was disconnected at once.

How can that be possible? They told me the cleanup was perfect. She was unaware of what destiny had in store for her that day.

Martha Serrano's past knocked at the least expected time. All these years, she tried hard to overcome the unforgettable events of her life, yet today they were right in front of her face, mocking her.

Martha's father was called 'el jefe' in the city of Tijuana, Mexico. He was the boss of the people who disobeyed the law, and eventually, it brought danger and tragedy to the family. Martha and her mother never approved of his activities and stayed away from his business. There was a persistent danger lurking behind and being members of the family of el jefe, they were constantly under protection… whether they liked it or not. It was a need – not a choice.

Martha taught English at a local school. When Martha's mother passed away, her father visited her more often although there was little communication between them. The coldness in their relationship never faded away.

When 'el jefe' was murdered, his loyalists asked Martha to join the organization, the idea which she strongly despised. She declined all the protection as well. She got married and was soon blessed with a beautiful daughter – a precious little angel, whom she named 'Sofia'.

Martha's husband vanished when things went rough because of less income and more expenses, and the additional responsibility of the new child. *Typical man! Wants everything easy.* Martha was unperturbed…she had her baby.

When Sofia was in her teens, she confessed to Martha about a young man she was in love with. Martha gasped, "This is not your age to have affairs, Sofi!"

"But mom, Marco loves me, and I love him too!" pleaded Sofia.

"You stay away from that man. I know what these men want from a girl like you!" She was anxious about Sofia's capricious behavior.

One evening, when Martha returned late from work, a letter awaited her. "Mom, I am leaving, I know you will never approve of Marco, but I cannot live without him. You always wanted to see me happy... believe me, I am happy!"
There was no address or phone number.

Martha searched for Sofia fruitlessly for months, and drained with anxiety, she appealed to the loyalists for the first time. They located Sofia in no time, not too far away. Martha was upset with Sofia for the pain she had caused, but when she noticed Sofia's pregnancy, her anger disappeared and gave way to an overwhelming delight of becoming a grandmother. She forgave and took Sofia in her arms.

Despite sensing something amiss, Martha found Marco to be normal, and Sofia seemed cheerful and contented. But as days passed, Martha began to receive Sofia's distress calls.

Marco abused her verbally and physically, came late at nights and mostly drunk. She was unaware of his profession and was treated cruelly when questioned. Martha's heart was drenched. She tried to counsel Marco, but always got rude responses. The physical abuse became intolerable, and with a child on the way, Martha was anxious. She approached the loyalists, they refused to intervene – it being a family affair. Martha was unable to sleep for nights; her Sofi was suffering.

One fateful night, when the situation worsened, Sofia called her mom. Martha drove as fast she could. On reaching, she found Sofia tattered – her clothes were torn in places and lips were swollen. Marco was heavily drunk. Martha restrained herself, "Marco, you should not hit your pregnant wife!" They were in the kitchen and Sofia shivered in fright.

"What you gonna do about it? She's my wife. I'll do whatever I want!"

"Calm down Marco, we will talk in the morning when you feel better."

"What you gonna do in the morning? You, old bitch! I provided your daughter all that she needed. Now she will earn for me, I'll sell her." Marco caught hold of Sofia by the neck and banged her against the wall.

"Marco!" screamed Martha. Unable to see her Sofia being tortured, Martha pushed Marco away but then saw a metal in his hand – a knife. In a flash, something happened. It was either her criminal genes, or her motherly protective instinct – horrified shrieks from Sofia brought back Martha to her senses.
The last thing Martha remembered of him… was his painful and pleading eyes.

"He will never trouble you hereafter," Martha wiped her palms on her dress.
Sofia was terrified on seeing Martha's coolness. Martha washed her face and hands in the kitchen sink. She wiped the blood on the granite kitchen top as if she was cleaning spilled coffee.

"Get your mama a new dress," instructed Martha.

Sofia walked upstairs slowly, still shaking in shock.

Martha called the loyalists, "I need a cleanup." She spoke their language. The man on the other side paused for a while and spoke, "It will be done but you need to scale the wall."

"Scale the wall!"

"Yes! Things getting tough here. You need to be away."

"What about my Sofi?"

"Since she is alone now, we will take care of her. She can do whatever she wants to and we will protect her."

"How do I contact her?"

"You will never call her, she will call you, and we will always call you. You will be gone forever!" He continued, "Now hurry! You leave in a few minutes, wall getting crowded nowadays."

By the time Sofia brought a new dress, the decision was made. Soon, there was a car waiting for Martha outside. "I need to leave," Martha pulled the fresh clothes over herself as tears shimmered in her eyes.

"Where are we going, Mama?" Sofia was not sure – whether to feel relieved or miserable over the turn of events.

"You aren't going, I'm leaving...alone."

Sofia sobbed, "Mama sorry, it all happened because of me and now I will be all alone without you."

"Don't blame yourself Sofi, things just happened, I am not leaving you alone. You can call me anytime; I will be on the other side of the wall."

It had been 18 years since she last saw Sofia. They did speak a couple of times a year. Sofia was doing well – her boy was all grown up. Little Marco excelled in studies and wanted to be an office supervisor. The loyalists protected them and kept Martha informed. *People I hated all my life are my saviors now.* But today's call left Martha wondering.

Martha's phone buzzed again. It was Devki. *Let me take care of this child for now!* thought Martha and answered the phone.

"Any update on Saira?"

"Not right now. I am trying… should hear something soon."

Chapter 8

Jayesh and Martha's suggestion seems to be valuable, but can I really help anyone through my talks?

Devki went back to the time when she won an inter-collegiate speech competition in Kanpur. On a different occasion later, she addressed a public meeting on the importance of women safety – the event was still vivid in her mind– the standing ovation still resonated in her ears. The spectators applauded relentlessly for a few minutes. The organizers admired her powerful speech and the way she motivated and connected with the crowd. When she happened to listen to the recording of her speech later, she was astonished to hear an entirely different voice. Her friends had often commented the same.

Perhaps I can still do it. But how? I can hardly speak now. Besides, how can I help when I myself am in need? What if my identity gets revealed? I cannot afford to take that chance! The very idea of returning to India gave Devki chills. The Police would still be looking out for her. The vision of getting arrested, the prison, and the condition of her daughters without her, terrorized Devki.

Yet, could this be my chance to liberty? Would it be possible? She recalled her college initiatives, through which she visited rural areas to educate and motivate women on various welfare schemes and self-employment, and how she encouraged the men to quit drinking. Her seniors remarked that she possessed a natural talent for communicating and winning over people.

Those were different times… that Devki was someone else – bold, confident, optimistic and pragmatic; now she cannot stand for even herself. She cannot speak a whole sentence, let alone delivering and recording speeches. *The Saurabh episode was just a fluke, which came out of the blue. It is easier to preach than to practice.*

Why me? There are better speakers in the world. Why Devki? Why Ian? I shouldn't have agreed to go with Martha for cleaning in the first place. I should stay hidden, away from all the attention; this idea is dangerous. I need to take care of my daughters. I need to keep them safe.

*****

Devki looked at the twins, "So, any ideas?"

The little girls slumped their shoulders, "Don't know mommy!"

"Why don't you help us?" little Saira danced her eyebrows.

Devki cleared out the table for the kids. "This is your school assignment and you have to do it. Think hard, you will come up with something."

Mini pressed her forehead and pretended to think; Saira was more talkative and was always onto something; they were the favorites of their teacher.

Gagan walked into the room and spotted the two little ones on the table with their books. "What are you guys doing? And if you are trying to study, then sit on the chair and not on the table!"

"Daddy we have to work on a Project." 'Project' seemed a heavy word for both the little girls and made them proud.

"Ha-Ha, what project?"

"Our teacher has asked us to dress-up and enact an inspiring character," said Saira. "And she also said we must choose an Indian since our parents are from India."

"Interesting! Could you think of someone?" Gagan pulled a chair next to them. He always enjoyed a chit-chat with the kids.

"That's what we are trying to work on," Saira hit her forehead with her palm.

"Saira, that's not the way to act!" Devki disciplined her.

The girls doodled aimlessly on the paper and hummed some song. Suddenly Saira's eyes gleamed and she raised her hand, "I know!" Her eyes shone in pride.

"Someone from India?" Gagan tousled her hair lovingly.

Mini pushed her, "Tell me, tell me first!" Saira whispered something in Mini's ear and they both giggled. Gagan was amused and looked at Devki. Her eyes were stuck on the kids.

Saira moved her head from left to right and then left and sang her words, "Yes, yes, yes...I know, I know."

"And who can that be, tell us too!" Gagan raised his eyebrows.

Little Saira picked her wooden rule in jubilance and announced, "LakshmiBai, the brave Queen of Jhansi!"

Gagan was thoroughly surprised, "Gosh! How do you know about her?"

Mini proudly added, "The other day Mom told us her story. The Queen was brave and fought with a sword." As Mini completed the sentence, both the sisters jumped from the table and pulled their rulers like swords and pretended to fight.

"You guys are hilarious." Gagan cheered and slapped the table. He caught their arms to calm them, "Okay, okay! tell me what else you know about Rani LakshmiBai of Jhansi."

Both the girls sat on Gagan's lap. Mini pushed Saira, "You say first."

Saira pushed the bangs of hair away from her face, "Rani LakshmiBai was a brave Queen. She fought for what she believed in."

Gagan admired the little one's knowledge, "Aha! And what did she believe in?"

Saira continued, "She believed in freedom, in the freedom of her country. She fought for the rights of her son."

Mini followed at an equal pace, "You know she tied her son on her back and fought with the mighty forces of the British."

"She was not afraid of anyone and fought with swords in both hands," Saira extended both her hands as if holding swords.

Mini added her piece, "And she jumped from a high wall to save her boy."

They jumped from Gagan's lap and played their sword fight again.

Devki trembled in sweat. Gagan looked at her, "Now what's wrong with you?"

"Nnnn nothing jjj thought about the Queen and what she might have gaga gone through."

"Relax, the Queen is long gone, there are no brave Queens in this world now."

"Bbbb but the war is not yet over," murmured Devki in an inaudible voice.

Gagan shook his head. He was used to not understanding Devki. *I need to fight, for myself, for my daughters and for the world around me* she whimpered.

*****

The next evening, Martha called Jayesh and confirmed that Ian had agreed to do the recordings provided they could be done during the day.

Ian had one condition – no one should ever know about her

identity. No address, no phone number, no photographs…nothing. This world should never know about Ian, as if Ian never existed in the real world.

Also, she would need an appointment with the speech therapist.

Jayesh agreed.

Chapter 9

Jayesh Patel was an honest man with simple values. He had a flair for identifying opportunities. His parents were originally from India but moved to Uganda to pursue their business. During the political turmoil in the seventies, they left Uganda and made the United States their home. They had infused Jayesh with their strong principle – 'The purpose of one's life is to serve others and a good deed is always rewarded with good returns'. They made a decent fortune in various small-scale businesses. Jayesh followed their footsteps and earned respect in his community.

Jayesh found a unique talent in Ian. She seemed to possess a strange power and passion in her voice, yet, he did not fail to notice an uneasiness in her demeanor. *I will do whatever I can to bring her talent out to the world.*

He owned an old, run-down building, located on the far side of the downtown. It had some vacant office spaces, and he let out one of those to Ian and Martha. He arranged for some basic furniture, a couple of refurbished laptops, and a few recording equipment.

It was a small office with two rooms but had the provision for expansion. The space was adequate for Ian, and Martha had arranged everything with Jayesh's support. The front of the building was made of stones, and the interiors were all wooden. It attracted fewer customers and Jayesh hoped it would yield better returns in future.

Though Devki agreed to record the audios, she required a lot of support and encouragement, which Martha provided in abundance. It was decided that they would come to work in the morning after the kids and Gagan left and return before they arrived. Sessions with the speech therapist enhanced Devki's confidence.

Devki was excited – it was her first office visit and when Martha parked her car outside the building, Devki's eyes widened in surprise, "We will be working here!" She was delighted like a child. Martha nodded with a smile and added, "And remember, once inside, you are Ian."

Jayesh was already in, inspecting and making sure everything worked as expected. He was replacing a light bulb, and was up on a small ladder, he looked down at Ian, "It's all yours from now. You should know what to record and how to record."

"I don't know where to start from," Ian reviewed her desk and chair. She ran her fingers around the edges of the table.

"You can record whatever you want to share with the world." Martha kept her purse on the other desk. *This will be my place.* Jayesh and Martha had discussed earlier that Ian should decide on the topics; after all, she knew more about speeches than them.

Jayesh spoke while stepping down from the ladder, "Remember, you taught Saurabh that one should speak with passion and from his heart. Likewise, reach out to your inner self and see what you always wanted! What you want to achieve! What message you want to convey to this world!"

Ian looked blankly at him for a while and sat cross-legged on her chair. "Ye Yes!" Devki in Ian's Avtar exhaled.

Martha left her desk and walked near Ian. Both Jayesh and Martha exchanged glances. Martha leaned over Ian's desk and looked deep into her eyes, "So, what is it?"
Jayesh moved forward, "What do you want to teach this world? What is your calling?"

Ian sat straight on her chair and spoke, deliberately trying to control her voice, "Mmm Mannn evo evolved from the bbbb beasts but the evolution is nnn not complete. We are ss still in the process. There is still an animal in each one of us."

Ian caught the edge of her table tightly as if trying to hold it from slipping away and spoke again, "Wawawa wonder why a man harms another man. Wawa why is there vvv violence in this world? How can we get rrr rid of all this suffering? I don't care for mmm money, nnnn name or ffff fame. All I strive is for frrrr freedom… freedom for the entire mankind in body and sou soul." Ian almost shrieked across the room.
Her neck muscles strained, and she panted hard. "I I caca cannot speee speak!"

Jayesh was stunned, "Your feelings about abuse and people sound intense – any relative going through this?"

"A clo clo close friend suffering." Ian avoided his eyes.

"Those are wonderful thoughts. You will make a great motivational speaker. Wish we had recorded that!"

Martha clapped with enthusiasm. "What are we waiting for? This is our first day! We have fine content, let's perform our first recording!"

Ian rubbed her palms together and bit her lips. She closed her eyes momentarily but didn't experience any comfort. Her heart raced in anxiety. She focused on a topic which she had planned the previous night. She usually prepared her speeches in her mind instead of writing them down.

With her lips closed, she repeated the name 'Ian' to herself, memorizing it. *I should never make a mistake of referring to myself as Devki.*

Ian took a good posture on the chair, leaned forward, adjusted her headphone, "I ..I…thth u thisss thiss." Words failed to come out of her mouth.

Seeing her embarrassment, Martha smiled warmly, "It's okay. A little fumble is alright dear."

Ian tried again but mumbled, "Ddd d dearrr f ffffff frien," she choked. She tried again, "Liiii lili fff life iss a jourrr," her face turned red but missed her words.

"Drink a little water and try to relax," Jayesh suggested, handing over a cup of water. Having heard her speeches earlier, he was confident about her.

"Take some deep breaths," Martha suggested.

Ian took a sip from the cup, took a couple of deep breaths, and closed her eyes. This time she tried harder, veins popped on her neck and forehead, her hands shook though words ceased to come out. She slammed her hands on the table.

"You are a little nervous Ian. You are doing this for the first time."

"I caca cannot do thi this!" cried Ian. She dropped her head on the table.

"No worries dear, we will try again later," Martha gestured Jayesh to wrap up.

The first day was over.

*****

Ian visited the speech therapist twice a week, when Gagan left to work early for his meetings. After a couple of visits to the speech therapist, the team gathered again to record.

Jayesh tried to put Ian at ease, "Don't worry even if we

cannot do it today. We aren't in any hurry, and moreover, it's for your sake. We are only helping you." Martha could agree no more.

There was complete silence in the room. As Ian took her seat, her heart raced. She did not want to fail this time. She cleared her throat and spoke on the microphone, leaning on the computer, "Thi thi thsss Ian. Hahiii hi frr frrriends,"

She squealed and slumped into the chair, "Sorry I raai raised high hhh hopes in you. I am not good att all. I am not good!" tears swelled in Ian's eyes.

Something is seriously wrong! thought Jayesh. Ian's speech at the house still echoed in his ears. Jayesh had read somewhere that people with speech problems stuttered more in front of their family and close friends. Perhaps Ian would perform better in the presence of a stranger. Also, an expert in the field of recording would be a favorable addition to the team.

Jayesh suggested, "Don't lose heart. A friend of mine is a professional recordist. Unfortunately, he is out of work now, I can inquire if he'd be willing to work with us."

"That will be great, but will he respect our privacy terms?" asked Martha.

"Certainly! He is my friend and we can even ask him to sign a non-disclosure agreement."

Ian sighed, "I gaga guess no harr harm in trying."

*****

In the evening, Jayesh met Mike at his apartment and discussed the recording job. Both had worked together on a volunteering project for a school, after which, they stayed in touch and became good friends. Jayesh respected Mike, he knew his job well. Though not financially successful in his career, Mike had a great deal of experience in sound engineering and recording. Jayesh discerned the importance of such a knowledgeable and trustworthy individual at this hour.

As the conversation was coming to a positive conclusion, Mike had only one question, "Why this secrecy? Why doesn't the speaker want to be recognized? Haven't heard such a thing before!" Jayesh was about to answer but Mike continued, "More than privacy, it sounds like we are concealing some secret, but why?" Mike narrowed his eyes on Jayesh, "What am I going to record? You know that I don't record any adult stuff."

"Of course, I know! I too don't fully understand the need for this secrecy – I just respect it. I hope you'd accept it too."

The next day, Martha and Ian were already at office when Jayesh walked in with Mike. Ian had a glimpse of Mike – he was tall, blonde hair and blue eyes. His white shirt was tucked haphazardly in his faded blue jeans. His physique showed the time he had spent in the gym. Ian smiled. Mike didn't care to reciprocate. Jayesh did a quick introduction.

Mike started to elaborate on his credentials and experience, when Martha stopped him, "We don't know anything about recordings, so we believe whatever you say."
Mike grinned over the joke.

"Also, we cannot pay you anything …at least not right now," Martha added.
Mike raised his eyebrows as he turned toward Jayesh.

"They are starting out… will welcome your guidance."
Mike looked at Ian. *Jayesh regards her as highly talented.* "Okay! Will see what I can do." Mike carried some recording equipment with him, he arranged them on the table to test Ian's voice. "Let's see what we have in here."

Mike took a headphone from his bag and approached Ian. He gently pushed Ian's hair behind her ears and fixed the headphone around her neck. The gentle touch of Mike's fingers induced shivers in Ian.

Mike walked in front of Ian and raised his right thumb, "Alright! Start!"

Ian adjusted her top and began, "Thh thh thiissss Ian!"
What the heck! thought Mike. "What happened? Is something stuck in your throat? Clear your throat and try again!"

Ian felt conscious in his presence. She tried again, "Thhhh hissss I…I…ddd."
Mike wrinkled his forehead as he looked at Jayesh and Martha. Jayesh had uttered nothing about this problem the previous evening.

Martha tried to clarify, "She struggles to speak sometimes when she's nervous."

"Why nervous? You are hiring me, not the other way around. Try again!"

Mike had a strange effect on Ian. For no reason, she

blushed. *What's happening to me?* She took a deep breath and tried again. No matter how hard she tried, words did not emerge from her mouth. She pressed her teeth hard, her face turned red. With her fist clenched, she banged on the table with frustration, but no words came out. She wept like a little girl.

Mike looked at Jayesh with cold eyes, "Can I have a minute with you?"

He ushered Jayesh outside the office. "Is this a joke? So, this is your award-winning speaker. She cannot even speak a word!" He pressed his temples in disbelief, "You got to be kidding. I am out of here now. Thanks for wasting my time." He pushed Jayesh on the chest.

"I am not kidding. She is a gifted and natural speaker. I have heard her speak and I swear I've never heard anyone like this before. She coached my son too." Jayesh continued, "I don't know what happened to her. I know she stutters but when she delivers her speeches, she transforms into a great orator, someone out of the world." Jayesh continued to tell Mike about his first meeting with Ian. How Ian presented her speeches in his house; how she walked around as if covering a stage; how she spoke with confidence and poise. She refused to record her speeches, but he persuaded her.

Mike listened attentively. His anger transformed into curiosity. "Interesting!" He stood with fingers under his chin for a few seconds, "Back in a minute!" he said and ran toward his car. When Mike returned, there was something in his hand.

Ian was still sobbing with her face on the table when she heard Mike's voice, "Excuse me, Ian."

She raised her head, "sasasa sorry I wasted your time. I caca can nnn never do this. Will nev never try again!"

Mike didn't say a word to anyone as he changed some configuration on his instruments. He finished his work and leaned closer to Ian, "Give it another try, for my sake, since I have come all the way to hear your speech. But this time, come out of your desk in the open and try this wireless mic."

"No No I cacaca cannot!" protested Ian. She did not want to be embarrassed again in front of the man toward whom she was feeling attracted.

"Please try once, for me," Mike took her hand. Ian wiped her tears, took a large gulp of water and moved out of her chair.

She walked to the center of the room following Mike. He adjusted the mic on her ear.

"And for your topic," said Mike. "Tell us anything, whatever you want – it can be the places you visited or people you met. Pour your heart out, the topic is trivial at this time."

Ian took a deep breath and closed her eyes momentarily. She opened her eyes and sized her audience – 'Mike, Martha, and Jayesh'. Their faces went blurry for a second and came back. She felt confident and at ease. The earlier discomfort vanished. "Dear friends, this is Ian!" her resounding voice shattered the silence of the room.

As Ian conquered the assembly…*Oh my goodness! Who is she? I was about to miss this wonderful voice!* thought Mike.

Ian's long blue skirt followed her as she walked. She was not looking in any particular direction, she was immersed in her own world. The voice was different, she was different. Her thick black hair and beautiful eyes were mesmerizing. Her hair moved on her shoulders as she walked. And her voice …Mike was stunned with the entire show – the voice, delivery and content. As Ian finished, Martha and Jayesh clapped and cheered.

Martha's eyes gleamed, "So, what do you say now?"

Mike's mouth fell open in disbelief, "Oh my gosh! This arse can earn millions!" he spoke without thinking. For a moment everyone was shocked but soon busted into laughter.

Ian looked embarrassed. She turned and gave a long deep look at Mike – her eyes took his breath away.

Mike now understood the reason for the privacy clause mentioned by Jayesh earlier. *This beauty and talent needs to be treasured and protected.* He smiled to himself, "Let me know what agreement I need to sign."

*****

Multiple visits to the speech therapist improved Ian's voice. The therapist remarked that Ian's speech defects were not by birth but from impressions of something that occurred in her past. She would improve with practice, though her speech problem could resurface at any moment. Stress was not good for her. She should stay away from any kind of tension and depression.

Martha was concerned. *What could have happened in Ian's past?* Ian neither opened up nor answered Martha's questions. Martha asked her to visit a psychiatrist but Ian refused.

Chapter 10

She walked across the backyard and turned on the faucet once again – in a false hope to get some water. A few drops of water dripped and stopped. Neeta inspected the buckets one by one, only to find them all empty.

She turned back toward the house, "Amma! Amma!" The house was old and in dire need of repair. The cement, holding the structure, had cracked at many places and exposed the bricks underneath. The roof was made of tiles, which had broken long back and leaked during rains. It was sagged in places, unable to bear the burden of time. There were a few dry pots of plants in the backyard awaiting care but when humans themselves struggled for water, plants got no priority.

Neeta shouted again, "Amma!" The whole house shook with her scream.

A woman as old and tattered as the house appeared at the entrance of the house. She mustered all the love and affection in her voice, "Now what happened my dear?" Her words failed to pacify her angry daughter.

"No water again," howled Neeta. "I'll be late to work for the third time this week. Do you understand how hard it is to get a job and if I keep going late, my boss will fire me!" Neeta cried at the last sentence.

"God will show some way!"

The old lady called in a low voice, "Munna! Go fetch some water for your sister!" A boy in his early teens appeared from nowhere and ran out in the open courtyard. He picked one of the empty buckets and ran outside the house.

Munna first approached the public water supply at the road crossing; it was already crowded. Being the hottest month of the year, the groundwater was at its lowest point. He thought for a moment and decided on the next course of action. He knew the importance of his sister's job, their livelihood depended on it.

Neeta stood fuming in the backyard for ten solid minutes before her little brother returned with a bucket of water. If it were other times, Neeta would have chided him for being late, but today she knew how far he might have traveled to get the bucket of water.

Neeta grabbed the bucket and rushed toward the bathroom but stopped at the entrance. She looked back at her mother. The old lady understood her dilemma – a strong wind had started and the curtain covering the entrance blew violently.

It was a challenge every day, to take shower in a bathroom with no proper door.

"You don't worry my child! I will stand at the entrance."

Once inside, Neeta pulled the curtain as much as she can. She hesitated momentarily. She could hear the voices of men conversing outside on the street. But today was an important day – a big chance, and Neeta wanted to be part of it. She undressed quickly and took a small plastic container to scoop water from the bucket and poured water on herself.

Neeta looked at her naked image in the old mirror that hung on the wall. She had stopped complaining to God long back. Her tears dried years ago when her father died and being the eldest, she was burdened with the responsibility of feeding her family of four – two brothers, the mother and herself.

Neeta looked at her reflection in anger and distaste. "These days will change. I will change my life," she murmured and poured more water on herself. Soon Neeta got dressed in a faded red salwar-suit and walked out of the house.

"God bless you my child," called the old lady from behind. Neeta didn't care to look back. She looked forward to her day at the office. Her boss had notified her earlier about an important call with a client.

*****

Neel Kanth Dubey aka Neel's thoughts and ideas were different from others. The college degrees on his letterhead read M.A., LLB. though he could only faintly recall what he studied during his tenure in Bundelkhand Degree College. He had a dream of establishing a successful career in the small town of Jhansi.

Neel believed that every individual on this planet had an interesting story and an intriguing past. Every soul had its own journey. When he started his own detective company, people ridiculed him, but Neel was confident that in the coming years his company would do well.

Neel had a small office in the old part of the town. He had three employees – two men and a young lady. The boys were his distant relatives and the girl was referred by a friend. He paid them according to their skills or perhaps their age because none had any exclusive skill. They could not acquire any other job and therefore ended up with Neel. A week's training was provided to them, which involved watching crime related TV programs and movies.

Neel landed on a few assignments now and then, which usually involved verifying a groom's background before the wedding or performing a background check on a new hire.

His staff respected him because he had more knowledge or perhaps, he watched more detective movies than them. Over the years, Neel had been waiting for a good opportunity and at last, he got one – a phone meeting with a foreign client, which could mean a bumper assignment.

Someone from the USA had promised to call him. He had spent the last evening reading and researching on how to handle international clients. He made a note of all the important points –
–*Never be late to a meeting,*
–*Don't address anyone as Madam or Sir,*
–*Be organized, write down every detail,*
–*Speak slowly,*
–*Be good at English,*
–*And lastly, never to lie.*
The thought of an International client made Neel happy. This was a golden chance to make money and he was ready to face it.

Neel arrived early at his office. He was a thin man of small stature. His straight and thin mustache was long, reaching the end of his cheeks - making his pointed nose more prominent. He looked much younger than his age. Jhansi's summer was at its worst, the temperature soared to 105° F, yet he wore tight pants, a coat, and a tie. He was the boss. He also had to dress well because of the call from a foreign client. He believed good dressing would boost one's confidence. His polyester shirt was wet with sweat. His thick black hair appeared darker and shiny under the coat of mustard oil. With the heat, thin streaks of oil dripped on his forehead and made his face oily too.

There was no A/C in the room, yet Neel was glad, at least they had the power supply for the antiquated fan to run. Most of the time, the town was out of power. His three employees were present to support him in the discussion – Sarang, Manish, and

Neeta, equipped with notepads, pens and a calculator.

The phone rang at the appointed time. Sarang picked the receiver on the first ring – it got disconnected. "Let it ring a few times before you answer!" growled Neel.

The phone rang again. Sarang let it ring exactly thrice and pressed the speaker button.

"Hello!" the female voice came through the phone's speaker.

"Hello Madam!" all four voices answered at once. They all jumped from their chairs in excitement.

"Can I talk to Mr. Neel Kaand Dobey please?" There was a struggle in pronouncing the name.

Neel waved his hands asking his teammates to be quiet. He took a deep breath, "Yes, madam. Neel speaking here from Jhansi, India." Neel forgot all his notes.

"I heard great things about you Mr. Neel kaan…"

"Madam, you can call me Neel." *Where did this lady hear about me?*

"Thank you Neel, and no need to call me Madam, you can call me Martha." She continued, "Listen, Neel, I have an important assignment for you."

Three notepads opened instantly. "Go ahead, Madam…I mean Martha, I am listening," Neel nodded toward his assistants.

"I need you to write down a message and deliver it to someone in Jhansi. Can you do it for me, Neel?"

Delivery message, that's it! "Absolutely. Give me the name, address, and message."

"Before I do that, I need to know how much you will charge for this task." Martha had no idea how money worked in the offshore town.

Neel chuckled. He was a shrewd businessman, who knew all tricks of the trade. "Before I could tell you my fee, I need to know all the details of the case – the address where this message needs to be delivered, etc. so I can calculate the expenses."

"Okay, that's fair," Martha narrated the address on the speaker. It was noted on all three notepads.

"I also need to know to whom this message will be delivered, because, sometimes that may affect the cost."

Martha rolled her eyes on the other side of the phone. "Ok.

Her name is Saira Jamal."

"Age?"

"May be late thirties."

"Religion?"

"How does that matter?" Martha was losing her patience.

"It matters in this town."

"You are smart, can you figure it out yourself? Now give me your fee!"

"Seeing the address, I can tell you that it will cost a lot!"

"Can you give me an exact price?" Martha was annoyed with all the questions.

"Let me calculate," Neel pulled a calculator in front of him.

Sarang had already calculated the expenses based on the address. He spontaneously presented it in front of Neel, trying to impress the boss. Neel frowned on seeing the estimate. He stared at Sarang. *You need to estimate in a different way for a customer from America.*

Neel scribbled all the details. It was a 30-minute job, – he estimated one full day. The address was at a ten-minute walk from their location, instead of a shared auto ride, he estimated a private cab, added lunch and coffee to the estimate, padded the expenses a bit more.

Boss is a genius thought Sarang.

Martha heard a lot of keys being punched on a Keyboard or a calculator. Finally, Neel's voice came on the phone again, "It will cost you forty dollars! But most of it is going into the expenses," he added quickly. All employees looked at their boss in appreciation.

Forty dollars! Is that all? thought Martha. She took a little pause, "Forty dollars, are you sure you aren't overcharging?"

"No ...Not at all!" Neel sounded loud, offended by the allegation. "I never lie or overcharge. You can ask anyone in this town. People will vouch for me!"

"Hmmm," Martha had just wanted to test the water. "Don't worry Neel, I believe you. But you should do a good job." She was thinking while speaking, "The letter should reach only Saira and no one else! Make sure she is alone when the message is delivered!"

Though Devki had not asked Martha to be secretive while

contacting Saira, Martha was judicious to keep it discreet based on their earlier conversations.

Neel's eyes narrowed. His detective brain had questions. "Can I ask something? If you have all the details, why not just send her a letter from America? Why go through us?"

"You are smart Neel. I will enjoy working with you, but for now, do as I tell you."

These Americans are weird. They have heaps of money to waste on things as mundane as this. "Alright, as you say. Now give me the message."

Martha narrated him the message, which read, "Saira, your long-lost friend is looking for you. Please send your welfare and contact phone number. D."

The phone was disconnected soon after Martha made a note of the bank account details from Neel to transfer money upon completion of the task.

"Who will do this job?" Neel looked at his team which had been listening to the chat intently.

"I will do it!" Sarang sprang from his seat. He was excited at the prospect of a private cab ride and a lunch.

"Fine, let Neeta accompany you since this involves a female. Make sure you take a shared auto-rickshaw or just walk. Also, there is no need to eat outside since you usually bring your own lunch."

"But...we charged ..." Sarang tried to protest.

"That's alright. This is our company's money. Our company needs money to grow," snapped Neel. "And if you guys will do a good job, you may receive a bonus after a year."

Neel thought for a minute. *This is my first big project and assigning this to an apprentice may compromise the task.*

He halted his thoughts, "Okay, change in plan. Neeta and I will go for this assignment and you guys take care of things here and wait for my instructions."

Neeta had stayed silent all along, the reference to her name prompted her to speak. "This looks like a small job – delivering some message to someone?"

Neel looked at Neeta assertively. "It seems to be a small job, but no one will call us from the USA just to deliver a small message. There is something more to it... some mystery."

Chapter 11

After initial hiccups Ian made appreciable progress on her speeches. The speech therapy and Mike's support improved her skills and soon a few recordings ensued.
She learnt new recording techniques from Mike. He came to work regularly despite being unpaid. He increased his hours and took charge of the recordings and creating audio files. Jayesh handled the expenses, which he assured to recover once the audio sales gained momentum. Jayesh and Martha managed the sales and office respectively.

Martha acted as a manager and the communication channel between Ian and the rest. She picked Ian up in the morning and dropped her off before her family returned. She quit most of her cleaning jobs, but managed to work at Devki's house, even while Devki was recording her speeches at the office. She hoped that their new venture would turn into something huge. She liked Ian and wanted to do everything she could for her.

Ian was given a free hand and she recorded whatever she wished and whenever she wanted to. Whenever she hit upon an idea, she was keen on recording it as soon as time permitted. Others worked around her schedule; she came to work as and when needed, except when a kid got sick or Gagan worked from home. She managed the secrecy of her outside world from her family. She did inform Gagan that she would go with Martha occasionally for some grocery or emergencies, to which he consented.

*****

Mike pushed the door with his elbow, carrying coffee cups in both his hands and a file under his arms. The very presence of Mike turned Ian's cheeks red.

"Here you go," he placed the coffee mug before Ian.

"You made coffee… for me!" asked Ian.

"Why? Don't you drink coffee?"

"I love it, nothing better than a coffee in the morning."

"Then why are you so surprised at this? Hasn't anyone made coffee for you earlier? Besides, you're my boss, I need to take care of you."

Yes, no one has ever made coffee for me. No one has ever asked how my day was. No one has ever taken notice of me. Ian turned silent.

"Ok, so this is what we have today," Mike flipped the pages of the file, "you need to record a speech while I fix your previous one."

"Martha and Jayesh are not available today, so you need to act as my audience."

"Oh, do I?" Mike rubbed his chin. "I thought we should work parallelly today, your day is already short!"

"Hmm. You know I cannot speak without someone in front to address."

"Okay, no problem. My work can wait. I'll be one for today, but you should practice speaking alone too."
Ian grinned.

"But again, why can't you work after 3 pm?" asked Mike. "Isn't it too much luxury considering the amount of work we have in here?"
Ian narrowed her eyes on him.

Mike rolled his eyes and raised his hands in defense, "Okay, okay... sorry. Forgot I'm not supposed to ask any questions."

*****

Jayesh honked and came to a screeching halt. The car in front of him stopped abruptly. He shook his head in despair, the traffic was treacherous during rains. An accident on the freeway forced Jayesh to take an internal route, and it didn't improve his speed. Heavy rain and thunder created a traffic nightmare. A few trees had fallen by the side of the road. The traffic moved at snail's pace. Jayesh checked his watch again, *Ian will be in office only till 3 pm.*

Martha and Ian were about to leave, when Jayesh rushed in. He had been away for weeks, trying to market Ian's speeches. Water dripped from his head to toe onto the floor, but it didn't seem to bother him. Jayesh's wet figure startled Ian and Martha, they distanced themselves and covered the papers on the desk.

Jayesh slumped on an empty leather chair and shook his head, with small droplets of water splattering all around him, "Sorry friends, you're all doing a great job, perhaps I'm not doing mine well."

All eyes were locked on Jayesh as he addressed Ian in

regret, "I know your talks are amazing, but I am unable to sell them!" Jayesh wiped the dripping water from his chin, "I did sell a few, but I don't know how to promote your audios! Big advertising would need a lot of money!"

Martha handed over a roll of paper towels to Jayesh. The heavy clouds outside made the room darker.

Ian spoke in a low voice, "We hav have to reach out to people."

"As more and more people will listen, they will spread the message," added Mike.

Jayesh dried his hair with the paper, "How? How do we reach these people?"

"Ga ga give it for frr free!"

"What!" Her idea exasperated Jayesh.

"Yes, give the aaa audios for fff free in schools. Ppp publish them for free through online channels too."

Martha broke her silence, "When people have nothing to lose, they will get the audios. We can advertise on a radio station too."

Jayesh's chin dipped to the chest, "I am sorry." He dropped the wet paper towel in the dustbin. "This is business and we cannot survive if we give things away for free." Jayesh continued, "Everything costs – this office, utilities, CDs, transport. Forget about us but Mike has not been paid for months!"

Mike waved his hand, "Don't worry about me right now."

Jayesh exhaled and edged on his chair, "I cannot continue. Sorry, I have already invested a lot, it will be difficult for me to go on like this."

"So, you no longer believe in Ian?" Martha questioned.

"Aw! Come-on! Don't get me wrong. I do believe in Ian. Every time I hear her speak, I get goosebumps, yet if we are unable to sell soon, things will get difficult."

There was a momentary silence in the room. Ian pushed her chair and walked near the window. It was pouring outside, nothing was visible. "I understand," said Ian. "We ddd definitely need money. Sorry to ppp put you in such a situation!"

"No, it was me. I told you to start all this," repented Jayesh. "I thought it will all be too easy."

Ian gazed through the window – the skyline was covered

with fog. Ian spoke as if talking to herself but loud enough for others to listen. "Although this is a business, it's a dream, it's a desire." All three looked at Ian intently, she turned, "I don't desire for anything but freedom – freedom of thoughts and freedom for people. The business may or may not survive, but desire should and will find its way."

Feeling guilty, Jayesh gave a slight nod – less water splattered this time.

"You guys showed great confidence in me. Martha, remember you told me that I have to do this for people suffering from abuse!" Martha looked down.

Ian continued, "Now how can we let them down, just because we don't have the money? We are hel helping people. We must find a way. We need to reach out to people."

There was complete silence, no one had any answer to Ian's question. After a few minutes, Martha looked at Jayesh. "I don't know how much money is required but I can arrange for some."

Mike moved forward, "I can contribute too."

"I wish I can…," tears appeared at the corner of Ian's eyes.

"Don't worry Ian, we will handle this," said Martha. She looked at Mike, "Thanks for your offer, I will work with Jayesh and if needed, will contact you."

Jayesh looked outside and stayed silent for a moment, trying to convince himself. He turned toward Ian, "I respect your thoughts, I will redraw the numbers again. Will work with Martha and see how much longer we can sustain." He continued, "But whatever audios we have so far, will go for free to schools, libraries and wherever we can upload them."

Ian looked at Martha, "Th Thanks, Martha." Martha reached out and held Ian's hands in affection. Ian looked at Jayesh, "I will be forever in-debt and…"

"Don't say anything, Ian. We are all in this together."

By the time Ian and Martha came outside, the rain had ceased, and the sky showcased a beautiful rainbow. In the parking lot, the rainwater slowly gushed out in the underground drains. Ian's eyes smiled. She missed Jhansi.

Chapter 12

Jhansi is a small city in Northern India, with a population of roughly 1.5 million. The town is known for its brave Queen – Rani Lakshmibai, who fought against the British forces in the 1800s. The Queen's fort still stands majestically in the center of the city dividing the Old and New parts. During the olden days, the city was within the four gates. With the passage of time, the gates aged, and traffic flowed between the old and new sections of the town.

Neel's office was located in the old city and the address he received from Martha was in the newer development of the town called Sipri Bazar. Neel and Neeta took an auto-rickshaw and reached the destination soon.

Neel wore a blue t-shirt and jeans. Neeta was dressed in a purple salwar-suit, hair tied in a long ponytail and a crossbody bag hung on her shoulder. They sweated profusely in the scorching heat of May. They were anxious, although it was only delivering a message – they had to be careful.

There were numerous houses lined next to one other. Some houses were separated by a narrow alley, while the others were joined by common walls – there were no numbers or nameplates on the doors. Neel looked around and noticed some street vendors. *These are the people who can confirm any address!* Neel approached one of them and showed him the address. He pointed at the fourth house across the street. It was a double-storied house with a bright green wooden door. The door was shut.

Delivering the message to Saira confidentially was a challenge now. They loitered around for a while, when a little hope arrived in the form of a vegetable cart. The vendor yelled out in all directions to make his presence known. Neel and Neeta rushed toward the cart and pretended to check the vegetables.

Five minutes passed…a little girl stepped out of a house, covering her hair. She carried a list of items and quickly picked the vegetables needed, offered exact change to the vendor and vanished behind the closed doors. A few mins later, an old man stopped by and bought some potatoes after haggling endlessly on the price. A younger lady opened the door from another house, scanned the vegetables, and turned back dissatisfied.

Neel hoped someone would step out of Saira's residence but the door didn't open.

The unforgiving sun burned them.

Afraid to knock on the door, Neel scratched his head, and a glint of hope lit his eyes; he scribbled something on a piece of paper and showed it to Neeta.

Her eyes widened in horror, "If we are caught, we will be in trouble!" Ultimately, there seemed to be no other option. It was stifling hot, and they could not stand in the sun forever. Neeta agreed reluctantly.

They climbed the three steps to reach the entrance door and Neel knocked on the door of Saira Jamal's house hesitantly.

"Who is it?" a man growled from inside.

The effect of the voice and their anxiety jolted the two. "It's... it's me, us," stammered Neel.

A man in his late forties opened the door. He gave a piercing look at both and growled again, "What do you want?"

"We are from the electricity department, need to check your meter."

The man frowned and looked at Neeta, "Haven't seen a lady coming to check the meter?"

"This is a new policy," said Neel. "Since ladies are alone at home during the day, it is a government order that a female employee must accompany a technician."

They both flashed their badges. *No one bothers to scrutinize the badges. Most people are satisfied with some Identification.*

"The Government doesn't provide us electricity but keen on checking the meter," the man grunted and moved aside. He was mad for no reason.

Neel and Neeta stepped inside the house, "What to do sir, we are only servants, following the orders."

"The meter is at the rear of the house. Follow me."

The house was long, with rooms next to one another. They crossed all the rooms to reach the other end of the house. Their pulse raced; they had taken a big risk. Neeta clasped the message in her hand. If she spotted Saira, she will deliver the message, hoping it to be discreet and it doesn't startle Saira.

Both detectives followed the man and came to a small courtyard. A woman was sitting in one corner, chopping vegetables, which were spread on a small table. She smiled at Neeta. Two kids were busy playing. *She must be Saira.* Neeta squeezed the paper containing the message in her right hand. It was folded inside a handkerchief.

The man pointed toward the electricity meter, which was fixed on a wall at a height on the right corner. Neel spotted a small wooden box to climb, and soon reached to the meter. He had no idea what to do next. He wished that the man would go away, and Neeta could throw the message at Saira.

The man sat in another corner on a small desk, working on some machine. Neel played with the meter, "Sir, do you happen to have a small screwdriver?"

The man frowned, "What kind of a repair man are you to come without any tools?"

He offered the screwdriver which was lying on his table. "Not this one sir. I need a smaller one," said Neel. The man shook his head in frustration and walked out.

Seizing the moment, Neel signaled to Neeta, *Come-on fast!* But Neeta couldn't make a move. Neel panicked. *Come on... are you crazy?!*

The lady raised her eyes and spotted the two strangers signaling each other. The man returned soon with a screwdriver. Neel was furious – the moment was lost.

Neeta's brain worked fast, she had to do something. *What if this lady is not Saira?* "Can I have a glass of water?" she asked.

"Sure. It's too hot!" the lady spoke for the first time. "Have a seat."

Neeta sat on a plastic chair which was lying in the sun. She gasped. It burned her bottom. "Beautiful kids," Neeta sipped the water slowly. The lady smiled in response.

The kids were running in circles. Neeta caught the little girl by her arm. "What's your name?"

The little girl looked at her mom for approval. "My name is Shama...Shama Jamal."

"What a beautiful name! And what's your brother's name?"

"His name is Mubeen."

Neeta placed her fingers under the chin, "How smart!" She challenged the girl further, "and what are your parents' names?"

The girl chewed the edges of her frock, "Father's name is

Shakeel and mom's name is…" She thought hard, "Mom's name is Sabina."

Sabina! Did the little girl make a mistake?

"Are the names correct? You will get a candy if they are right!" Neeta searched her bag – hoping to find a candy inside. She looked at the lady, who nodded in agreement.

"You are a smart girl, let me get a chocolate for you."

Neeta was lucky to find two small candies. "This is for the intelligent girl who knows all the names of her family!" Neeta handed over the candies to the girl. "And make sure to share it with your brother."

Neel stepped down from the box and dusted his hands. "My work is done here."

"What's the meter reading?"

"This is a maintenance check, sir, the reading will be taken by someone else."

They rushed out.

"What a close call!" Neeta heaved a sigh of relief as she walked beside Neel on the way back.

"If this is Sabina …then where the hell is Saira?"

Chapter 13

The audio sales soared. Within months, Ian's speeches became the bestsellers at online retails. The idea of giving the audios for free worked, and when Ian's speeches were broadcast over the local radio stations, orders swelled.

People admired her talks and admitted how they experienced a life-change by listening to Ian. She touched hearts. She gave people simple, yet highly influential messages with sincerity and compassion, and this made them closer to her despite being invisible to them. Listeners found a friend and guide in Ian.

Over the months, Ian's audios became a regular feature in schools and college libraries. People talked about Ian but were unable to gain any details on her whereabouts. Jayesh and the team launched a website to market the audios, which prudently had no reference to Ian.

Ian's fans grew large in numbers and were curious to know about Ian. A local newspaper published an article on Ian's speeches and mused on her identity. Jayesh's website was listed as only a retailer, leaving no clue about Ian.

As activities increased, Jayesh expanded and modified the office space. More employees were hired. The newcomers were Jayesh's close contacts but were oblivious of Ian. They took charge of packaging and shipping.

Recordings were always done in strict confidence in the presence of an audience. Everyone knew what it took for Ian to record a perfect speech. She had to stand in front of an audience, who usually were Martha, Mike or Jayesh. Once a speech was recorded, it went through the process of testing and voice cleaning. Mike played a major role in all the recordings.

Since speech sessions did not occur every day, Ian was present only when needed, but she yearned for the time she could spend there and found reasons to visit the office.

Martha, Jayesh, and Mike pondered about Ian concealing her identity. Martha knew to some extent, but she stayed discreet about it. Ian's secrecy was the highest priority and it was followed with absolute compliance. Jayesh discerned how much the sales would multiply if only Ian would come out in the public, but he respected Ian's privacy and restricted himself.

People had a faint idea that Ian might be from Atlanta since her audios were mainly shipped from there, but nothing else was known. Jayesh and Martha worked hard in promoting the audios. It was a message that they wanted to spread, as far as possible.

Martha quit her cleaning jobs and joined Ian fulltime. Jayesh dedicated himself less to his other businesses – Ian's work kept him busy. Ian and Mike spent a great deal of time together at the office. Mike wanted to make Ian's voice perfect.

*****

As Devki sat in the car with Martha, she fidgeted with her wedding ring. It bothered her again. *I need to buy a new one soon,* she removed it and placed it in her clutch purse. Martha watched silently.

"I will be away for a while, need to take care of some stuff this morning," said Martha keeping her eyes on the road. She drove fast since the morning traffic was light.

"You know how much you're required here?"

"I cannot avoid a few things and Mike will be there to assist you anyways."

"Yea, as if Mike will know everything I need," frowned Devki. In her heart, she was cheery that Martha will be away. "The guy is a nerd. He is always busy with his machines, speakers, headphones!"

"I guess that's what we've hired him for! Isn't it? Do you expect anything else from him?"

"Fine, I can handle without you." Devki pretended to be upset.

Devki, as Ian, walked into her office; the work provided her comfort and security, the kind of comfort she lacked at her own house. *This will be my home till 3 pm.*

Mike was at work as usual with his shirt sleeves rolled till elbow, headphone on the ears, and eyes shut. He ruffled his hair with his fingers as he listened intently to one of Ian's speeches. *This guy works too hard. Does he ever sleep?* An image of Mike sleeping carelessly on a bed flashed in front of her eyes. She killed the thought before it could take roots.

Ian made deliberate sounds with her shoes as she walked toward Mike, but he hardly noticed. Ian reached his desk and knocked. Mike opened his eyes, "I was thinking about you."

"I am listening," Ian controlled her smile.

"You know how you can make this speech more effective – by speaking from your stomach."

"From my stomach!"

"Yes, if you speak from your stomach, your voice will sound deeper. This voice is fine too, but that will have a better effect."

"Are you kidding?" Ian placed her hands on her hips, "I've heard about speaking from the heart but speaking from the stomach – I'm hearing this for the first time."

Mike removed the headphones hanging around his neck and placed them on the table. "No, seriously, you should take out all the air from your stomach, by squeezing it and blowing the air faster out of your lips and speak after that. In this way, the voice will come from deep within."

Ian eyed him warily.

"Ok look here," Mike lifted his shirt.

Devki's eyes were glued on Mike as he squeezed his perfect abs inside and blew the air out by circling his lips. He blew and sucked the air in and out, in and out. *Oh God, this is too much to handle in the morning* thought Ian.

"Okay I'll see to it!" Ian blurted and sprinted to her room. She slumped on her chair and took a deep breath. *What's happening to me?* She suddenly remembered her ring, opened her purse and forced it back on her finger.

As she looked up, Mike was at the door, forehead wrinkled, "What happened, did I offend you in some way?"

There was no answer.

"I don't understand! You behave strangely sometimes. I was trying to tell you something new and you walked away!"

"I am fine, I was thinking about the technique you showed; you can never offend me."

"That's better. Remember, speak from here." Mike patted on his abs. A thin smile adorned Ian's lip.

"Do you want me to show you how?" Mike walked toward Ian.

"No!" Ian blurted out and folded her arms across her chest. "I will work on it myself."

"Ok cool, try that and I will get your coffee in the meantime," Mike walked away.

Ian sighed in relief, but the devil was back soon. He handed over the coffee mug to Ian and took his position near the door.

Mike stirred his coffee, "We have to edit your last week's speeches, need to remove some of the background noise. We might have to re-record some portions," he strained his mind on the unfinished tasks. Ian hid her face behind the coffee mug.

"Can you work a little late today?" asked Mike.

Ian looked away, "No, I cannot stay after three."

"Oh yes! You have to take care of your family and kids," said Mike as if recalling something. He added, "You know what… it's good that you're already married and have kids, otherwise you're so busy with speeches now that you would have no time for a date!" Mike laughed at his own joke but Ian could not get it.

There was a sound at the door and Martha walked in, "Sorry guys, hope I'm not too late."

"VIPs are never late," joked Mike.

"So, what are we doing today?" Martha always kept the handle of the schedule and things around the office. Mike quickly brought her to speed. Martha dusted her desk and shuffled around the papers.

"Why are you so busy?" asked Ian.

Martha waved a bunch of papers in the air, "Because of these…Invoices need to be paid, checks waiting to be deposited and a list of supplies to be bought."

Ian's eyes warmed up.

"When business grows… Martha's work also grows with it. And with Madam Ian being invisible most of the days, all the load falls upon poor Martha." She bowed in front of Ian.

Ian raised her right palm as if blessing her. The women cracked up on the joke.

Mike returned to his work, leaving Ian and Martha to themselves.

Outside, Mike listened to one of Ian's speeches and found something odd in one. He listened to it again. His forehead furrowed.

Mike listened to Ian's recorded speeches multiple times before giving them a final approval. Sometimes he was away during recordings, therefore reviewed them later.

He was listening to one such speech which was recorded a few weeks earlier, when he noticed some interruption. Who is it? Mike tried to listen closely. The voice was not clear. Mike removed the background sound and focused more. It was Martha's voice.

She said something which was not audible. It appeared as if Ian was finishing a recording when Martha cut in and the recording abruptly stopped.

What the hell! Mike was upset with the unprofessionalism. Where should be complete silence when Ian recorded. He was frustrated when he couldn't figure out what Martha was saying. Mike cleared the sound further and listened. Though the voice was not yet clear, he heard something like Deva or Dave. *Was Martha on the phone, talking to someone outside?*

It did sound like Martha talking directly to Ian. *Why is she calling her Deva or Dave or Div?* Mike thought for a second on what it could be and later slapped his forehead. *Oh, Martha is calling Ian 'Diva'. That makes sense, she is a Diva.*

Ian's behavior confused Mike. He knew she was married yet she gave mixed signals to him. No family pictures on her desk, but that was not unusual…some people don't keep family pictures in their office. Her dressing was quite odd too. No matter what season, she was always buttoned-up till the chin. Sometimes she is in a pleasant mood but otherwise, she stays aloof and seems nervous about something. She constantly looked at the door as if someone is after her.

Occasionally, during recording, a mere touch of his hand startled her but at other times, she herself seemed to be drawn toward him. There were days when she was unable to record at all. When he was able to relax her, she produced better results. And the look… the look she often gave him, tickled his spine. He knew why a girl would give that kind of a look to a man.

Sometimes she is in a pleasant mood but otherwise, she stays aloof and seems nervous about something. She constantly looks at the door as if someone is after her. Occasionally, during recording, a mere touch of his hand startled her but at other times, she herself seemed to be drawn toward him. There were days when she was unable to record at all. When he was able to relax her, she produced better results. And the look... the look she often gave him, tickled his spine. He knew why a girl would give that kind of a look to a man.

Mike enjoyed her company. He carried her thoughts with him after work. The whole secrecy about Ian's identity intrigued him. No one was allowed to contact her. There was no phone number. The only person who can ever contact Ian outside working hours was Martha. *There is something more to Ian.*

*****

Mike looked at the hard-working people in the room, "The weather looks excellent today. Anyone interested in joining me for dinner?"

Ian kept herself busy in the notes. Martha peeked over her glasses, "Meee!"

Mike knocked on Ian's table, "What about you?"

Ian continued her attention on the notes, "Sorry I'm never free in the evenings."

"Ok, no problem. Martha and I will go for dinner and make you jealous tomorrow." said Mike.
Martha laughed and squinted at Ian, but she hardly took heed.

It was almost seven in the evening when Martha and Mike sat at a corner table in a Mexican restaurant. Drinks and appetizers were ordered. This was their first meeting outside work. They talked about work in general. Martha enjoyed her favorite drink of Tequila with lime juice. Mike relished it too.

Mike nibbled on the chips, "How long are you acquainted with Ian?"

"Don't know, feels like a long time," sighed Martha.
Mike took a quick look around the restaurant. It was someone's birthday and the servers were singing the birthday song.

"I enjoy working with Ian. She's a true professional," said Mike. "Do you think Ian Scovich is her real name?"

"Don't know man!" Martha played with her glass. "People have all sorts of names. It's only a name." Martha changed the topic, "Been to Mexico anytime?"

"No, but want to visit India, I dated a girl long back ...she was from the South. She told me wonderful stories about the country."

"Hmm…interesting. So, what's your status now, dating someone…married?"

Mike ran four fingers down his hair. "Nah…too busy with work. Never got interested in marriage!"

"What about you?"

"I was married once." Martha pushed the salsa away.

"What about Ian…she's married …right?" inquired Mike.

"Yes, she's married. You're asking way too many questions about Ian…remember your agreement…want to get fired?" Martha laughed loudly, trying to sound funny.

The place got crowded as they left the restaurant.

*****

There was no moon in the sky. It was a dark night and it was darker in the room. Devki squirmed under Gagan's weight.

In her mind, her own voice was echoing,

"Dear friends,

This is Ian.

Break your chains. Break the things holding you down.

You are a soul passing this world for a higher destination.

No one can touch or harm a soul.

The soul doesn't need any attachment. The soul doesn't yearn for any worldly things. It only yearns for liberation.

So, my friends, liberate yourself!

You owe this to yourself! You owe this to Ian!"

She was preparing her next speech.

Chapter 14

The room was silent. Neel rubbed his forehead and reviewed his own report from the previous day's events. Although they failed to find Saira at the address given by Martha, he was pleased their attempt was executed with less than five dollars. He was impressed by Neeta's initiative and quick thinking.

Intending to check her out, Neel threw a casual glance at her. No ring on the fingers, no red dot on the forehead and no bride's chain around the neck.

"You did an excellent job for a newcomer," Neel's lips parted displaying his white teeth.
There were no red stains on his teeth. They were sparkling white – no signs of tobacco use – a rarity in that part of the town. Neeta smiled too.

Neel was initially disappointed that the message could not be delivered, but as he thought further, he brightened. *This shows there's more meat in the case.* His eyes gleamed, as he spoke like an expert, "This is an important case."

Everyone leaned closer in excitement. Neel continued, "From the message we got to deliver, we can see that our client is looking for Saira, but there was no Saira at the given address. This shows that we have more work."

Neel adjusted his tie, "And now I need to make an important call to Martha." He looked at his watch. "Can you guys please step out for a while?"

The whole office comprised of a single room. Sarang, Manish, and Neeta left the room and stood in the open, with no shade. Neel was unable to bear the sight of Neeta standing outside in the blistering heat, "Okay, you guys can come in, but don't utter a word when I am on the phone."

Neel dialed Martha's number, avoiding the speaker this time.

"Hello." Martha's voice came in.

"There is good news…and bad news!" Neel had seen enough movies to create dramatic dialogues.

Martha's happiness could be sensed over the phone. She had not expected it to be this easy, "Give me the good news." She spoke in haste.

Chandraish Sinha

"Good news is that the address you gave us is correct!"

"And the bad news?"

"We couldn't find Saira in that house."

There was a long pause. "Then find her!" Martha's voice was loud.

The other people in the room stared at Neel, trying to guess the conversation.

"We can try finding her ...but it will involve a lot of effort and resources. It will cost more."

"How much?"

Neel had already thought of a big amount before dialing. "It's going to be one thousand dollars. One .... Zero .... Zero .... zero dollars."

Neel's voice came back on the phone slowly but crisp and clear, to ensure the amount was understood. He continued, "We need to do a lot of work – a great deal of searching and investigation will be required. We are not even sure if she's alive!" He wanted to get to Martha's sentiments.

There was a long pause. *Looks like I hit the target.*

Martha knew the importance of Saira in Devki's life. Why and how, she failed to understand, as Devki hardly spoke about her past and Martha did not wish to appear too inquisitive. Martha did realize some strong connection, some history between the two. People do have friends, but rarely does someone miss them as much as Devki missed Saira. Saira must be vital for Devki – to name her daughter after her.

Martha made several calls to people in India and they, in turn, called other people. She was able to reach Jhansi but things were not easy. It would have been easier to locate someone in the whole world rather than to connect to someone in a town like Jhansi. People whom Martha was able to contact did not speak much English and those who spoke English struggled to understand Martha's accent. Neel was Martha's only hope.

"Listen Neel!" Martha's voice came back flat and unemotional. "If you can trace Saira for me...I will give you five thousand dollars... five zero zero zero dollars!"

Neel's mind went blank for a second. He wanted to repeat out the number, but his voice failed to come out. He choked with excitement. $5,000 meant around Rs.350, 000.

80

For this money, I could find anyone. All the employees noticed the enthusiasm gripping over their boss.

Neel gulped quick breaths, "Okay… okay…sure. We'll search the heaven and earth to find Saira for you!"

"Glad to hear that!"

"Can you give us any other detail that will bring us closer to Saira? Like a photograph or a physical description?"

"Sorry, not much on that, there is no picture and I cannot give you any description because I myself have not seen her."

She has not even seen her! Neel bit his lips.

"The only information I can give you is that Saira lived at that address."

Interesting! "Her education?"

Martha thought for a moment. If Devki referred to her as a friend… "She studied at least till bachelors." Martha made an assumption.

Neel made a mental note of it. "If you don't mind, can you please tell me your relationship with Saira?"

"I am helping a friend… like you are helping me."

"And once we find Saira, what will you do?"

"Will talk to her."

Neel displayed all his teeth with a broad greedy smile. "No worries! We will start working on this right away. We will work day and night – will try every bit to get Saira for you."

"Great! I cannot thank you enough for it." Martha was ecstatic.

"Please arrange to send some advance so that we can continue our work." Martha disconnected the phone, satisfied and assured by Neel's genuine voice.

Neel took a deep breath, closed his eyes, joined his palms and thanked God. The juniors understood that their boss had hit a jackpot. Neel looked solemn. He took a few minutes to digest the information he had received.

He looked at Neeta with sparkling eyes, extended his arms, "My Saira!"

"What!" exclaimed Neeta.

Neel's face twisted as he smiled, "I have found our Saira!" All eyes were fixed on Neel, perplexed. "Yes, Saira's search is over!" Neel pointed at Neeta.

She was aghast upon perceiving what he meant.

"Noooooo!" she delivered the biggest 'no' of her life.

"Yes, why not?" Neel laughed again.

He pulled a chair and drew some aimless lines on a piece of paper. "See, the thing is simple. Martha has never seen Saira, and we don't know why she is looking for Saira. All she wants is, to find her and talk to her over the phone." Neel took a pause, looked around to gauge everyone's expression and spoke again, "So, Saira will talk to her. Saira can be whomsoever we want."

Sarang and Manish high-fived with excitement.

"This is deceit!" protested Neeta.

"This is business!" asserted Neel. "Do you know how much she will pay us for this? ...Rupees THREE LAKH FIFTY THOUSAND. Do you even know how much money that is?"

"No, I don't know Dubey ji...I've never seen this much money together in one place... ever!" Neeta's voice trembled. Neither of them had seen such a huge amount in their entire lives.

"This is a wonderful opportunity! In the coming weeks, we can get our Saira ready and all the money will be mine!" Neel immediately corrected himself, "I mean our company's. This will open doors to future possibilities." Neel flashed a smile at Neeta.

Her face was stiff, jaws clenched. Her respect for her boss diminished. She recalled her school going brothers – old mother – the damaged and unrepaired house; the bathroom with no door. She had to retain her job at any cost. "Whatever you say Boss," obliged Neeta feebly.

Neel was firm on his decision, "The next few weeks are crucial for us – we should prepare Saira for the client. Our new project starts tomorrow."

*****

The next day, Sarang, Manish and Neeta, arrived on time. Neel was already present, having reached early.

'Project: Creating Saira' adorned the whiteboard.

Neel slowly hummed a song. Sarang and Manish shared some joke and pushed each other. Neeta pulled herself along with the others. The temperature inside the room was still high though no one seemed to notice.

Neel knocked on the table to get their focus. "This project

82

is not all that difficult, since the meeting is going to happen over the phone." He looked at Neeta, "Yet, Neeta, you must feel comfortable."

"I don't!" pleaded Neeta.

Neel played with the pen between his fingers, "You see, acting is an important part of a detective's job. Even in olden times, the king's spies disguised themselves to infiltrate the enemy's camp."

"And who is the enemy here?" Neeta folded her arms to her chest.

Neel ignored Neeta and addressed the others, "Though this will be a telephonic conversation, I want Neeta to prepare well. She should feel like Saira from inside." He stood closer to the white board, "To start with, what are some of the traits of Saira?"

Manish raised his hand, "Her name is Saira!" He spoke for the first time, as he tried to get involved, not wanting to miss the big money. Neel returned a frown.

Sarang was next, "She is a Muslim woman."

"Yes ...go on."

Manish looked at his notes from the earlier discussions, "She is around 38 years of age,"

Neel nodded and moved the pen across the board. "She holds a bachelor's degree," and completed his thoughts. He looked at what he wrote and seemed impressed, "And that's all we know about her." Neel continued, "Most of these qualities are already in Neeta. She needs to dress and behave like a Muslim lady and she would be perfect."

"All you have to do is to practice saying 'aadab'!" Manish acted like a Muslim woman greeting someone. Everyone enjoyed Manish's acting. Even Neeta couldn't avoid smiling.

Although unnecessary, Neel advised Neeta to wear only salwar suits and avoid wearing pants and T-shirt. He also asked her to keep Saira in her thoughts and try to feel like her.

"I have never met or even seen Saira, how can I feel like her?" argued Neeta.

"Think about it as a movie," Neel spoke like an expert. "In real life, you don't see the characters like those in a movie, but you can still act and feel like them. I want you to get into the character of Saira."

They practiced every day. They even rehearsed how Neeta, pretending as Saira, will talk to someone from America over the phone.

In a couple of weeks, the team was ready, yet they waited for some more time. Martha called in twice to check the status and Neel updated her that the team was extremely busy. He detailed her about how they travelled to nearby towns and villages in search of Saira with the limited information they had, how they searched the local newspapers for the past 10 years and had not found any obituary naming Saira. Neel sent regular false updates to Martha, about their strenuous efforts in tracking Saira. Martha transferred some more funds to cover the expenses. Martha was satisfied with Neel's efforts.

After four weeks, Neel informed Martha that they have found Saira and scheduled a call between them.

The evening before the call, Neel sat in his office alone. He was slouched on the chair with his feet on the table. He thought about the past few weeks and smiled in self-appreciation. The team worked hard in preparing Neeta as Saira. Though initially Neeta required some convincing, she was fine later. Success was knocking at the door.

With more clients like this, his life will be settled. He will move to a larger workplace, buy a spacious house with a large lawn where his kids would play. The thought of home and kids brought thoughts of Neeta along.

Ah, Neeta! Neel sighed. He recalled the day when Neeta called him "Dubey Ji." Neel chuckled *Dubey ji*. Their names were so close Neel and Neeta. *Neel weds Neeta...*

Neel smiled to himself.

He checked his watch – it was late in the evening. *Time to go.* He looked around as if for the last time. *From tomorrow life will be different.* Once outside, he called Neeta's phone. An old voice answered ... Neel disconnected the call.

Tomorrow will be mine. The future will be mine. Perhaps I should propose to Neeta once Martha is convinced.

Chapter 15

The clock read 8 am in Jhansi. The streets bustled with people rushing to their workplaces. The main streets were packed with cars, scooters, motorbikes, autos, and tempos. People buzzed in all directions. Street Vendors sold hot breakfast consisting of samosas, kachoris and jalebis. People made beelines at the tea-stalls. Although the temperature was high, people preferred to drink hot tea over cold drinks. School students drove their bicycles zigzag between the traffic.

The historic city was young and alive.

The Old city was small with narrow by-lanes. Some alleys were so small that one can only walk through them – no vehicle can ever pass through. The market, with a wider road, had assorted shops – cloth stores, pharmacies, computer retailers, small clinics, all lined one after the other. With little space for parking, people left their vehicles wherever they could find a spot. Neel's office was sandwiched between a grocer and a tea vendor.

The detectives arrived at the office earlier than usual. The boys wore jackets – the sultry weather didn't seem to bother them. They were excited and anxious. Tea, coffee, cold drinks, and snacks filled the table, which were more than needed, but were ordered anyway. They were only four, but the place seemed crowded. Neel was in his usual suit and a tie. Standing tall, he felt like a winner already. Neeta wore a light brown salwar suit, matching her somber mindset. She twisted the corners of her top and looked outside the window aimlessly.

Neel addressed her, "Today is your day. You are on the camera, give your best shot!" He showed his thumbs up to her. Neeta's eyelids drooped, she clenched her jaw and looked at the floor in silence.

On the other side of the world, Martha was excited. She lived alone in her apartment. The initial days were tough and lonesome, but she gradually got used to it. With Sofia in Mexico and no known relative in Atlanta, there was no alternative. The evenings were difficult when she returned home from work, but in recent times, with Ian's work, her evenings were occupied too. There was something to be done every other day.

Martha was unable to stop smiling to herself from the time

she received Neel's call the previous night. *They have found Saira! God! Thank you!* prayed Martha. *This Neel is such an honest and hard-working man. Devki would be thrilled upon hearing this news.* She often inquired about Saira, and every time, Martha requested her to wait. Martha had not relayed the news about Saira to Devki. She wanted to talk to Saira first. Though Martha knew only a little about her, all this search made her feel closer to Saira.

Martha wanted to advice Saira on how to reconnect with Devki. *All this happiness should not take an emotional toll on her. Too much sadness or excitement could affect her.* Devki was onto great things and Martha didn't want anything to influence her. *It'd be great if Saira can agree to come to the USA.*

On both sides of the world, 5 hearts breathed hard in anticipation. Despite being thousands of miles apart – Neel, Sarang, Manish, Neeta, and Martha took deep breaths at the same time. It was Martha who dialed the number.

In an instant, it rang on the other side of the world, "Hello!" answered Neel.

"Oh Neel, you are the best friend ever. Thanks, and congrats to you and your team!" Martha's voice echoed on the speaker phone.

Her trust and excitement embarrassed Neel.

"Where is Saira? Saira! Saira!" Martha called as if she was physically present in the same room and calling out her close friend.

"Yea… Yes…Yes Madam," said Neeta putting her face close to the speaker phone.

"Oh, come-on! Don't call me Madam. I am Martha. You don't know me Saira, but I know you so well. You know there is someone who's dying to meet you!" Her voice crackled over the phone.

Neeta raised her eyebrows at Neel. He signaled her to just go on with the flow. The room fell silent. Only Martha's voice filled the room.

"We talk about you every day! You know whom I am talking about …can you guess…can you guess Saira?"

"No… no, I don't know Madam." Neeta's voice was soft and low.

"Ok tell me…. who in this whole world, would be so

anxious to meet you?"

Neeta was speechless. Her heart pounded hard. She could only muster, "Hmmm."

Martha's gut feeling told her that something was not right. *Saira doesn't sound excited. Is it because I am a stranger to her, but she must sound curious at the least?*

Martha stared at the receiver, and spoke again with a flat voice, "Saira …you there?"

"Yes."

"Tell me how many daughters were there." *Saira will know about Devki's daughters. Devki once remarked that they were neighbors.*

Neeta looked around for some reinforcement. Neel was dumbfounded and the others had no answer either. *Where did these daughters come from?* He showed 4 fingers to Neeta. They had to respond with some answer.

Neeta wiped the beads of sweat from her forehead. "Forr… Four."

"How many daughters did your friend have?" Martha persisted in a cold voice.

What! Which Friend? Neeta twiddled with her dress. She looked around – all faces appeared blank. Neeta stared at Neel. He did not have an answer either.

Displeased at the pause, Martha continued, "I am asking you something!"

Neeta blurted, "Three."

"What was your friend's name?" Martha was loud.

"Friend…friend madam, you know, I…," Neeta stammered. "I had no friend." She realized her gaffe in an instant. She had replied that her friend had three daughters and immediately declined on having any friend. Her mouth went dry in desperation. It was too late for any corrective action.

"Neel…Neel!" shrieked Martha. The whole room shook with her voice. Neel quivered in his place. "Where is Saira!!!" Martha demanded. "You cheat …you damned liar!"

Martha's voice seemed to target each object in the room. All the faces went sullen. "I thought you were a gentleman, but no, you have no regard for any sentiments."

Neel wiped his dry lips.

Martha continued, "Who is this girl? Some cheap drama queen? How can you play with someone's emotions like this? Tell me, Neel! Answer me!"

There was a small pause in the line. Neeta threw a glance at Neel in despise. Her eyes turned watery. She collected her purse and walked out.

Martha's face went distorted in disgust, "If you needed more money, you should have told me. If you didn't want to do the job, you could have refused. Why lie? Why cheat?"

Martha tried to control her breath, "Now what answer should I give my friend who waits for Saira every day?" Martha's words pierced Neel like arrows.

"You know how I found you? I searched all the local newspapers in Jhansi and only your ad was in English and only you were listed as a private detective. Am I getting punished for believing you, and not doing a background check on you?"

Martha's voice trembled, "Now where should I go? You killed our Saira, Neel…You killed my hopes!"

"No! No! I will not let Saira die!" Neel blurted out.

"Stop your lies!" Martha's voice blared, "I know someone from your place…a wonderful soul, I thought you will be the same, but you are a fraudster!"

Neel's face turned pale and his whole body shook with guilt. He had no words.

He somehow managed, "I will find Saira…. Martha…I will find her…this is my promise to you. I will be a trustworthy friend like you wanted me to."

"This is what you promised me earlier Neel!" Martha cried.

"I will find Saira this time, no matter what. I will find Saira on my own… you don't have to give me a dime. This is my promise to you."

"Then find her!" Martha slammed the phone.

By the end of the call, all others had left. Neel stared at the vacant room. He collapsed on his chair. He had never been insulted like this before. His ego was crushed. With elbows on the table, he caught his face between his palms and sobbed. All his dreams and ambitions were swept away in a moment. He thought about Neeta. He wiped his eyes using the back of his sleeves and dialed Neeta's number. There was no answer. He called again and again in vain.

He wept bitterly.

*****

Till late, Neel was proud of himself. He belonged to a family of soldiers. His great-great-grandfather had fought beside Queen LakshmiBai against the British forces in 1857.
His uncles fought for the Indian Army. His grandfather and father were community leaders. They were not rich but had earned a good reputation in the town. He had ruined it forever. No one had ever spoken to him the way the American lady had.

Neel slammed the office door in disgust as he stepped out into the street. He walked in the sun. He walked in the town till evening and into the night. He walked for days.
He wandered aimlessly in the crowded streets of 'Manik chowk'; he walked in the deserted streets of the town. No one noticed him, no one looked for him.

He visited the Queen's fort. He sat near the high wall from where the Queen jumped with her little son. She fought for her beliefs. He had let the Queen down. He begged for forgiveness.

He walked from dawn to dusk. He walked in the light and he walked in the shadows. He cried and screamed in the darkness. No one heard him. He was tormented by his own deceit. No one knew if he cried for Neeta or for Saira.

He called Neeta many times over but got no response. He tried calling Martha and there was no answer as well.

Neel wanted to be a detective although not by choice. After graduating, all he wanted was a job – any job. But in a country of a billion people, employment was a big struggle. While growing up, he heard his uncles and aunts discussing work. Jobs were scarce then, and they were scarcer 30 years later.

With three unmarried sisters and a sick father...where was the money? This was the only business he could do without any investment, but that should not be the reason for his betrayal. His misery did not give him the right to play with someone's feelings. He had no right to hurt the feelings of someone sitting across the table in his office or someone living thousands of miles away.

He was from the town of fighters, where people once fought against the mighty forces. Although it was more than 150 years ago, they still carried the temper and vigor. People of Jhansi still fought with their day-to-day problems with the same zeal and valor.

Neel stopped one day, either because he was exhausted, or because he missed himself. He visited all the religious places in town. He climbed the stairs of 'Kaimasan Devi temple' in the university campus. He took solace in the temple of 'Sakhi-ke-Hanuman'. He lit a candle in 'St. Jude's shrine'. *I will find Saira!* he promised himself.

Neel called Neeta's phone for the last time. It was answered after the first ring. No one spoke on the line. Neel didn't even know who was on the other side…but he spoke anyway,

"Neeta, I'm sorry for what had happened. I wanted to let you know that I will pursue Saira on my own. I won't trouble anyone. This is my fight!" and disconnected the phone.

A minute later, Neel received a text message on his phone. It read, "Dubeyji, I am with you in this fight or any other in future, as long as the fight is for a righteous reason"
Neel smiled for the first time in weeks.

Neeta dialed others. The next day, they were all present at the office, confident and optimistic. They were into this together. Neel nodded at them in appreciation and received smiles in return. He lifted the brown marker and wrote on the white board…

"Project: Finding Saira!"

Chapter 16

Little Saira hushed Mini by placing her index finger on her lips. Both girls tiptoed upstairs to Esha's room. The door was unlatched. Saira slowly pushed it, and it opened to a messy and disorderly living space. Bending their torsos in, both the girls peeped inside, to make sure the room was empty. The way was clear, both the young ones sneaked inside, still on their toes but taking longer steps.

The room had two beds by the sides of the opposite walls. One bed was spotless with its bedsheet neatly tucked in and the comforter folded. It was Kajal's, who was perfect in keeping things in order. The twins were not interested in her stuff. They looked at the other bed. It had piles of dresses, a crumpled bedsheet, and other stuff tossed around. Posters of shirtless rock stars were pinned on the wall. Books were lying haphazardly on the bed, table and the floor.

Their eyes beamed as they spotted Esha's side of the room. They placed their fingers on their lips and hushed each other again.

Devki was downstairs in the laundry oblivious of the little ones' mischief. Esha and Kajal had gone out to a teenage party, granting the opportunity to the twins to invade their room.

Both the girls paused for a second and moved toward Esha's closet. Her clothes fascinated them. To their surprise, the garments were neatly arranged on the shelves. Some were folded and some were on wooden hangers. The girls were awed seeing such an assorted arrangement of colorful clothes.

Saira pulled a red top from the hanger. The dress got stuck but with a little tug of war, it gave away, sacrificing a button.

"What are you doing?" whispered Mini.

"What do you think, I'm putting on the dress."

"No! Don't do that, she'll kill us!"

"Don't worry, she'll not be back anytime soon. We will put everything back like it was."

Mini too pulled a black skirt, it was too big for her waist. She threw it on the floor and picked another one, but it did not fit her either. She pulled out several skirts with the hope to get one of her size. In the meantime, Saira had put on the red top. It covered her from neck till ankles. She looked at the mirror and giggled.

"I want something for myself, nothing fits me!" cried Mini.

"Sshh! Skirts will never fit you, try some tops."

Mini pulled different dresses and at last settled on a black t-shirt.

They moved across the closet and pulled the draws one by one. They picked and tossed garments all over the floor.

Mini pulled a legging and spoke while trying it on, "Why does Didi call mom Devki?"

"Maybe mom is not her mom," said Saira.

"How can that be possible, there is only one mom in this house and she has to be everyone's mom. And if our dad is their dad, how come our mom is not their mom."

"Maybe, mom is an aunt to Didi," Saira pulled out an earring.

"Do you call aunt by her name? We call aunt Renu ...aunt Renu, but who knows, once you are in high school, maybe you can call elders by names?" Mini banged her head, "This is all so confusing."

They checked all the drawers one by one. In one of the drawers, Mini found a weird item. It looked like a slingshot toy or something to cover the eyes. She showed it to Saira, she was able to identify it. She had seen it in the magazines – it was a bra. Saira quickly tied it around her chest but it was too big. She asked Mini to tie a knot around her back.

In one of the shelves, they found some lipsticks. They were not sure if Esha was allowed to use makeup. They tried to apply lipsticks to each other, which ended in a lot of smudging and smearing across their faces.

Excited over discovering a pair of sunglasses in another shelf, Saira adjusted the large sunglasses on her eyes, "Do I look like an actress?"

When she got no answer, she turned back – her eyes met with two glowing eyes of Esha.

"Didi, it was ...I mean," Saira gulped the air. "Mini forced me to come here. I would have never come here on my own. God promise!"

Esha and Kajal had returned earlier than they anticipated. Kajal was still downstairs.

The twins were jolted by Esha's sudden scream. "Devki! Devki! Devki!"

Devki was back from the laundry when she heard Esha, and sprinted toward her room, followed by Kajal.

Esha was still screaming as Devki and Kajal entered the room and came closer. A look at the twins and the closet, Kajal gasped "OMG." The whole closet was in a mess, with loads of clothes on the floor, some half-hanging from the hangers, drawers open, with clothes pulled out and Saira and Mini in the midst of everything, wearing oversize tops, lipstick smeared all over the face and inners tied to their waist.

"Ssss sorry," Devki pulled the twins out of the closet.

"How the hell did these devils reach my closet?!" demanded Esha.

"I I ddd don't know. I was working downstairs…don't know hhh how they sneaked in here."

"Devki…how many times has Dad told you to take care of the house, and this is how you take care. All my dresses are spoiled…who will be responsible for all this?"

"I ap apologize for their mistake. Sss sorry it will never happen agg again."

Devki dragged the frightened twins out of the room, "Why do you spoil your sister's closet? Why do you do this to me? You guys don't let me be in peace."

*****

Kajal checked her closet, it was undisturbed. She was relieved but grim. *Those monsters didn't take any interest in my clothes!*

Esha assessed the damage to her things. She was sure Devki would easily clean all the mess. She recalled Saira's frightened face – wearing a long top, lipstick, innerwear, and glasses – *she looked cute and funny.* The kids' mischief made Esha smile… *And how this naughty girl blamed her sister!* Esha could only laugh.

Ever since the little ones arrived, the house was filled with joy. They were sweet little babies when they arrived and changed the gloomy atmosphere of their house. *The only good thing Devki did is bringing these dolls into the family!*

Esha was in her thoughts over the little girl's mischief, when she heard Devki yelling at the kids. *Oh my!* Esha rushed to the edge of the stairs, "Enough, cut it out Devki!"

The kids whimpered as Devki spoke in rapid rage, "All my pampering is spoiling you. God only knows what you learn at school. Today I will teach you how to behave."

Esha ran down the steps, "Stop it Devki, it's okay." Before Esha could guess anything, Devki whacked Saira and Mini on their backs. The kids wailed.

Esha's eyes turned wide in anger. "How dare you beat such little kids. You evil woman! Cut it out or I will dial 911 to call the cops!"

Drained, Devki slumped on the ground and sobbed.

Both the kids ran toward Esha and wrapped around her. They submerged their faces into her skirt and cried. "Sorry, Didi!"

"Hey, it's okay. I am not angry. When I was of your age, I was naughtier than this. You guys have done nothing compared to what I've done to my elders."

Kajal also came down and stroked their hair, "Come on guys, it's okay!"

Esha looked at the twins, "Now who wants to eat something...how about some dessert?"

The little ones wiped their eyes. Saira said, "Yesterday Mom made yummy rice pudding."

"Okay, so we will have that. Kajal can you fetch the bowls?"

Soon all the kids were on the couch relishing the pudding. "Your mom is bad to have hit you and from my experience I can tell you, all moms are evil!" Esha laughed with sarcasm.

The kids failed to get the hidden meaning but giggled anyway.

Mini licked her lips. "But she cooks delicious food."

Devki walked slowly toward the kitchen.

"And guys whatever happened today, will be our secret," said Esha. "No one needs to know what happens between sisters, not even Dad. We are a gang of sisters!"

"Yay!" the girls screamed, "we are a gang!"

Chapter 17

Devki was unable to go to work since Esha was at home, sick. She was cleaning the twins' room, when she heard Esha coughing. Devki walked up to her room, hesitated for a moment and knocked.

"Yes."

"Caca cannn can I come in?"

"What do you want?" yelled Esha, coughing intermittently.

Devi pushed open the door. The room was cluttered with tissues, text books, magazines, stationery, and clothes scattered all around. Small dumbbells and a hula hoop lay carelessly on the floor. It was a complete mess and looked as if a tornado had passed across.

Seeing Devki, Esha flared, "Never enter my room without my permission!"

"You are feeling sick. You wawa want me to make something hot for you?"

"I'm fine. Don't pretend to be my mom!"

Devki paused after such a welcome, but she had expected nothing less. "Why you aa mm mean to me? What did I do to you?"

"Nothing! If I need anything, I will let you know. Now leave."

"You want me to clean your room?"

"Leave, Devki!" Esha growled. *Where on earth did dad bring this creature from?*

*****

Esha was a 15-year-old junior high student. She was the eldest of the two daughters of Gagan. She was chubby, fair and had big hazel eyes. She liked colorful clothes and loved to party. Her teenage tantrums were known to the family and friends. People close to the family usually commented on her likeness to her mom, though it was never a compliment to her.

Esha could never forgive her mom. The thought of a mother usually fills a child's heart with love, but to Esha, it brought hate and disgust. The incidents of the past were still fresh in her mind.

The memories of her mother and her actions left an indelible mark on Esha's mind. It felt like yesterday, when they were a loving happy family – Mom, Dad, Kajal and herself. Kajal was too small to understand anything. Dad was strict but loving and Mom was sweet.

Esha remembered the stories her father read for her, and the mouth-watering meals mom prepared. Mom was caring, kind and understanding. They reached out to her for everything, until things started to change. Slowly everyone noticed a change in mom. She was often absent from home and mostly preoccupied whenever she was present.

Once, when Kajal was sick and her teacher tried to contact mom, she failed to answer the call. Gagan had to drive 35 miles from his work to pick up the child from school.

When they reached home, mom asserted that she didn't receive any call, unmindful of her oversight and her family's anxiety. Eventually such events became more frequent. Mom was busy most of the time. If she was at home, she was busy with her phone or on the computer.

One evening, when Dad returned late from work, and mom was busy with her social media interactions, Esha walked up to him, "Dad leave your job, please!"

"What! Are you serious? I can't, sweetie! I must work for our family, to send you to a good school. To give you this house." He looked at mom, "To pay for your mom's shopping."

"No dad, I don't need anything. I want you to stay at home."

Later when Esha was alone in her room reading a book, mom knocked on the door.

"You are my mom – you needn't knock on my door."

Mom slowly treaded across and stood beside Esha ruffling her hair, "Esha there are things, I wish I could explain to you."

"No mom, you cannot!"

Esha sobbed in her mother's arms. "What happened to you mom? Please come back! We all miss you!"

"I am with you…I am with you," which was all she could say.

Esha had no clue what was happening to her mother.

Another morning, when Mom was in the shower, Esha

snooped into her phone. There were texts and pictures which she couldn't comprehend. The texts and the weird photos of a stranger confused her; her instinct told her they were bad. She recalled how their English teacher had warned them about the perils of cell phones …she might have referred to such texts and photos.

Esha was uncertain how to proceed. Her small brain was unable to contemplate what was going on, but she understood that her father would be unhappy about all this. *Perhaps telling him will solve the problem,* but she feared her father's anger and what it might do to their family.

Her little brain took the decision.

Gagan was engrossed in his work one Sunday and Mom had gone shopping. Esha walked to her father, "I want to tell you something dad."

Gagan pushed the laptop away, "Yes dear."

"Dad, you need to take care of mom."

Gagan circled his lips, "I do sweetheart. That's why I work hard, but yes, I need to focus more."

"Dad, did you notice, mom's changing? She is out of home most of the time. We miss her."

"I noticed it too…she is spending too much time with her friends, spas, and shopping. Maybe she's tired or bored. Guess what, we'll surprise her with a party or a gift!" Gagan continued, "Got any suggestions?"

"Why don't you look at Mom's phone …that should give you some ideas," Esha peeked into her dad's eyes.

After a few days, Esha noticed a closed-door conversation between her parents. She clasped her fingers and prayed. A day later, they all went out to eat. *Mom and dad both look jubilant. Yay!* Esha was elated. She saved the family.

She checked her mom's phone whenever it was left unattended. There were no texts, no photos. All the older photos were gone. She sighed in relief.

Sadly, the relief was short lived. Much to the little girl's dismay, there were soon new texts and different pictures on her mom's phone. *Pictures of someone else! Oh! Oh!* Esha panicked.

This time Esha did not have to tell anyone. Dad knew it all. The closed-door conversation did not go well. There was no outing after that. Mom did not care for anything – neither for Dad nor for them.

People in dark suits came inside the house. Esha learnt the word 'lawyers' for the first time. They measured the house and counted everything they owned. Mom made many false allegations on Dad, but none were proved. Esha loved her dad because the last thing she heard him tell mom was, "You can take whatever you want, but leave my daughters with me."

She took everything and left them.

Things were never the same in the house. Everything changed, even Dad.

A few years later, *Dad married this…this Devki.*

Esha hated her from the very first day. She found Devki weird. Her dressing sense seemed awful. *Looks like she wants to look like a teenager!*
She looked at Devki still standing at her door. *She can never be my mom.* Esha jumped from her bed furiously and slammed the door right on Devki's face.

Chapter 18

It was a sunny morning in July, when Jayesh rushed into the office, sprinting in excitement. "Hey, guys! I have some great news!" he announced as soon as he was inside. "Till yesterday we have sold 60,000 audio copies!"

Hooray!! Everyone hi-fived one other.

Jayesh spoke to Ian, "Now it's getting difficult to manage, we should register a company – your company."

Ian recalled their first day at recording. They had barely imagined that such a day will come. "Yes, we should. Consult Martha and do as appropriate," said Ian.

"Well, if the responsibility is on me, what should we name it?" asked Martha.

"I don't know! Call it Martha Inc."

"Or better Ian and Saira," added Martha. Everyone laughed. They all knew about the long-lost friend of Ian.

Mike thought for a minute and leaned forward, "How about 'Ian Speaks'? This name will convey what Ian is doing and what people expect from her."

After a lengthy discussion, they all agreed on the name of the company as 'IMS LLC' with 'Ian Speaks' as the brand name. The company was soon registered with Martha as a CEO of the company.

The business multiplied over the months. Although Martha managed things more out of office, she never missed to pick up and drop off Ian. Mike took care of the recordings and supervised the packaging. He was mostly busy with his instruments and wires – he enjoyed working with them. He ensured that Ian's voice sounded perfect on the audio and removed small glitches in the speeches. He also suggested some relevant topics. He came early and left late, dedicating his entire time for Ian's company.

Mike intentionally helped Ian, often in adjusting the headphones, in her office needs, etc. Once she caught him smelling her hair.

"Cannot help it, they smell heavenly," Mike laughed.

He deliberately took chances to touch her hands. He touched her waist on the pretext of correcting her posture. Ian liked the attention and loved his soft touch.

Whenever they got an opportunity, they ate together. Ian avoided restaurants, they usually stopped by at Mike's apartment, which was not far from their workplace.

Ian yearned to come to office every day, but speeches were not recorded frequently and even if she did come, her stay was short.

"So, you mentioned about having an Indian girlfriend!" Ian and Mike were having a casual chit-chat. Martha was not in, and other employees had gone out too. They looked for such occasions for some private time. Ian sat across the table from Mike, who was arranging some equipment.

"What a question early in the morning! And I've told you that I 'had'! I don't have any girlfriend right now."

Ian bit her lips.

Mike leaned forward, "Your work doesn't give me any free time to date anyone." He looked at Ian. *God, she is so beautiful!*

Ian put her hands through her hair, "So, what language did she speak?"

"What do you mean which language?" Mike blinked in confusion. "With me, she spoke in English, otherwise she also spoke an Indian language."

"Indian language!" Ian laughed, "Do you know India has some 45 languages?"

"What!" Mike's mouth fell open.

Ian leaned forward and dangled her feet toward Mike, "So, how was she?"

"It was way back, I hardly remember her now," Mike moved closer. "But I do remember one thing."

"And what's that?" Ian flipped her hair over her shoulders.

"I remember she never had beautiful hair like yours," Mike extended his arm and touched her hair. "She never had as smooth and glowing skin as you do." Mike softly rubbed the back of his palm on Ian's cheeks and let his voice linger.

Their eyes locked, they came so close that they could smell each other. Their lips were inches away when abruptly Ian broke the gaze, "Ok time for work," she said hastily and jerked back.

"Hey wait!"

Ian hurried toward her room. She knew his eyes would

follow her and she smiled to herself. Mike looked at her from behind, the way she walked, the way her hips swayed. He was out of breath.

Mike tried to focus on his work, yet his thoughts were flooded with Ian. He continued shifting the speakers, though his ears craved for her sounds. He could still smell her fragrance.

He felt warm in the room and sweated hard.

He was repairing a speaker when he heard Ian's shoes. She walked toward the bathroom, which was located on the far side of the office. One had to pass a small hallway to get to the bathroom; the hallway was filled with extra supplies. Ian threw a glance at Mike, who was down on the table.

Once in the bathroom, Ian checked herself in the mirror. She pushed her breasts up, adjusted her dress, took a tissue and dabbed her face and neck. Droplets of sweat shimmered on her forehead and her heart raced for no reason. After a few minutes, she stepped out.

A look at Mike increased Ian's palpitations. Mike stood in the hallway, drenched in sweat, with sleeves pulled back, arms stretched out as if waiting to embrace a storm. There was no way out, he was standing in the center of the hallway.

Ian took tiny steps and reached up to him; she softly pushed him on the chest, "Mike please…" Ian was startled as Mike caught her waist and pulled her close to him. He slipped his strong hand into her thick hair and planted his lips on to hers.

Oh God! This is happening! was the last thing Ian could think. Mike's lips were crushing and imploring. He pressed his lips hard on hers. Ian fought back and kissed him with the same intensity. They kissed for minutes. Their tongues touched.

Mike pulled her back gently by her hair and looked at her uplifted face. Ian trembled in his arms. "No Mike," moaned Ian still holding him tight.

"I love you!" Mike whispered into her ears.

Before Ian could think of anything, Mike lifted her and placed her on an abandoned table. She kissed him hungrily. Her hands slid beneath his shirt and clawed his back. His hands moved like an expert and explored her body. He started to unbutton her blouse.

Suddenly, Ian became aware of her condition – her scars.

He will know everything. He will hate me.

"Mike…Mike, please stop!" pleaded Ian. There was no way of stopping him. Using both her hands, Ian pushed him off with full strength.

Mike trembled, "I love you, Ian, I know you love me too."

"I don't know, I don't know Mike," Ian's voice was low.

"I want to have you, Ian. I am incomplete without you… please complete me!"

"No Mike. This is not the time, you… you got to wait."

Ian slid beside him and scurried away.

Although disappointed, Mike did not wish to compel her.

They smiled at each other the whole day. Mike ordered lunch and they ate together. The love birds' little hide and seek was interrupted only when Martha arrived to pick Ian.

Chapter 19

Traffic was the only thing that bothered Martha about the place, the subway train did not cover the whole city and the traffic got heavier during the peak hours. Nevertheless, Atlanta was the choice of millions. The weather was mostly pleasant, without any harsh winters, although the place witnessed ice rains a couple of times a year. The city was forced to shut down during those days, because of lack of equipment to tackle the ice.

But winters were still away.

Martha drove absentmindedly, with the traffic getting heavier. At an exit before Devki's house, Martha texted her as usual, "Coming in."

"No." Devki's reply came swiftly. *Perhaps some kid is sick or Gagan at home!* Martha drove back to the office.

Mike was waiting for Ian. Speeches were delivered twice a month and he ensured that they met the schedule. Ian's fans queued for her upcoming speeches.

Noticing Martha enter alone, Mike fumed, "We need Ian here, where's she?"

Martha nodded, "Should be in tomorrow."

Later in the day, Martha received a text from Ian, with only two letters - 'Aw'. Martha couldn't make any sense of it. She knew Devki avoided texting or calling when Gagan was at home. Martha waited for the next day to call Ian; it went straight to her voice message.

Mike paced angrily, "Where's Ian? If she delays, we'll miss the deadline!"

He couldn't comprehend all the complications – why no one else could contact Ian and what was holding her back from her schedule. He had the least idea why Martha made a big fuss to call her.

Martha, Mike, and Jayesh waited patiently for Ian to no avail. Martha's calls went unanswered and texts were undelivered. Ian knew the importance of the speech-recording-days. She never failed; whenever she was unable to come, she informed Martha. Daunting thoughts clouded Martha's mind. *Has Gagan learned about Ian's secrets? Is Devki sick or injured?* After a couple of days, Martha decided to visit Devki. There was not much risk since

Gagan was acquainted with her.

Martha chose mid-morning when there was the least chance of anyone else at home. She hit the call bell and waited for a few minutes. There was no answer. She pressed it again and knocked on the door. There was still no answer. Martha rested her ear on the door – nothing was heard from within either. *Looks like no one inside.* Martha slowly circled the house and went to the back porch. *Not a soul!*

All doors and windows were shut. Martha returned to her car, waited for a few minutes and left, confused and disappointed.

They waited for days, without any news from Ian.

*****

It all started a few days earlier…

"What's the surprise?" asked little Saira.

"How can I tell you baby? It's a surprise!"

"Enough of your surprises, Daddy," said Esha. "Last time you gave us a surprise and we ended up hiking for hours on Kennesaw mountain."

"This time it's different," said Gagan. "Better pack your swimsuits."

"Swimsuits!" Saira and Esha's eyes opened wide in surprise. "We are going to the beach!"

Gagan dropped a red and blue colored brochure on the table, "We are going on a cruise. We didn't take a vacation for a long time, so this will be a family fun time!"

"Yayyy!" the kids jumped with joy.

Devki looked blank, "Can we go somewhere else other than a cruise?"

"No questions asked, we are going to Jamaica and Haiti for a week. If possible, we can stop by at Miami on the way back," he announced.

Anxiety gripped over Devki, she cannot afford to be away for that long, she tried again, "One week! That's a long while away from home." Her recordings were scheduled over the coming days.

"Now don't be a spoil sport, tickets are already booked, so get ready now!" ordered Gagan. "This was supposed to be a surprise. We are leaving tomorrow."

"And please wear something different," advised Esha looking at Devki, "You always wear this uniform of yours."

Devki avoided her eyes. "I …I feel cold. Remember I am from India, we are used to covering ourselves."

Everything happened in such haste that Devki had no time to inform Martha. Her heart ached for her fans and she felt guilty that she couldn't notify anyone at her office.

*****

The whole family drove to Fort Lauderdale, Florida to board the cruise. It was a luxurious cruise liner. Devki had never seen anything like that before. The ship was like a five-star hotel moving on sea. It had 15 decks with some 2,500 staterooms. Gagan had booked two balcony rooms, one for Devki and himself and one for the kids. There was a lot of food, drinks, and activities on different decks. The ship left the port at 5 pm in the evening.

Devki looked out from the balcony, the waves splashed against the ship as if teasing it. She saw the blue of the ocean meeting the sky in the distance. There was nothing for miles, only water. She could see dolphins gliding away far into the ocean. The setting sun soon turned the water glittering golden orange. She loved beaches right from her childhood.

Devki recollected her trip to Goa with her parents when she was a little girl, they had great fun. Devki remembered running across the beach and spending a great deal of time in the water. She loved the big waves, and when it was getting late, she pleaded with her father, "One more big wave Papa! Bigger than this one please!"

Devki was still deep in her thoughts when Gagan wrapped his arms around her waist, "We will have some good time here." Devki nudged him away, being familiar with his idea of a good time. Gagan kissed her shoulders and leaned forward to kiss Devki on the lips, she turned her face and the kiss landed on her cheeks instead.

"Honey, why the heck do you wear this same dress forever? It's hot and for God's sake, wear something lighter."

Devki stared at him for a moment and shifted her gaze toward the horizon, "No, I like it this way."

It was five-day cruise with three days on the sea and two days on land. There were plenty of activities to keep the patrons entertained. There was twenty-four hours of food, with different cuisines. The best part was finding the food one liked. All that food made them hungrier and it was a great pleasure to eat while relaxing by the sight of the ocean. Devki was surprised when she got her favorite Dal and rice on the ship. She least expected Indian food, but she had never taken a cruise earlier. Plenty of activities, a variety of musical programs and dance shows kept the patrons occupied. The kids enjoyed movies on the topmost deck. People were reveling with each other all around. Devki was pleased to watch her daughters enjoying the cruise.

On the third evening, after dinner, Kajal suggested that they should walk through all the decks to explore the liner. The ship was huge, with a lot more to see. They started with the topmost deck and proceeded to the lower floors. On the fifth deck, they came across the auditorium, where they had watched a Roller-Skating musical during the day.

"Let's see what's going on now," said Gagan.

As they stepped in, the theater was empty. Devki had failed to notice the enormity of the hall earlier and it appeared bigger when vacant. There was a stage in the center, around which a large number of red colored chairs were neatly arranged.

"Now who wants to play a game?" Gagan challenged the girls.

"Like what?" Saira's eyes widened.

"You see, there's no one here and it's unlikely anyone will come, so why don't we become actors and perform among ourselves?"

Kajal scanned the place. "Wow Daddy! Brilliant idea! And we have a mic also. This will be great."

"That's awesome!" said Esha clapping, "Where do we start?"

"I'd suggest we go to the stage, and speak something, perhaps introduce ourselves or showcase our talent, whatever, like acting, singing or dancing."

"Yes, yes." Saira and Mini jumped in the air.

Saira raised her hand. "I'll go first." *She wants to be the first one every time!* Devki sighed.

Gagan adjusted the lights and sound using the knobs on the side of the wall.

Saira held the mic in front of her face, "I am Saira Mishra." The voice echoed and Gagan turned the knobs to reduce it.

106

Saira spoke again, "I am Saira Mishra. I like to play, dance and read." Her voice boomed in the empty hall.

"Read! Since when did you like reading?" Gagan guffawed. The family roared in laughter.

The kids went one by one and spoke about themselves. Kajal sang a song. Saira and Mini took the stage again and enacted a small play they had learned at school. Esha spoke about the new fashion look for the teens. Gagan also took the stage and spoke a few lines about himself and his achievements at work. Devki clapped for everyone.

"Now it's your turn mommy," Saira pointed her finger at Devki.

Devki crossed her arms. "Me? No way!"

"Come on, come on, mommy, mommy," the little ones cheered and Gagan joined them.

"I caca can't."

"Come on dear, play along with the kids, nothing serious," said Gagan.

"You can do it." Esha encouraged. Devki was surprised by her softer tone. *Perhaps the effect of this vacation.*

Devki walked up to the stage reluctantly and Esha handed her the mic. The mere touch of the microphone sparked new energy into Devki. She walked slowly on the stage and looked at the numerous vacant seats in front of her. She imagined an audience chanting her name, 'Ian! Ian!' She controlled the thought. Her knees trembled. She looked at Esha, Mini, Saira, Kajal, and Gagan. She forced her eyes to remain open. She missed her listeners.

"Go on," Gagan sat in the front seat.

Devki looked at Gagan. She pitied him. *One who thinks himself as the most powerful, is, in fact, the weakest, since he hides his insecurities.* Gagan failed to notice the fire in Devki's eyes which were glaring at him.

Esha looked at Devki. *She looks so nice. She would look beautiful if she takes a little care of herself. Why does she cover herself this much? She is always into extremes. Earlier she wore short skirts and now she wears such long ones. A little change in dress would make her look gorgeous.* Esha brushed off her thoughts.

Devki raised the microphone to her chin, "Hi Friends, this

is… Dd Devki." It was a forced voice.

"I..i frr Att attt." Devki pretended stuttering and took quick breaths faking it.

Gagan snickered, "Okay guys, it's over now. Time to catch some sleep."

On the fifth day, the liner returned to Florida. Gagan had next planned for a Miami and Key West island trip. Although Devki enjoyed the time out with the kids, she was anxious about her absence from recording.

*****

"I am back," the text message popped on Martha's phone. Martha rolled her eyes, after receiving the first text from Ian in two weeks. She wanted to relay a series of questions, but kept it brief with, "Ok. When are you coming to office?"

"Tomorrow."

Two weeks was a long time. The speech schedule was delayed for the first time. Ian's fans were disappointed. Some lost hope and concluded that Ian stopped her speeches forever. There were messages all across requesting Ian to come back. The delay was only a couple of weeks, yet it felt like ages for Ian's regular listeners.

Mike and Jayesh were upset, but Martha hushed them. There must be some reason. No one uttered a word to Ian.

Chapter 20

Neel looked at what he had written on the white board, 'Project: Finding Saira!'

He sighed and turned toward the others seated around the table, "Finding the footprints of Saira is not going to be easy." He continued, "Sarang and Manish, you should visit the 'Danik Jagran', daily newspaper office and request them access to their older newspapers. And Neeta, you should assist us in the research. You are the only one who could slip into Saira's shoes – try to grasp her mental state on that night and guess her move."
They all nodded.
Sarang, Manish, and Neeta discussed among themselves and headed toward the local newspaper office.

Neel looked at his diary and planned his next actions. *A visit to Saira's neighborhood should yield some information.* He checked the address once again, 'Chamanganj, SipriBazar'. Neel marched straight to the place, this time with a different mindset, looking for some clue, hoping to stumble upon some tip. It was located near the old railway bridge. A water storage tank and a Tonga stand were the landmarks. Tandon road ran perpendicular to the water tank and lead to the row of houses in the neighborhood.

Once in the locality, Neel familiarized himself with the surroundings. Numerous shops were lined on both sides of the street. The watch showed 1pm. Neel looked around and stopped at a tea stall at the corner of the street; the shop keeper was busy serving his customers. Neel ordered tea, which was served in a glass that had lost its luster ages ago. At another store, he stopped to munch on biscuits and at another, he bought a pen. He strolled around looking for some clue.

As he surveyed the street, Neel noticed a small barber shop, 'Menhattun haircutting salon', the neon sign glittered in red. Neel cracked a smile, *the owner must have thought of Manhattan of New York but had no clue of the spelling.*

Neel entered the shop and spotted a barber attending to a customer.

The man smiled, "Welcome to Keshav Das palace."

Keshav Das had long and braided hair, extending up to his lower back. He was in his mid-fifties but looked older than his age.

Earrings and rings in each finger gave him the look of a magician. While working on his customer's hair, he elaborated on international politics like an expert.

His tongue and scissors moved at a great speed. He seemed to be an encyclopedia, having information on everything and everyone.

"So how often do you travel?" asked the irked customer, peeved by the barber's blabbering.

Keshav sighed, "The love for this city never let me go out of the town."

Neel couldn't avoid laughing. *Hasn't stepped out of the city but has the knowledge of the whole world! Wonder if even the newspapers publish these news items!* The previous customer left and Neel was the next victim in the salon.

"You seem to laugh too much!" said Keshav. "Perhaps I gave you some reason for it."

"I'm amazed with the depth of your knowledge, that too without even leaving this place!"

Keshav squinted, "These are bits of news, you don't have to go anywhere to get them…they come to you!"

Neel took the chair before the mirror, "Okay! Okay! If you know everything, then tell me how much you know about this neighborhood!"

"Keshav knows everything, nothing passes by here without my knowledge," he thumped his chest.

"Then tell me something interesting. One of my friends is looking for a house to rent, I am checking a few places to see what works well for him."

"Is he new to Jhansi?!" asked Keshav excitedly. "Tell him that 'Major Dhyan Chand' was from this town!"

Aww! Neel yawned. *Who doesn't know about Dhyan Chand, the great hockey player?*

"Tell me something which no one knows. How is the locality? Are people friendly out here? What's special about this place? Neel pointed toward the houses across the street. "Tell me what cooks behind these doors."

Keshav started like a tourist guide, "This is an old place, most of the houses were built in the late fifties. Earlier, the houses had thatched roofs and I heard there were some cowsheds too, but things changed over time. Cow sheds have long gone, as generations passed, people reconstructed the houses."

"Hmm…"

Keshav sighed, "This was a peaceful place for long, but things changed one day."

"Really? What happened?"

Keshav's hands rested momentarily on Neel's hair as he focused.

He looked straight with a furrowed forehead and then started, "You know," Keshav broke the silence, "A few years ago a woman vanished from this neighborhood!"

"Who was she?" Neel turned on his chair.

"Her name was…Sa…sara…saro…" Keshav wrinkled his forehead, "I think her name was Saira."

Neel found it hard to hide his excitement, "Uh-Oh! Why did she vanish?"

Keshav spoke, recalling the olden times, "She was a nice lady. I remember seeing her when she came to this place soon after her marriage. I ate the milk cakes she distributed on some occasion." Keshav moved his palms on Neel's hair, "Not much was known about her maiden family."

Neel shut his eyes to gain more focus.

Keshav pointed in the general direction to the group of houses in the far end and spoke again, "She got married to Shakeel. He is a rascal and she was so sweet."

Neel could hear the sound of scissors close to his ears as Keshav continued, "She helped many families here. She taught the kids in the community, assisted in marriages and birthdays. She helped the young and old. She was there for everyone, but…" Keshav shook his head in disgust, "When she was in trouble, no one was there for her."

"What kind of trouble?" Neel's heart raced. He wished he could have recorded the conversation.

"That Shakeel was already an idiot. He beat her on small pretexts, but the real problem started when she did not get conceived."

"How do you know all this?"

"This is a small place. When something happens, people obviously notice!" Keshav frowned.

Keshav's hands paused as he meditated on his thoughts further. After a brief silence, he spoke again, "I heard that the doctors declared that she can never bear a child. Shakeel's family planned to get him married again – Saira was the roadblock in their plans."

Neel edged on his chair, Keshav pushed him back on the Chair's backrest and continued on his hair.

"Beautiful Saira was destroyed," Keshav halted. "The whole neighborhood knew how she was tortured by her husband and in-laws. People often spotted her with a swollen face,"

Oh, Saira! Neel Sighed. "Why did he not divorce her?"

"Ha! Divorce!" chuckled Keshav, "That would have costed them a huge sum and reputation in town. For them, it was better if Saira ran away on her own or died."

Keshav's voice cracked as he continued, "Saira died every minute. She had nowhere to go. No one was expecting her, no one wanted her."

"And then?" Neel's heart crunched for Saira.

"What will happen to such a girl…one night she vanished."

"Where, when?" In his anxiety, Neel closed and opened the strap of his wristwatch.

"No one had any clue. The Police were called. There was an investigation, but nothing came out of it. Some people hushed that her husband killed her but there was no proof."

Neel sat still in the chair.

Keshav shook his head in despair, "Shakeel waited a few months for things to settle and later got remarried."

Oh, God! Please keep Saira alive. She must not die! thought Neel.

Neel got up, "What do you think happened? Did her husband kill her?" Keshav pushed him back on the chair and spoke like a critic,

"Shakeel is undoubtedly a mean guy, but I don't think he would've gone to the extent of killing her. Perhaps she ran away or something else happened to her. Since no one looked for her, she was forgotten."

"Weird…how strange can someone's life be!" Neel let out his breath, he hadn't realized he was holding.

The conversation was coming to an end.

"Still this is not the weirdest part of this story!" whispered Keshav in Neel's ears.

Neel was confounded. Keshav beamed on seeing his customer's expression. He was proud about the way he unfolded the story and kept something for the end.

"What else is there? What's the other part?"

"On the same night, another girl disappeared from the neighborhood too," Keshav whispered again looking around as if someone may overhear them.

"What!"

"Yes, she was the next-door neighbor of Saira. She was the daughter-in-law of the house and was not known by many. The members of that household were private people. No one talked about them, they were rich and well-connected."

Neel's eyes popped with this new information.

Keshav continued, "The son was decent and didn't talk much, but his wife was cunning. She robbed them of cash and jewelry and absconded with his two babies."

Neel's face lost its color.

Keshav had more to say, "After she left, the house was more open to others. They cannot take the grief alone after all. That poor husband cried for weeks for his daughters."

Keshav paused and stared outside as if thinking of the past events. "Unfortunately, a few years after the incident, the whole family died in an accident."

Keshav looked around and whispered in Neel's ear, "I think, these two cases are linked."

"Which two cases?" jumped Neel, trying to comprehend this new information.

Keshav slammed his forehead and sighed on Neel's foolish question, "Perhaps Saira's absence has something to do with that other girl, who seemed to be criminal minded. But what can we say…these are just speculations."

Neel made a mental note of all the important points and looked at himself in the mirror. He had been too engrossed in the discussion that he had failed to check his hair. Horrified, he looked at Keshav and again at himself in the mirror. He was nearly bald!

"Keshav! What the hell happened here?!"

"Sorry sir, the story grew longer, and the hair got shorter!"

Keshav grinned.

*****

Neel rushed to his office. The team was back too. The juniors exploded into a roar seeing Neel's new hairstyle. Neeta was the first one to speak and explained that no useful information could be obtained from the newspaper office. Neel shared about his interesting meeting with Keshav.

*****

It was late at night. Neeta lay awake. She checked her watch. The time was 12.30 am. She contemplated her next move. She deliberated a little more and at last dialed the number. After many rings, the phone was answered. Neeta relayed the information to the intent listener, and they both promised to secrecy and disconnected the phone.

The next morning, the sun was friendlier than usual. Neel and team discussed various options. The pressing question was – if Saira did leave her house, where did she go? Who was the other girl who lived next door and what was the connection between them? *Is Saira still alive?*

Neel insisted. "Let's assume for now that she's alive since we have no evidence of her death!"

Neel was drawing a map on the board, when the phone rang. Neel hit the speaker phone, puzzled, "Hello."

"Hi Neel, this is Martha". It was several weeks since Martha spoke to him. With his mind occupied by Saira, Neel almost forgot whom he was working for.

He went blank on hearing Martha's voice. "Martha I'm sorry for what happened last time," Neel spoke in haste, fearing she would disconnect the call soon.

"That's okay!" said Martha. "You promised me that you will find Saira. Did you start on it?"

"Yes, and we've got some useful information." Neel narrated their approach and all the progress to her. Martha was receptive. She appeared surprised when Neel mentioned the possibility of another girl with Saira, although Neel couldn't give any further details to her.

"Now that's some progress. I will transfer the money to your account soon."

"You don't have to send any money, I promised you that I will do it on my own. I made a mistake and I should compensate for it."

"That's all right my dear. Humans make mistakes and everyone deserves a second chance. Also, I'm sending money to speed up my work. Keep me posted on the progress," said Martha and disconnected.

Neeta looked at her toes and smiled.

Chapter 21

Esha banged the book against her forehead in despair. She hated economics assignments. All the other subjects were manageable, but economics was "Argh!"

The deadline to submit the assignment in her class approached, but she was nowhere near completing it. Gagan wanted to help her, but with his tight schedule, he was unable to devote any time for her. He had got a new position in his company which involved longer hours of work.

It was late in the evening after dinner. Esha worked on her school essay while cursing under her breath and jolting her books.

Gagan stared out of his laptop, "Watch your language!"

Devki was loading the dishwasher. "I think I can help you."

"You! Ha-ha!"

"Yes, why not?"

"If I get an assignment on cooking and cleaning, I sure will come to you!" Sarcasm overflowed in Esha's voice.

"Cooking and cleaning are my areas of expertise now." Devki wanted to make the environment light. "But I have other specialties too."

"Like what, name one!" Esha mocked as she continued to work on her assignment.

"Like I'm a postgraduate in management with distinction and an economics topper."

Esha's mouth fell open. She looked at her dad – he nodded.

"So, you did receive an MBA – Master of Business Administration?!" uttered Esha in disbelief. A few years earlier, Esha had heard from some relative that her Dad's new wife was a Management graduate, but she did not understand then and cared less.

Esha raised her eyebrow. "When did you do your MBA, in 1957?... Times have changed now!"

"Well, my college days were not that far and once an MBA, always an MBA." Devki continued, "Also, Keynesian theory of Employment will not change from my time to yours."

Esha kneeled on the couch and raised her head to stare at Devki. *This lady knows her stuff.* Esha observed Devki – *she looks different.* Esha noticed her on the cruise too. The usual turtleneck kind of top was there…but a longer skirt replaced the mini skirt; she wore flats instead of heels; lesser makeup revealed her real beauty. Her speech was coherent of late. *Why the hell did she wear those horrible dresses earlier?! She's changing.*

"For now, I can manage on my own!" Esha grabbed her books and walked toward her bedroom. *I will not give in to this woman, a pretend mom after all!*

Gagan sighed, "Don't know what happened to this girl. Her grades are falling, and she's brazen. She's become worse in the last few years!" He closed his laptop.

"Have you heard about Ian? Heard her motivational talks are useful for kids," said Devki.

"Ian," Gagan rubbed his temples, "Yea, someone did refer this name at my office too. I'll check it out."

Gagan noticed Devki adjusting the cushion over the couch. "What are you up to?"

"What does it look like?" Devki avoided his curious glances. "I am going to sleep."

"You will sleep here …not in the bedroom?"

"Nah! I feel like sleeping on the couch tonight. And I'll be watching TV for some time. Don't want to disturb you."

Gagan stared at Devki who was already placing the pillow and a sheet on the bigger couch. *She's changing of late. She doesn't care much about what I say. The way she dresses has changed too. The other night, she pushed me away saying she was exhausted. What's happening? And why? Perhaps she's spending too much time with that Martha. Her stuttering has reduced too.*

The changes occurring in Devki made Gagan uneasy. *I need to do something before she goes over my head. Maybe she forgot who wears pants in this house!*

Gagan turned in his bed as he lay awake. There was no sound of the TV. Devki slept like a baby on the couch.

*****

The date to submit the assignment drew closer and Esha hadn't made any headway. She hated the very idea of asking help from Devki but could not figure out any other solution.

A few days had passed, the family had finished dinner, and was relaxing before the television.

"What would happen if I don't complete my assignment?"

Esha talked to herself loudly.

"You will get an F grade!" said Gagan. He was too tired to get involved into anything.

Kajal was flipping channels on TV and the little ones were busy on their mobile devices.

"Stop that TV!" screamed Esha. She snatched the remote from Kajal and switched off the TV. "I am trying to study here, and you guys are disturbing me!"

Gagan wrapped his laptop. "Okay! At least I will not disturb you!"

Devki addressed the little ones, "It's time for you sweeties to go to sleep and stop harassing your sister!"

The little ones looked annoyed but understood the tense situation. They walked to their bedroom...eyes still glued on their tablets.

Esha threw her books on the table. "Who cares about these silly demand and supply graphs! No one bothers about these things in today's world. I don't know why the teachers insist on this! I don't care if I fail!" she talked to herself.

"Do you want me to help you?" asked Devki.

"No need! It is not as easy as you think, and I'm not even interested in this subject."

"Let me see...where do we start?" Devki pulled the books closer to her.

Esha blew out her cheeks, "Suit yourself!" and slapped the assignment paper on the table. As Devki read the questions, Esha switched on the TV. Devki took a fresh sheet of paper and started writing and drawing the x-axis and y-axis. Esha glanced sideways at Devki and noticed her being fully immersed into the books. She slowly reduced the volume for Devki to work undisturbed.

Devki opened the laptop after her paperwork. Her fingers smoothed on the computer, leaving Esha gawked – for she had only seen Devki chopping vegetables and doing household chores. Esha looked at Devki's fingers on the keyboard, her hands, her hair, her face, and dress. *She isn't that bad! But why is she helping me? Perhaps out of spite or wants to show how small I am and how big she is. But she has this look which ...which moms usually have. Soft, loving and understanding.*

Esha despised her thoughts. "Stop it...stop it...I say!"

"It's near completion. I wrote pointers for you to follow and ..."

Esha snapped the laptop to close, "I said I'm not interested in this subject. I don't need any help. If needed, I'll do on my own." Esha collected all her books and computer and hurried to her room.

Devki smiled – even in her anger, Esha carefully folded Devki's work sheet and took it along.

*****

The whole class applauded as their teacher spoke highly of Esha's work.

"This is precisely how it should be structured!" admired Mrs. Hancorn. Later, she told Esha, "If you focus like this, no one can stop you from earning excellent grades and entering into a reputed college."

It had been long since Esha received such positive feedback at school. She held her head high, proud of herself and her stepmother. Esha rushed home after school, excited and elated.

Devki was at home as usual. *Does she go out anywhere at all?* thought Esha.

Esha looked at Devki with soft eyes, she had an unusual feeling, which she could not describe. Esha bit her lower lip, paused for a second, "Thank…thank you Devki."

"Thank you for what?" Devki raised her eyebrows in surprise.

"Thank you for helping me! I was highly appreciated!" Esha twisted her face in embarrassment. She had never spoken to Devki like this before. This was a rare occasion.

Devki waved her hand, "Oh, it was nothing; in fact, I scribbled something, but it was you who did a brilliant job in expanding the thought."

Esha smiled.

"If you still want to thank me then keep your bags and shoes in place once in a while – that'd put me in less trouble."

"Yes, of course, we all should!" Esha continued, "Can I ask you one more favor? Can you accompany me when I am learning to drive? I sometimes go with Dad but he yells at me almost every time."

"Yes dear, anything for you."

Devki liked both Esha and Kajal. She sympathized for the mental agony they had gone through but also understood that she could never be accepted as their mother. She was called by her name, nevertheless, she was slowly making progress in scoring their hearts.

Esha and Kajal spoke regularly to their grandmother and aunt Renu, who showered them with utmost love and affection.

Devki also spoke to her in-laws quite often. She respected them for their support, but it was evident that they were trying to cover-up Gagan's shortcomings by turning a blind eye. They were making her emotionally weak, to be mellowed in front of Gagan.

Devki was able to apprehend everyone's emotions, but there was none to understand her feelings. Gagan's treatment toward her was terrible. He had no respect for her. He was rude during the day and abusive at nights. He had eternal complaints and demands, but, whom could Devki complain to or confide into?

She had sleepless nights feeling anxious about her daughters. *What if something happens to me, who will take care of them?* She was terrified by the thought of returning to India. Things which had occurred in the past gave her a cold sweat.

Chapter 22

It was late in the evening, "Got some mails." Gagan threw a handful of envelopes on the table, some open and some still sealed.

Devki looked at one of the postal mails that was marked 'USCIS- U.S. Citizenship and Immigration Services.' It was from the visa department.

Gagan relaxed on the couch and folded his arms behind his head, "These people keep on asking some documents from me in support of your visa application."

He stretched his legs on the table, "They always need something or the other, I am tired of them. How many documents can I send?" He looked at Devki a little longer and continued, "Should we do all this work when you don't even like being here?"

Devki squirmed by Gagan's stare. "Who wo sasa said I don't lik like being here. I love it here," She winced, her older way of speaking surfaced.

Devki's dependency on Gagan for her visa became his trump card. "Don't know...will see to it later!" Gagan tossed the mail into the trash bin.

Devki stared at the bin – a ticket to her freedom. "You u look ee aa exhausted...I will cook something nice." Gagan did not care to respond, he simply walked to his room to change.

Shortly after, Devki walked in. Gagan lay in bed, his eyes closed and resting.

"Shall I ma mmm massage you...," whispered Devki, walking toward him in a short skirt and high heel boots. Gagan's eyes opened half way and then closed.

As Gagan slept, Devki walked toward her closet to change but the door didn't budge. She had accidentally latched it from inside earlier. The only way left for her was to go out of the room and open it from the other side. She slowly came out of the bedroom and carefully closed the door behind her.

Esha was flipping channels on TV – the sound of the door upstairs made her turn back. She saw Devki holding her shoes in one hand and adjusting her skirt with the other. A look at Devki filled Esha with disgust. Devki could not take Esha's glaring eyes.

This lady will never change. Esha threw the remote on the ground and walked out of the house.

"Esha wait, I wish I can explain!"

Esha slammed the door.

Chapter 23

Finding Saira was a self-imposed mission for Neel. He wanted to find her to remove the blemish he had thrown upon himself. Martha had smeared his face with the word 'fraud'. He was not a fraud – he was trying hard to make his ends meet.

He learnt a great deal while searching for Saira. He was becoming a true detective. His curiosity grew manifold after each step. *Where did Saira go!*

After gaining substantial details from Keshav, Neel made the local police station his next stop. The staff were acquainted to him through his earlier visits, usually for background checks on prospective hires or grooms.

"What's the point in looking for documents on that woman?" inquired the constable. Work was never a pleasure to him. He was responding to Neel's request for the details on Saira's case. "Why do you show interest, when her own family didn't bother?"

"As a detective, I look for unresolved questions," explained Neel taking a sip of his tea from a small plastic cup.

"Interesting!" said Constable dryly and raised his eyebrows. "You can look at the files but make sure you don't increase any work for us. This is a cold case, and no one turned up asking for the lady and we have many other urgent cases to chase – cannot reopen this old crap."

Neel scanned the heavy-set constable. The buttons on his shirt seemed to struggle for breath under his large pot belly. *Other cases to chase...ha!* chuckled Neel.

The Constable ushered Neel to a large room at the back of the building through a narrow passage. The room was loaded with files and papers; several wooden filing columns occupied the space. Each column had a name and number. The room had an aura of a library. There were hundreds of files, log books, clipped papers in the shelves. Lots of paper lay scattered on the ground too.

Two clerks sat behind a metal desk, busy in making some entries in big registers.

How on earth will they locate Saira's file in such a mess! The Constable pulled out three or four registers, his forehead wrinkled as he checked the entries.

Neel grew weary on seeing all the clutter, "Don't you have a computer?"

"Mr. FBI, you are standing in a small police station in Jhansi, not in a metro!" the Constable cracked at Neel. Everyone laughed at the joke.

At last Saira's file was located, *Phew!* sighed Neel. It was a large folder, with pages like bank ledgers. The size of the document was disheartening. *It will take hours to go through all these pages.*

"Will you allow me to call my assistant?" asked Neel. "We can go through these documents faster and won't take much of your time."

"You can take these files to the room outside and call your assistant. It's fine, as long as you are done by the end of the day."

Neel immediately called Neeta – the only person he could think of, for such a work.

Neel sat outside in a smaller room, with the thick file on the table. The monsoon rains made the room hot and humid. Sweat dripped from Neel's head onto his cheeks and chin. He wiped his face profusely with his sleeves.

Neeta arrived soon. It had started to rain unexpectedly and caught her off guard. She wore a light blue tight-fitting salwar-kurta which got drenched in the pouring rain. Neeta attempted to dry her hair with her dupatta and wrung the corners of her top. Her wet figure left Neel mesmerized. Enthralled by Neeta's beauty, he pulled his shirt with two fingers and blew some air inside. Neeta turned red at his action.

Neel opened the thick file and took half of the pages out from the punch-hole. He handed the file to Neeta and got immersed in the other half. The file contained pages of investigation details regarding Saira's disappearance.

The testimonies of Saira's husband Shakeel and her in-laws irked Neel. Shakeel had stated how much he loved and missed her. His parents had asserted about their cordial relationship with Saira and that there was no reason for her to run away. There were statements from neighbors too, all of which refuted anything abnormal in Saira's life. Neel fumed with anger after reading all the lies. If he had not received first-hand information from Keshav, he would have considered them all to be true. He made notes of everything that seemed important.

Neeta skimmed through similar pages. She read and flipped each page but found nothing useful. She was about to give up when something caught her eye.

She read through it twice and thrice and called Neel to come over.

It was a testimony from an auto-rickshaw driver named 'Ram Bharose'. He had recounted seeing Saira with another woman at around 1am on the night when Saira disappeared. The ladies had asked him for a ride but he refused since he was exhausted and off shift.

The Police interrogated him but couldn't validate his story. His statements were later disregarded as a hallucination of a drunkard. He seemed to be the last person to have seen Saira.

Neel was excited for having landed on to a critical information, at least they gained something useful after rambling through the piles of sheets. He searched for Ram Bharose's address or contact number but in vain.

It was way past five in the evening when Neel and Neeta finished their probe on Saira's documents. The sun dazzling after the showers, provided no respite from the heat.

"Your work timings are over, but if you like to have tea with your boss, you are more than welcome," suggested Neel as they walked out of the police station.

"Why Dubey Ji, offering only tea after such a tiresome day? And who would want to drink tea in such a hot weather?"

Neel smiled at her. "How about some fruit juice instead?"

"Yes, some juice and also something to eat, I am starving!"

Neel took his chances, "Or maybe dinner?"

"We still have time for dinner, first let me quench my thirst and will see about dinner later."

Neel grinned as they walked toward a juice bar. No girl had ever gone out with him. He had never asked a girl out in his life, considering himself unfit for the honor. Neel halted abruptly as Neeta stopped him in the last minute by pulling his hand, a car sped by in front of him. "Look out for the traffic Dubey Ji!"

*****

Neel dialed Martha, early next day. "I have an update," said Neel as soon as Martha came on the phone.

"I'm listening."

Neel narrated his visit to the Police station and about his new discovery regarding an Auto driver.

Hmm… what's this auto? Perhaps a cab! thought Martha.

"But the police have rejected Ram Bharose's claim since he is drunk most of the time," added Neel.

Martha paused for a minute. "This is the only lead you've got so far. I would suggest you locate this driver and have a word with him. Will it be too taxing?"

"Shouldn't be a big problem. I'll inquire about him with other drivers. He must be known for his drinking."

"Good luck!"

Chapter 24

Finding Ram turned out to be easier than Neel had thought. When Neel and Neeta inquired about Ram Bharose at the auto stand, "Oh, that drunk and imbecile Ram," reacted one auto driver. "Is he in trouble? I knew one day he will knock someone in his inebriate state."

On assurance that Ram was not into any trouble, they directed Neel to some local bars. There were some ten unkept bars, lined one after the other. Neel checked the bars one by one in a hope to spot someone like Ram. It proved difficult to search for someone without a picture or an identification.

Finally, outside one dilapidated bar, Neel noticed a haggard and old drunk man in a driver's uniform. The khaki colored uniform looked old and wrinkled, much like its owner. Neel motioned Neeta in the direction of the man and whispered slowly. "Looks like our search is over."

"You take it from here," said Neeta. "I cannot stand this place. The smell is nauseating!"

"Okay, you make a move, I'll catch up with you later."

*****

Neel got himself seated next to the drunken stupor, lying on the sandy unpaved ground. To reassure his conclusion, he looked around and shouted, "Ram!"

"Eh?" the man responded immediately.

Neel smiled, "I'm going inside the bar, want to accompany me?"

There was excitement in Ram's eyes, but he resisted. "Do I know you? Why are you offering me?"

If this man could talk to the police, he will be interested in talking to others too.

Neel whispered in Ram's ears, "I am looking for someone and I hope you can help me."

"Me!" sneered the old man, "People call me a lost man."

"Only you and your knowledge can fulfill my need!"

The man looked at Neel with suspicion, "What do you want?"

"I am looking for a woman and..."

"Woman! What do you think I am? A pimp?!" the man

laughed shamelessly, hitting the bare ground with his palms. The dust on the ground entered his nostrils and he coughed.

Neel looked at him in distaste. *How do I get him to talk?*

He moved a little closer, "Can you help me in that missing woman's case? We need a hero like you."

"Which...which woman?"

"The woman who went missing on that night. Her name was Saira, I think you were the last one to see her. Do you still remember her?"

Ram squatted on the ground. "How can I forget anything like that? Such things don't happen every day, but if you talk about it, people think you're a fool."

"I don't think so, that's why I came to you."

Ram stared at Neel with his red eyes. The strong smell of alcohol from his mouth revealed his recent intake. He spoke in a low voice, "You want some information on that Saira murder case?"

"Murder!"

"Yes, murder! The world thinks that she ran away but no one knows she was murdered!" Ram flapped his feeble arms. "I tried telling everyone, I told the police too. They never cared to listen to me and ignored me as a drunkard." Neel tried to hush him. Ram coughed and spoke again, "I was the last one to see her, still, no one believes me. Do I look drunk and insane to you too?"

"Not at all!" said Neel trying to quieten Ram. Neel looked deep into the man's eyes, "I need a drink, are you coming along?"

Ram nodded and picked himself up.

The bar was small, with a thatched roof. It was late in the afternoon and the place was less crowded. The anticipation of a drink shook Ram's limbs. It was only a few hours since he had a drink, but his body was already craving for it. Neel ordered a bottle with two glasses though he didn't plan to drink.

The sound of liquor being poured into the glass, played music in Ram's ears. His cheeks flushed red as he looked greedily at the glass and took a large gulp and one more.

Finally, he spoke, "I don't drink often, since you seem to be a nice guy and it is about the lady." Ram took another big gulp of his drink.

"You are amazing!" Neel tried in vain to keep himself

away from the smell of the cheap liquor. "So, what were you saying?" Neel leaned forward. "Where did Saira go?"

Ram took quick gulps out of his glass and licked his lips, "She did not go anywhere, she was killed!"

"What?! Why do you say that? She may have gone away!"

"Did they ever find her? ... No, and that's because she was murdered."

"In that case, who killed her?" Neel sat on the edge of his chair – eyes glued on Ram.

Ram looked around suspiciously and took a few more gulps. His experienced eyes measured the quantity left in the bottle, "I will tell you, I even told this to the police…"

"What?"

"Saira was murdered by a woman she accompanied that night!"

"What!" Neel tried hard to grasp the whole thing. He recalled Keshav's comment on the other woman who vanished the same night as Saira.

"Yes. The other woman was a criminal, the whole neighborhood knows about her, still no one wants to talk because she was from an affluent family."
"Who was this other woman?"

Ram continued, "This other lady was Saira's neighbor. I didn't know then, but later heard from others. She ran away with her two babies and a lot of money. She is the one who murdered Saira too."

Neel was unable to grasp the new information. "Why would she do that, and how do you know about it?"

"I don't know why she killed her," Ram contemplated and sat back on his chair, "Maybe because she didn't want any witness, or it could be for money."

"Money! But…" Neel's voice was cut as Ram continued, "I was there!" Ram slapped his chest, "but was unable to save her." Ram produced a fake cry without tears.

"How can you be this certain that the other lady killed Saira?"

Ram frowned, "Because these eyes have seen everything." Ram pointed at his eyes and in his drunk state, put his own finger in his eyes and winced with pain.

"Did you see her killing Saira?" Neel's head was about to explode.

"My eyes never miss a thing. There was an exchange of money between the two women. Saira gave away all her money to this lady. She wanted to leave, and tried to run away, but that horrid woman stopped her and pulled out a weapon from under her dress."

"Weapon! What weapon? Did you see her kill Saira? Why didn't you intervene?"

"See, I told you everything and now you don't trust me. You are like those policemen who don't want to believe me. Did you also take some bribe from that other woman's family?"

"Did you see where this woman went after the act?"

Ram moved his head in denial, "Saw her running in the direction of the railway station. That is all I know!"

"Why didn't you save someone getting killed in front of your eyes?" Neel almost cried.

"I die of guilt every day that I couldn't protect that poor lady. I was tired because of my 12-hour day shift and I am an old man; got scared of the weapon." Ram hid the truth that he was too drunk to even move.

"Okay, okay," said Neel. "If Saira was killed, where is her body? No one ever found her corpse."

"I told you what I knew." Ram's whisper changed into a yell. He pushed the chair behind him, but his feet were unsteady; losing his balance, he stumbled under his own weight first onto the chair and landed on the ground with a thud, knocked out.

Neel couldn't believe what he had heard moments ago. The details given by the drunkard were unbelievable, *can this guy really be trusted? When no one believed Ram's account, not even the police, on what basis can I consider it to be true? We're searching for Saira as a needle in a haystack. Martha doesn't have much details about her either.*

It is obvious from Martha's calls and persistence that Saira is important to her and Martha is looking for Saira on behalf of someone else; who could that be? Perhaps this was the other lady with Saira? Neel abandoned the thought. He must not make wild assumptions. *I have no option other than to follow Ram's account.*

131

I have at least something in hand, I should investigate further on this.

Saira was accompanied by a woman… possibly her neighbor – a woman with two babies. Saira had no money and got killed in a scuffle or robbery. The other woman ran in the direction of the railway station. If she boarded the train, where did she go? There are thousands of possibilities, but, above all, can a woman carrying two babies kill someone? And if she did, how did she dispose off the body? Weird! Neel was drained. *I better share this with Neeta and get her input.* The last thing he had anticipated was Saira's death. *I should relay this information to Martha as soon as possible.*

Chapter 25

Time flew as if it had wings. Nature displayed the change by using its vibrant colors. Beautiful red, orange and yellow leaves carpeted the ground. The trees shed their leaves and promised to grow new ones soon.

Devki, as Ian, worked on her speeches with absolute commitment. Her talks brought joy to her listeners and she hoped one day they will bring freedom to herself and her daughters. Ian produced one magic after another and earned acclaim everywhere. When Jayesh informed about her audios getting international attention, Ian was filled with awe. *Something which I was so reluctant to start, is now crossing boundaries!*

On a crisp beautiful morning, Mike and Ian were the only ones at the office. Martha had gone to a meeting, and the other employees were outside for a big consignment.

Ian was rehearsing an upcoming speech. "Don't lose the power given to you by God!" spoke Ian to the audience who was none other than Mike.

Mike blew a kiss at Ian, "You Miss! Give your power to me!" He moved forward, kissed her neck and earlobes. Ian blushed red.

"Stop it, Mike, let me do my work," Ian stroked his hair. Their relationship had only grown stronger after the previous incident.

"Hey, come on! You're working forever, grant some time for love too." Mike took her in his arms, "Shall we go to my apartment?"

"Not now Mike, got a lot of work to do!"

Business had grown much over the months. Ian and Mike behaved like normal colleagues in the presence of other employees, but they looked for an opportunity when no one was present.

"You are shameless! Lifting your boss like this!" said Ian coyly, her face turned red with the thrust of blood. Her neck rested on Mike's shoulders.

"I'll show you in a minute, who the boss is!" Ian jittered seeing the hunger in Mike's eyes. He untied her hair and smelled them. He moved her hair to one side and kissed the side of her neck. Soon Mike's hands were on her top, trying to unbutton it.

Ian got hold of his hands in the last minute, "No...No Mike stop it!" she panicked.

Mike ignored her pleading and continued.

"Stop it, Mike!"

"Why...why should I stop?" demanded Mike, "Don't you love me? We've been together for a long time now!" Mike threw his hands in the air. "I haven't seen you full till now. Why don't you let me? What's stopping you? Answer me!"

She sat motionless with watery eyes. She yearned for Mike too but was left with no option.

Mike stared at her from a distance. "I want you, Ian. I want the whole of you. I want to see your full body, everything, every spot, and every mole!"

"I don't understand what difference it makes!" pleaded Ian. She tried to grasp Mike's hand, but he moved away.

"It does make a difference to me. Why you don't give it to me? I don't ask you any uncomfortable questions, I want you." Mike turned back, "Here, everyone has to sign some secrecy agreement and I am okay with it, but don't you think I deserve more than others? Don't I have the right to know everything about you?"

"Give me some time!" begged Ian.

"How much time and why?"

"As much time as I want."

"I know you are married and have kids, but where do I stand? What's our future? What's going on around you that requires all this secrecy?"

Ian stared at Mike for a moment, her lips quivered, she turned back and stormed into her room. Mike followed her but Ian slammed the door. Mike tried to push the door in vain, it was latched from inside.

"I ...I am sorry," said Mike.

Ian's muffled voice was heard outside. Mike hated himself for behaving like a jerk.

During lunch time, Mike knocked on Ian's door but there was no answer. He called her on the desk phone, it went unanswered. Mike winced at his behavior. *She is so sweet, and I am so rude, but why does she behave like this?*

Martha returned late in the afternoon. As she walked in, she juggled with her purse and documents. "This place is sometimes too silent for a recording studio," commented Martha and looked at Mike.

Though Ian and Mike never confided in her, Martha knew something was cooking between them. She was happy for Ian. Despite knowing less about her personal life, she was convinced that Ian deserved extra love and care.

The room was locked. Martha knocked twice and called. The door opened. Ian appeared at the door with a puffed face…

Hmmm! She's had a good deal of crying! This was not unusual to Martha. She was aware of Ian's mood swings. She would cry or laugh for some reason or no reason at all.

"Time to go boss." She kept all the files on her table. Ian left her chair without any expression. "You are doing awesome," Martha pointed at the documents on the table trying to lighten her mood. Ian did not respond. She walked silently toward Martha's car and took her seat.

The boisterous traffic couldn't penetrate into the dead silence inside the car.

Martha sensed Ian's uneasiness, "Are you feeling okay?"

"Martha, did I tell you how much I appreciate you around me?" Ian failed in her smile.

"Okay! This is news to me," tittered Martha.

"I am nothing without you. You are everything to me." Ian sobbed.

"I am always with you dear, but what happened, why don't you tell me? You'll feel light, maybe I can be of some help."

"I know! Devki doesn't exist without Martha."

"Hey better make it Ian. Let Devki go."

Ian laughed after many hours.

Chapter 26

Martha answered the phone on the first ring, she was anxious for some positive news.

"I have an update," said the caller. "I was able to locate the auto driver and got some intriguing piece of information."

Martha pressed the receiver hard on her ears. "Tell me...tell me...fast...quick!" She did not want to miss out a word.

"Before I go on, I'd like to warn you," said Neel. "It's tough to believe this weird guy, I mean this auto-driver; even the police did not pay any heed to his testimony."

"Testimony!"

"Yes, the police report says he was the last one to see Saira, yet the police never bothered to follow his lead."

Martha took a deep breath, "Okay. Tell me whatever he told you." She opened her drawer and looked for a pen and paper to write on.

"This guy mentions the presence of one more person with Saira on the night she disappeared." Neel took a dramatic pause and continued, "A woman with two babies."

"Another woman," Martha listened attentively. "I remember you telling me about this lady earlier too."

"Yes. This guy has witnessed all. That woman had two babies and she ran away on the same night too."

"Hmmm, a woman with two babies," Martha chewed on Neel's words, getting curious. Devki had never discussed much about Saira. *If there was another lady with Saira, who could it be?*

"According to this eyewitness, there were two women that night. One had to be Saira and another lady...a neighbor of Saira. It seemed that they were running away from something or someone."

Martha's brain churned the information, *One more woman... with two kids. Whom could it be? Neighbor?* She thought for a minute. *Could it be Devki herself?*

"Also..." Neel interrupted Martha's thoughts.

"What ...what else did he say?"

"He says the women were in some desperate situation, the other woman took all the money from Saira and..."

"And?"

"And," Neel paused, hesitated for a moment, "The other woman might have killed Saira."

"What!" gasped Martha.

"We need not believe all that he told," said Neel unconvincingly. "These drunkards hardly know what they are talking about."

"Did he say where the other lady went? Didn't the police arrest her?"

"I asked him the same, he says she ran toward the railway station. The Police may have never found her."

A sudden chill swept over Martha. She recalled the day when Jayesh had asked Devki to record speeches and Devki had hesitated. When Martha inquired why she was so scared…Devki had said …Martha could still recall Ian's exact words – "Do you know how hard it is to hide when police in a different country are looking for you? Do you know how it feels not being able to go to your country or call your family?"

And the name Ian Scovich, Martha thought hard, *who can come up with such a strange name?*

When Martha asked Devki who Ian Scovich was, Devki had said, "Some Russian Mafia."

Has Devki been fooling me all along? Why the hell was she this persistent in the search for Saira? Is there something more to Devki's story, something sinister?

A maze of thoughts ran across Martha at lightning speed. Her mouth opened out in a cry… the sound died behind her vocal cord.

Oh…my… God! Did Devki murder Saira?! Did she deliberately put me on this task to learn if the cops were still looking for her back in India? Martha's knuckles were in her mouth.

She tried hard to compose herself, "How is that auto driver so confident about the murder?" She wanted more affirmation.

"He has seen everything that night. He stated that Saira was, in fact, running away from that woman, but she stopped Saira and pulled out a weapon from under her dress. This guy is the only one who saw Saira last."

"Oh God!" Martha cried.

"I will still suggest you not to believe him. These addicts

can hallucinate anything. Even the police weren't convinced! There's no information about Saira's death in police records, if at all this lady had killed Saira."

What to believe and what not to! There was something more to the story.

As far as I know Devki, she can never kill anyone in this world, but do I know Devki at all? She is always elusive about her past. Martha cursed herself for being stupid and used. She knew nothing about the actual Devki.

How can I be so gullible? I believed whatever information Devki gave me.

"What do you think about this lead, Neel?"

"I...Me," Neel hesitated. "Based on the facts, this guy has been recorded by the police. And the way he described the events, it does look like he was there. Also, the story about the other girl vanishing the same night, has been confirmed by others too...so I think..."

Martha cut him off, "What do you think, tell me fast!"

Neel's voice cracked, "I think, at least some part of the story is true."

Martha breathed heavily over the receiver.

Neel sensed a delay, he paused and continued, "Do you know this other woman? Is she your...?"

Neel heard a click and the line went dead.

Martha's face hardened. *I will get to the bottom of the story. I need to find out who this real Devki is.*

*****

Martha texted other employees to take a day off, citing some urgent repair work. She next hit the road to pick Devki up from her house. It was still early in the morning, Martha waited at a gas station not far from Devki's house and later drove to her house.

Martha gunned the engine as soon as Devki took her seat. Martha stayed silent during the drive. Intrigued by her silence and coldness, Devki asked, "Everything okay?"

Martha cared not to respond and kept driving. As they approached the office, Devki noticed the empty parking lot.

"Is no one coming in today?"

"I gave them off!"

"Why? What's going on Martha, won't you tell me?"

Martha swirled the car into one of the parking slots and brought it to a screeching halt. She looked blankly out of the windshield, "I need to give you some important information."

"Is something wrong?"

Martha stepped off the car and walked in haste toward the building, Devki sprinted behind to catch up with Martha's pace. The silence during the elevator ride was torturous.

Martha stopped in front of the entrance and gestured, "After you Madam Ian."

"What's this Martha? Why all this drama, tell me what's going on?"

"Have a seat, I have some news for you." Martha latched the door behind her, not wanting to take any chance, despite the place being empty.

Ian guessed the gravity of the situation. She took her seat and edged forward over the desk.

"Tell me now, I'm ready!"

Martha glued her eyes on Ian, "We found Saira." She scanned Ian closely to catch her reaction.

"What!" Ian bounced from her chair. Martha did not fail to notice the happiness on her face. Ian ran toward her and held her arms. "Oh Martha, only you could have done this. I had lost all hopes. I missed Saira terribly all these years. You'll not believe what a gift this is for me. I can never thank you enough for this. I was scared that Saira might be... might be..."

"Dead?" Martha cut her off.

"What!" Devki's eyes widened as she covered her mouth in horror.

"Yes," Martha moved away from Devki, "Yes Saira is dead. Murdered!"

"No... don't say that!" screamed Devki. Her painful voice shivered, and tears streamed down her cheeks. She was standing close to Martha, her expressions of shock and sadness clearly visible.

"Did they kill Saira? Oh God! Tell me Martha this is not true." Martha moved away. She had witnessed many such dramas in the past.

"They?" Martha mocked. "Who are they? She was killed

by a woman…her friend." She looked at Devki with disgust.

"What! Who killed Saira? Tell me who killed my Saira!" shrieked Devki.

"She was killed by a woman with two babies... her neighbor. Any guesses who this lady could be?"

Devki lifted her hand and clasped her throat lightly in shock. She was unable to comprehend Martha's accusation. She managed, "Martha, please…"

"Cut it out," Martha pointed a finger at Devki. "You killed Saira. You Devki… you killed your friend!"

A little yelp escaped from Devki's lips. She stared at Martha, "Me!"

Martha spoke rapidly, "Yes you. It's all over Devki. I know everything now. You were the last person with Saira that night. There is an eyewitness too, so stop pretending."

Devki trembled in shock as she whispered, "Me…Will I kill Saira…?"

Martha ignored her, "Now you tell me, Devki or Ian Scovich, whatever your real name is. Tell me what happened on that night. What the hell transpired in Jhansi?"

Devki took quick short breaths.

Martha tapped hard on the table, "Who was Saira and why did you murder her? I want to know everything and right now!" She continued, "That's why you were scared ...weren't you?"

Deep down you were scared that someday Saira's story will close on you ...right? … Your fears were correct dear. You were looking for Saira and here she comes knocking at your door."

Martha trembled in anger. Tears welled in her eyes, "You better tell me now…the truth. You owe it to me." Her breath shuddered, "I looked upon to you as my daughter Devki! Why did you use me like this?"

Devki shook both her hands gesturing 'no', but it had no effect on Martha.

Martha yelled again, "I want to know your present and past…everything!"

Martha gave a hard stop.

Devki wept in silence. She remained in her place, "Yes, you deserve to know everything. You are my world – how can I hide anything from you?"

Martha stared as Devki unhooked her blouse buttons one by one. She took off her blue top and dropped it on the floor. She then took off her bra and stood half naked in front of Martha. Martha's eyes popped in horror. There were scars all over Devki's body. From waist all the way to the neck. It looked like an animal had chewed on her body.

"This is my present." Devki's tears broke free and tumbled down her cheeks. Devki turned her back toward Martha, "And this is my past."

There were scars all over her back too. It appeared as if someone had lashed her with a whip or a belt. There were cigarette burn marks all over.

"Oh My God!" Martha panicked in horror.

Devki turned toward Martha trying to hide her emotional outburst but tears flowed as an unbroken stream. "Now listen to everything Martha. You have the full right to know."

Devki turned the pages of her past as Martha listened in dismay. "I... I was raped on my first night," started Devki with some hesitation.

"My first husband was Sudhir. I was married to a man, who looked gentle from outside but in reality, was a psychopath. He took great pleasure whenever I cried and begged. He cut me off from my family and friends."

Martha squirmed in her chair.

"On my first night, I came to know that he had an affair outside marriage. He married me because he needed a victim to satisfy his urges and his family needed money for their business.

Sudhir hated me, he thought I was spying on him. He blamed me for his separation from his girlfriend. My in-laws disliked me, as they felt I didn't bring enough wealth from my parent's house."

Martha's eyes were glued on Devki. It was difficult to see her, but she forced herself,

"Go on my child, tell me everything," said Martha in a heavy voice.

Chapter 27

Devki drifted in memories back and forth, past and present. It was a full moon night of July, many years ago in Jhansi. Devki was eagerly waiting for Sudhir, her newly wedded husband. The first night after the wedding was special in every girl's life, and so it was for Devki too. She was in her bedroom – it was a large room, painted in muted colors with a king size bed in the center. The bed was decorated with flowers and garlands, seeing which she blushed.

Devki checked the time again, the wall-clock read 10.30 pm. *When will Sudhir come?* She looked outside through the window – decorations were still up. The serial lights which adorned the large house seemed to smile and celebrate with her. Little did she know that these celebrations were going to be short-lived.

She heard the waiters clearing the plates and dishes; chairs being pushed. A faint sound of people chatting came from below. A few kids were still playing and chasing each other. She was excited for the night.

Devki was twenty-three then. She had already made significant accomplishments for her age, won numerous awards since childhood in speech contests and debates. She was an obvious choice for anchoring her school functions, birthday parties, and other public functions.

She obtained her masters from a reputed Management college where she was highly appreciated. In her first job, her communication skills and client dealings were greatly valued. She desired to have her own business but continued in her job for the much-needed experience.

She wanted to be successful in the business world, but when Sudhir's family approached her parents for a marriage proposal, they couldn't refuse.

Sudhir seemed to be too shy for the size of the business he owned. He sparingly spoke when his family met hers for an alliance. He kept his head low throughout the evening. She fell instantly in love with the man who seemed gentle and warm.

That night as she waited patiently for her new husband, Devki was lost in dreams of her future. She might have to accompany Sudhir to office soon. He would look upon her for assistance. She will take his business to new heights. She will create a perfect balance between her work and home. Devki smiled to herself.

Perhaps in the near future, the company would be renamed "Sudhir-Devki & Sons". Devki blushed at the thought of 'sons'.

Sudhir's family appeared displeased about the wedding and the gifts she had brought from her maternal home, though her parents had taken immense effort to perform her wedding in a grand manner. She was confident that Sudhir would respect and love her parents as his own.

Devki looked at herself in the mirror and adjusted her makeup. She looked stunning in a green traditional attire of lehenga-chunri with loads of jewelry. She thought of changing into comfortable clothes but postponed the thought – *let Sudhir see me in this dress first.* She wanted to see her effect on him.

She paced across the room slowly as if walking on a stage. She had won on many podiums in her life and she will win today too. She measured her steps and walked to the center of the room. She sized her audience, there were only inanimate objects today – a bed, two side tables, a dressing table, and a few teddy-bears on the far table. Instinctively she closed her eyes momentarily and opened them again. Her audience went blurry for a second and came back crisp. She was at ease.

Her voice filled the room, "Dear friends, I am Devki Sudhir Saraswat, Vice-President-"

Her thoughts were broken by the knock at the door.

Her heart raced. It must be Sudhir. *What should I do? Do I open the door with dupatta on my forehead, do I hug him first? Should I play hard to get?* She got confused, though her married friends and aunts had detailed her what to do.

There was a knock again. With trembling hands, she opened the door.

Sudhir leaned on the side of the door and made a feeble attempt to smile. He pushed his way in. Devki's heart pounded with excitement. Sudhir looked the same – towering and handsome. She forgot all she had prepared for this nuptial union. Her face flustered red.

Sudhir took a few steps forward but stopped – his walk was wobbly.

Hmm! Looks like mister has taken a drink!

She smiled, "No worries dear, let me give you support!" and held his arms.

Sudhir took her into his arms and pressed Devki against his chest. He crushed and suffocated her, but she managed to free herself.

"Hey dear, control yourself!" Devki said playfully. Sudhir again lurched at her trying to get hold of her hand... she stepped back.

"Not so easily," Devki shook her index finger mischievously. "First apologize for drinking and coming late to my room. I am now the queen of this house, so you better behave!"

Sudhir struggled to reach her, the alcohol in his system made his gait unsteady. Devki put a finger on her lips and gestured, 'No' to him and giggled in love. She turned her back to him, enjoying the playful flirting.

Suddenly Sudhir grabbed her from behind by the waist and planted passionate kisses on her. Before Devki could save herself, Sudhir picked her up and threw her over the bed.

Her head hit the headboard of the bed and she winced in pain, "Ouch! Come on Sudhir, take it easy!"

But he was not listening. He ripped open his shirt, caught Devki by the leg and pulled her toward him. In no time, he was over her. His red swollen face laden with the heavy smell of hard liquor was over Devki's. He caught her dress from the shoulders and tore it away.

Devki squabbled under him, "Sudhir... please ...please slow down."

Slap! An unexpected blow made a muffled sound escape from her lips. She heard twice, the sound of her cheeks, as they slammed against the back of his palm. The marriage ring in his finger made a deep incision on her face.

She heard him speak for the first time that night, "I don't want any drama." He spoke in a heavy and hoarse voice on her face.

His hand covered her mouth tightly. Sudhir won over

something that was his own anyway...

It was all over soon.

When Devki came to her senses, the sound of Sudhir snoring was the only thing which made her aware that she was still alive.

It looked like someone had torn all the garlands and plucked all the petals away. The flowers which adorned the bed a few hours earlier, lay worthless on the floor. Her broken bangles were all over the floor. Devki's cries brought no sounds.

What she encountered that night was never explained to her by any of her aunts or friends. She had heard that some men get impatient on their first night. *But still, my experience ...is this normal? Maybe it is!* she argued with herself. *Maybe he was a little impatient. It was my fault; I shouldn't have teased him for long. Men will be men after all.*

Sudhir's naked back was toward her. *He doesn't know me yet, after all.* We've *not spent any time together; this is the problem with these arranged marriages. Maybe, as I will live and spend time with him, he will learn to respect me. There is nothing unusual about this episode* Devki tried to convince herself, though a feeling of disgust prevailed.

A shiver ran through her spine as she glanced at him. Devki felt an excruciating pain. A piece of glass from her broken bangle had pierced her wrist. Her hands quivered as she pulled it out and a few drops of blood dripped. The glass scratched her delicate skin. She wept silently.

It was her first scar.

Devki drifted to unconsciousness, which was disturbed by a sudden buzz on the mobile phone that lay on the side table. The illuminated screen displayed the arrival of a text message. It must be from one of her friends, Devki thought, as she picked the phone but immediately realized that it was not hers although it looked similar. By then, she had mistakenly viewed the appalling messages.

There were two... from someone named Sonal.

'Missed you, darling!'

'Did you nail that bitch last night?'

Images of the past made Devki uncomfortable. Her thoughts were muddled, she was clouded whether she was in

Atlanta or Jhansi. She rubbed her eyes and looked around.

*****

Martha listened, leaning against the wall as Devki continued. "Sudhir detested me. He hated my voice; he hated my looks, but that didn't stop him from crushing me every night." Devki sobbed. "I hoped things will improve after the birth of my twins, but it just worsened."

Martha moved forward and patted on Devki's hand.

"I was beaten several times. I was starved even when I was pregnant. Perhaps he thought killing me was a better option than divorce to keep his respect in the society." Devki blew her nose into a napkin and continued, "I was restricted to my room for days…scared for myself, scared for my daughters. I lost my voice – the one thing I loved the most…I lost it!"

Devki paused for a quick breath. "And even if I could speak, who was there to listen to me?" "Except…except for Saira…my neighbor."

Martha clenched her fingers in her mouth to stop herself from crying loudly. Devki continued, "Saira herself was in a difficult situation, but her condition was at least better than mine. When she realized that I was captivated in the room for days…she would play songs for me."

So that's the secret behind those songs! thought Martha.

"When I was pregnant, she would manage to flip small packets of food into my room. I've often heard cries from Saira's house but couldn't do anything for her!"

"Oh, Saira!" whispered Martha.

"Later one day, Saira overheard my husband and family planning to kill me and my newborn babies. She saved me risking her own life. She helped me escape."

Martha sobbed as she took Devki's fallen clothes from the ground. "What happened after that?"

"I got no information on Saira, but I soon heard that my husband and his family filed a police case against me. They accused me of kidnapping the babies and robbing them of cash and jewelry."

"Oh Lord!" gasped Martha.

"Later I met Gagan, my current husband. I thought running away from India would save me and my daughters, but…" Devki's voice trailed off.

"But what?" Martha leaned forward. Devki stared at Martha. No words came out of her mouth, in desperation, she sobbed incessantly.

"Don't say anything, my dear, don't say anything!" cried Martha.

"Now tell me, Martha, could I have killed Saira? Saira saved my life, saved the life of my daughters. I owe my life to Saira. I cannot even think of harming her!"

"I am terribly sorry Devki for suspecting you," wept Martha.

Martha recalled her earlier conversation with Neel, "But where did Saira go? She certainly vanished on the same night as you and what about that auto driver? He said that you had pulled out a weapon from under your dress. This is too specific to ignore."

"I had no weapon, Martha. If I had, …" Devki's voice trailed.

"Was there any other woman beside you, whom that auto driver mistook for you?"

"I don't know who this guy is and what he saw. We did approach one auto, but the driver was too drunk to drive."

Devki folded her fingers on her forehead to recall the night and with a flash, it came to her. "Yes! I do recall now. This guy seems to have sharp eyesight!" Devki's eyes gleamed. "Saira did give me some money and I did pull out something from under my dress, but it was not a weapon but a notebook with a list of phone numbers and contacts, which I had collected during my captivity."

"List of phone numbers?" Martha was confused.

Devki spoke rapidly, "Yes. In my confinement, I was losing my senses. I jotted down whatever I could remember – phone numbers of relatives, help-line numbers, etc. and before escaping, I gave that notebook to Saira so that she can use them."

"Oh, and this ass, since he was drunk, did not see what you had taken out, and made a story about Saira's murder to get some attention."

"That means Saira is still alive!" Devki clapped. Sorrow

soon changed to joy as both women caught each other's arms.

"I guess, if she disappeared on the same night as you, she must have called one of the numbers and planned her escape."

"Yes...yes," Devki jumped again in delight.

"Do you remember those numbers, by any chance?"

Devki's shoulders dropped, "No. It was way back."

*****

Martha paced around. "Few things still don't make sense."

"Like what?"

"Like, if there was a Police case against you, how was it possible for you to travel out of the country?"

"It's a big country...no one noticed. I didn't stay with my parents at Kanpur but moved to Ajmer to my relative's house, where I was in the hiding. I met Gagan there and everything happened so quick."

"Did you ever talk to the Police? Did they ever interrogate you?" Martha's brain was exploding with questions.

"No, I did not. I was on the run, but my ex-husband and in-laws threatened my parents constantly about how the police were looking for me. They even demanded money in return for the withdrawal of the case."

"Exactly, that's all it was!" Martha thumped on the table.

"What do you mean?" Devki looked at Martha with blank eyes.

"Tell me, are your parents still receiving those calls?"

"I don't know. I stopped calling my parents for fear of being traced."

Martha explained, "No one can travel out of a country if they have a criminal case against them. I mean, they can come, but it isn't that easy. It's my assumption, that there was no criminal case against you after all. Your ex-husband would have gained nothing by filing a case against you."

Devki crossed her legs and listened to Martha.

"They called your parents, perhaps to frighten them so that you don't charge them for abuse."

Devki was taken aback. "I had never thought of it. It was usually my in-laws or Sudhir who harassed my parents about the Police."

"Okay, we'll discuss about that later." Martha was still not satisfied, "And why are there scars all over your body that you need to cover them? You wear this dress to hide these scars, don't you?"

Devki nodded. "Oh, these are, these are rewards from my current marriage." Devki hesitated.

"What!"

"Gagan loves biting and hurting when he makes love to me."

"What the...!" Martha shocked like never before.

"I should have known it, when I got acquainted with him," Devki's voice lingered.

"What do you mean?"

"When Gagan proposed to me, I confided in him of my past and about the scars on my body caused by Sudhir. I expected a sympathetic response from him at the least but..."

"But what," Martha was exasperated.

"He, sort of smiled and winked and said, 'Some people like to give or take scars during love making.' I failed to understand him then but later realized what he meant." Devki fought back her tears.

"What kind of love making is this...by hurting someone."

"I asked him if he would still love me, he replied, 'Oh Yes, you are a frightened little doe. I will love you and care for you forever. We will have lots of fun. Just take care of my daughters.'"

"So, he likes rough love, I will give him some rough below his belt." Martha showed her fist.

"Can you believe this Martha? I had to go through this twice in my life."

Martha wiped the trickling tears from her cheeks, "If you escape from a misfortune once, there's no guarantee that you'll not face it again. I'm sorry God has been unkind to you."

Devki clenched her teeth.

"We will resolve all this one day, first let's find Saira with the new information you just gave me. Wish you had told me all this – much earlier."

Devki nodded.

Chapter 28

It was a usual afternoon, Devki was at home, waiting for the kids and Gagan to return. She was in the living room, reading a magazine, when she heard a car pull up near the house. *Looks like the kids are back early.* Esha drove to school occasionally, after earning her driver's license, and sometimes her classmates picked her up. Kids of her age were excited to get their license, which paved their way to freedom.

Devki expected the familiar sound of the door opening, but she heard none. She continued with her reading with all ears on the door, but when no one entered, her curiosity turned into anxiety. She walked over to the kitchen window overlooking the driveway. As she looked out, she spotted an anonymous car parked on the curb not far away from her driveway, under the shade of a maple tree.

Whose car could that be? She squinted to see if she could spot any passenger in the car. She peeked further and noticed someone familiar – it was Esha in the rear of the car. *What is she doing in the backseat and whose car is this?* While Devki was still contemplating, she saw another head moving in the backseat and this time she noticed a male figure.

"This doesn't seem right," Devki spoke to herself. The boy was kissing Esha. "Oh my God!" Devki gasped, and rushed out of the house, taking longer steps. Once near the car, she knocked on the tinted window of the car fiercely, and screamed, "Open the door, open the door!"

The occupants of the car were startled. Esha glared at Devki through the window. As the window came rolling down, Devki noticed a boy who appeared older than Esha.

The boy looked at Devki but spoke to Esha, "Who is she?"

"I am her mother!" said Devki in a stern voice.

"Mother?"

Before anyone could utter a word, Devki instructed, trying to sound polite, "I invite you inside for a cup of tea. We can learn more about each other."

The boy spoke to Esha, while still looking at Devki, "You said you have no mother."

"She is not my mother. She is some…some woman who

150

lives in our house."

Devki interrupted, "I am married to Esha's father."

She insisted again, this time jerking the door open, "Either both of you come inside the house or Esha, step out and let the guy leave."

Esha stepped out of the car adjusting her dress. She was enraged. The young man looked at Devki and displayed all his teeth, "Thank you ma'am for the invitation, I don't drink tea." He stepped out of the car, took the driver's seat and turned on the ignition. He looked at Esha, "Sweetheart, don't wait for my phone call!"

The car was gone.

Esha stomped in, while Devki followed her. Once inside, Esha turned toward Devki, "You are not my mom and stop pretending to be one!"

"I am your mom Esha…whether you like it or not. I will not let you get spoilt away like this."

"Spoilt away… ha, look who's talking!" mocked Esha.

"Don't judge me …you don't understand a lot of things in this house."

"I understand one thing clearly…that you can never be my mom!" She was still hurt over how her biological mother had cheated on them; how she never bothered to even call them after the separation.

"Do you think that guy is fit for you? If yes, then why did he run away?"

Esha glared at Devki and pointed a finger to speak something but Devki cut her off,

"Listen to me Esha, this is not your age to hang out with guys. Focus on your studies and pick your friends wisely."

"Huh!" Hatred and teenage meanness took over Esha. She wanted to slash out sharp and hurtful words. She walked near Devki and spoke on her face, "Mind you, Devki. Stay out of my business… otherwise…otherwise, I will make your life miserable. I'll put so many allegations against you that my dad will whip your clever ass."

Devki's expression changed from good to bad and then to ugly. She glared at Esha.

"So, you do know what goes on in this house." Devki's

voice pitched higher, "Do you realize what you said? Do you think that it is okay for a man to whip a woman's ass? Answer me!" Devki took a quick breath, "Do you think it is okay for a man to torture a woman only because she is physically weaker than him?"

Esha fidgeted with her clothes nervously, regretting her words. She was angry, yet, she never meant to say all those words, "Devki …I …"

Her voice was cut by Devki's loud voice, "Is it okay for a man to take advantage of a woman only because she is dependent on him? Answer me!"

Esha was shocked, she had never seen Devki in such an avatar.

Devki took deep breaths to control herself. After a long pause, Devki spoke again, "I think it is my mistake, not yours."

Esha sighed.

"If I treat you as my daughter, I should set an example for you." Devki's eyes illuminated as if she was having a eureka moment. She continued, "I had never thought of this before. I am living this …this kind of life for my kids but if I am setting a wrong example for them, how good can that be?"

"I am not your daughter," Esha spoke in a low tone and squeezed her eyes shut, scared of receiving another scream from Devki.

"I love you and Kajal like my daughters. You may find it hard to believe though. I know how much you have suffered at this age for no fault of yours." Devki continued, "You kids need to be protected…emotionally and physically." Devki slumped onto the chair…unable to bear the emotional burden. Esha stared at Devki as she sobbed.

"I…I am sorry," whispered Esha slowly kneeling on the carpet before Devki.

Devki's face displayed signs of resolution. "Not anymore. I need to be a role model for my daughters…for you. Things need to change now." Devki walked toward her room.

"No, No Devki…don't do anything stupid…please!" pleaded Esha. Devki kept walking. "Please mom!" begged Esha.

Devki stopped for a moment and turned to look at Esha. Tears formed in Esha's eyes.

Devki walked away.

Chapter 29

It was a sultry morning in Jhansi. The hot weather usually extended until the last quarter of the year. Manish and Sarang arrived early at the office. They had received a text message from Neeta the day before, late in the evening – 'Dubeyji has an update on Saira.'

Neeta felt miserable over the dismal news. She had least expected that their project would come to such a tragic end. *It would be better if Neel himself conveys the message of Saira's demise to the team.* They had all put their heart and soul into the task and would be dispirited by this information.

Neeta was pouring her tea into the cup when Neel walked in. *He looks pleased for the news he is about to deliver.*

Neel's gestures were deliberate as usual. He walked in the center facing his three teammates. He looked behind at the white board, which still read, 'Project: Finding Saira.' Neel picked the marker, looked around, and changed the content, 'Project: Finding Saira – Continued.'

They were all puzzled but Neeta was even more confused.

Once Neel got all eyes and ears, "For the past few weeks, we have spent a lot of time researching on Saira and our recent exchange with one Mr. Ram Bharose gave us an impression that it is futile to look for Saira because she may be dead."

The boys gasped.

"As luck would have it," Neel continued with a short pause, "after I updated Martha about this development, she did her own research and concluded it to be otherwise. There is some truth in the auto-driver's version, but it is not entirely accurate."

"Really!" jumped Neeta, "This is the best news ever!"

"Yes, it is true that there was another woman with Saira on that night, but she would have never killed Saira."

Neel filled everyone on his meeting with the driver Ram Bharose and the later snippets of his phone call with Martha.

Neeta was unsure, "How can Martha be certain when we have an eye-witness for the killing?"

"Martha is one hundred percent sure. How, I do not know." Neel took a pause, shrugged, and continued, "She told me not to worry about it, at least Saira's companion could have never

153

murdered her."

"Hmm, so, what next?"

"Now we must probe further. We've gathered some new information and hope it'd provide more clues in finding Saira."

The group was silent but elated with this new development. Neeta had more questions, "Okay, say, we do find Saira this time, why on earth would she trust us? Don't you think she will be paranoid on seeing us, strangers, looking for her? Will she not panic and run?"

Smart, real detective. This is exactly what he had asked Martha. Neel smiled in appreciation, "Martha will give us a clue which Saira will believe, but she has a condition."

"What's that?"

"The clue will reach us only when we are in front of Saira or when we are certain to have found her!"

"Wow!" said Sarang. "Another layer in the story."

Neeta pinched the tip of her nose – she wanted further assurance. "What about Ram, he saw some weapon used by that other lady?"

Neel chuckled, "This guy is imaginative. There was no weapon. This lady gave Saira a list of phone numbers and contacts of some helpline agencies."

After moments of thought, suddenly Neeta banged on the table with excitement, "Bingo!

Things are clearing up now!" she couldn't conceal her elation.

"Like what?" all voices echoed.

"This other lady was Saira's friend and they knew each other well. And now I can guess for whom Martha is working." said Neeta.

"For God's sake, can you say it clearly!"

"If you analyze a bit, it's pretty simple… Saira and this other lady were spotted together by our auto driver. If they were strangers, they will not be working in unison and exchanging stuff. Moreover, the woman had given phone numbers and contacts to Saira… perhaps she wanted Saira to take flight too. This shows a similarity in their situation…Saira did not go with her, otherwise, the lady in question will not be looking for Saira."

Neel was catching up, "You are saying the woman who

accompanied Saira, is the one trying to search for her?"

"Exactly."

"How can you say that?"

"It's quite evident. Martha approached us, here in Jhansi…who will do that? – someone with a connection to Jhansi. Martha is keen on finding Saira…it's not Martha who is looking for Saira, but Saira's friend. And Martha's assurance that Saira's companion did not kill Saira, makes things crystal clear."

"Huh!" Neel could not produce any other sound.

"I think on that night – this other lady did reach the railway station and caught a train and eventually landed in the USA. And after many years, when she thinks that the dust may have settled, she is looking for her lost friend."

"Oh, my!" Neel and others were in loss of words.

"Now we have to figure out where Saira went since she didn't go to the railway station with her friend," said Neeta.

Neel looked at her in admiration, *How intelligent, what a deduction! An expert detective!*

Neeta was jubilant, "So, where do we start? Can we have the list of those helpline numbers?"

"Our client has no phone numbers," Neel played with the pen, "but still it shouldn't be difficult to figure out. Most of these numbers must be of common places."

"Okay," Neeta rubbed her palms together. "So, we start from square one, but well assured that Saira is alive."

"How can we be so conclusive? When in so many years no one saw Saira, she never turned up, perhaps someone else killed her," said Manish without foreseeing the impact of his words.

Neeta scowled, "Saira is alive because we have no reason to believe she's dead! Never utter such words in future, otherwise, you will be dead for sure."

After all the commotion died, the attention turned to Neel for directions. Neel eyed Neeta, "You have done some wonderful analysis, no words to describe. You are the only woman in our team, your direction helped us so far. Remember you once acted as Saira."

"A failed actress," laughed Neeta.

Neel continued, "Now based on your theory, try to contemplate what Saira would have done on that night with those contact numbers in her hand, with no future back home and her friend leaving her." Neeta tried to follow Neel's suggestions.

He spoke again, "Try to feel like Saira. Get into her character again. Imagine what Saira would think and do."

The other guys looked at Neel, "What about us?"

"You guys, investigate today's and older newspapers, search the telephone directory, call your contacts. Look for local or national helplines that assist abused women." The duo scribbled some notes and discussed.

Neeta paced around the room... leaned against the wall for some time, tapping her forehead with the back of a pen. Neel's eyes were on her. He hushed everyone. *Saira is at work now.* Neeta was lost in her own world.

After a while, she approached the door, "Need a walk, see you guys in a while."

Neel hurried, "Shall I join you?"

"No, I want to be alone."

Once outside, Neeta looked at her secondhand scooter – finding Saira had benefited her.

Should I drive my bike? Neeta dismissed the thought and decided to take a stroll in the sun.

*****

Finding Saira was not about money – it was about survival. Locating Saira meant a new roof above the head and food in the stomach, but more than money, Neeta was concerned about Saira now. Whatever she learned about Saira, made Neeta sympathetic about her. *Poor lady. She's undergone undue suffering. Why the hell is no one concerned about her? Every human being has someone in this world, but Saira has none.* Neeta's heart ached for Saira. *Where did she go! I will find Saira, not for money but for her.*

Neeta strode around the nearby streets, deep in her thoughts and soon found herself standing in the main intersection of Sipri Bazar – Saira's neighborhood. She had come here often in the recent months. The market seemed over-crowded at that time of the day.

'Feel like Saira', Neel's words echoed in her ears. She chuckled – *I am not Saira.*

She stood under the shadow of the huge public water tank

and watched the traffic move in both directions. Girls from the nearby 'Arya Kanya' School passed by, holding each other's hands, giggling and laughing playfully. Neeta smiled. She had studied in the same school many years ago. Teachers patiently guided the smaller kids on the road. *Saira might be a teacher*. With her helping nature, she would have made an exceptional teacher.

Neeta looked around and comprehended her surroundings. She studied the different roads and streets in the vicinity. The road across led to Saira's house on Tandon road, the house which they visited earlier to deliver the letter. If Saira had taken an auto that night, she should have come through this straight road.

Neeta looked around and noticed there were many autos and tempos waiting for passengers. As Neeta placed herself in Saira's shoes, she thought harder on what she would have done that night. *She would have come through this straight road along with her friend. She would have stood at this same spot and looked for some means of transport, and this is where that auto driver would have spotted them.*

Neeta looked around to figure out where the intersecting roads led to. The road on the right went straight to the railway station. "It's unlikely for Saira to have taken this road," Neeta spoke to herself; *otherwise she would have gone along with her friend.* Another road behind the water tank led to the Railway bridge, but it was a dead end, some old railway coaches lay rotting there. No one would go there.

As Neeta studied the direction of the third road, her thoughts were disrupted by the sound of a bus honking. Her mind was preoccupied with Saira, she failed to realize that she was standing in the middle of the road. She scurried aside. The bus driver gave her an angry look, as he skillfully maneuvered the bus around her. Startled, Neeta looked at the rear of the bus… as if the bus carried her with it.

Neeta suddenly jumped with excitement and raised both her hands in the air and shouted, "Yahoo!" She knew where Saira would have gone and what she might be doing. She instantly looked for her phone, but she had left her phone and bag at the office. She hurried toward a paid phone. She had no money to pay for the call but assured the phone operator that her call was urgent, and she would pay for it later. He obliged.

Neel answered the unknown number, "Hello?"

"This is Neeta."

"Neeta!" Neel jerked, "Thank God! Where are you? You have been away for hours, no one knows where you are. You left your phone here and …"

Neeta smiled at his anxiety, "Okay, Okay, I'm sorry but I think I know where Saira is."

"What, where, how, did you meet her, is she in town?" Neel threw a volley of questions.

"No, she is not in Jhansi, right now, I am not absolutely sure where she is, but my gut feeling tells me I am right."

"Great! Awesome! Come here immediately and let's discuss about it."

Chapter 30

It was nearing five in the evening, when Neeta arrived at the office. The floor was littered with papers and phone directories.

"We found twenty-five reputed helpline agencies. We called them but got no news about Saira."

"That is because Saira did not call any of them." said Neeta. The whole team gaped at Neeta who spoke with an air of confidence, much like a stockbroker who had insider information.

"How in the world do you know this Neeta? Tell us now, whatever you learnt on Saira," Neel became impatient.

Neeta explained, "Okay, this is my assumption but let's see how it goes...so, on that night, Saira had no plans to leave because, if she had planned, she would have left with that other lady and Ram Bharose would have reported differently. But after her friend left, Saira must have desired for her liberty too, as no one cared for her anyway. Moreover, she would be in trouble the next morning, when her friend's absconding would come to light."

Neel leaned forward with hands on his knees.

Neeta drew a rough layout of Sipri Bazar on the board with different roads to explain Saira's position on that night. "For some reason, she did not opt for the railway station, otherwise she would have accompanied her friend and we will not be discussing this."

Neeta added a picture of a bus and paused looking at her drawing and extended a pointed arrow from the bus, "And at that moment, a bus from some nearby town arrived. Saira boarded the bus."

Neeta enjoyed the curious looks of the others.

"And where did this bus take her?" asked Neel.

"This bus could have taken her to 'Shivpuri', the next good-sized town from Jhansi, about four and a half hours away." Neeta relaxed and twisted her knuckles. She sipped some water' breathed deeply and heaved a sigh. All this imagination and story-telling excited her.

Sarang was unconvinced, "And what made you think that she's gone to Shivpuri? She could've gone anywhere – Mumbai, Delhi or Calcutta. Why only to Shivpuri?"

"First, her location makes this a plausible route. Also, considering that she was alone, with no money, the bus conductor could have sympathized on her and allowed her to travel for free but for a short distance only. Besides, she has lived in Jhansi for a long time – she would've decided to stay closer," concluded Neeta.

Neel folded all fingers under his chin, "And what would she be doing in Shivpuri?"

"She can do anything, but she would possibly be a teacher. Teaching matches her personality and the company of kids will keep her happy. Remember, the barber too had remarked that she taught kids in the locality."

She is so smart. She covered all the points from different angles. Neel felt proud to have her in his team.

There were mixed responses, but Neel was confident about Neeta's deduction.

"I believe your theory," Neel said. "And this is the best presumption we have right now. What next? Whom do we contact in Shivpuri?"

"No one! I'm going there by the next bus tonight, to look for her."

"What!" The word echoed from all the other three.

"Yes, I cannot be away from Saira now. I can feel it... I can feel Saira. She is nearer now." She looked at Neel, *Believe in me, please!*

Neel was more than pleased. *Brilliant! This girl has changed my life and everything around me, ever since she joined my team.*

"Okay, if you feel so strongly, we'll go to Shivpuri by the next bus. I will go with you."

"You can accompany me and tell Martha to keep her message ready for us because we are meeting Saira soon!" Neeta showed her fingers as if shooting at a target.

"Ok Neeta you go home now and pack your essentials and I will do the same, we will meet at around 9 pm near the bus station."

"Saira didn't pack anything when she left, so I will not pack, and neither will you!"

"Alright, what do we do with our vehicles?" Neel said. "And we need to reserve a room in case we need to stay overnight."

"We'll keep our bikes at the Bus station and will think

about the hotel once we're there. Anyways we'd be back by tomorrow evening."

Neel rose from his chair, "Whatever you say madam, you are the boss now!"

As Neeta apprised her family about her travel plans, Neel gave instructions to the others and called his home too.

Once outside, Neel noticed Neeta mounting her red scooter. Sitting on the vehicle, she raised the accelerator. Her hair waved carelessly in the air and covered her beautiful face. She shrugged them off by shaking her head. Her shoulders and torso looked strong – her small waist firmly settled on the seat. She took her black scarf and tied it over her face to save it from the smoke and dust. To Neel, she looked like an avatar of the Queen of Jhansi mounting her horse.

Neeta kept the engine at full throttle, turned sideways toward Neel, "Dubeyji ready for a ride?" and sped away.

Neel came back to his senses. He kick-started his bike and swiftly followed Neeta who was darting between the traffic. Neel was in his thoughts again. From being a timid junior, Neeta had transformed into a skillful detective. She has proved to be an asset in every step. *I would be nothing without her.*

He was doubtful of Neeta's assumptions and whether they were on the right track, but he wanted to move forward at least for Neeta, for her untiring effort and determination. A strange feeling took over him. *I love Neeta.* Before finding Saira, he wanted to find his love.

Neel chased her bike, she was several lanes ahead of him, but he drove furiously, zigzag between other vehicles and was soon behind her.

A red traffic signal came up and Neeta stopped. Neel came to a screeching halt beside her.

"Neeta…Neeta!" he yelled over the sound of the traffic.

"Yes, Dubeyji." Neeta looked at him, both bikes roaring.

"Will you marry me?" Neel shouted over the traffic.

"What!"

Neeta's face showed shock and bewilderment. Neel was unable to figure out if she was pleased or annoyed.

"Are you out of your mind?" asked Neeta.

"I am in my senses Neeta. I love you. I cannot live without

you. Will you marry me?"

Neeta looked away escaping from Neel's gaze.

"What's that? Yes or No?" Neel grew impatient.

Neeta looked deeply into Neel's eyes, "A green signal!"

"What!"

Neeta pointed at the traffic signal, "You got a green signal Dubeyji!"

"What's that supposed to mean?" Neel tried to reach for Neeta's hand with his right hand.

"Make a move, before other vehicles run over you." said Neeta and was lost in the traffic once again.

Chapter 31

Ian was unsettled after the last argument with Mike. She was not sure if she was upset with herself or with him. She was overwhelmed by Mike's love, but her situation prevented her from moving forward. *I am married, and a mother of two...* she reminded herself repeatedly. Her life was in a complete mess. *Can Mike handle my past? How will he react if he sees my scars? He will be horrified; he will hate me forever.*

Martha did not see anything amiss – she was accustomed to Ian's behavior. She was aware of the reasons – Ian had a tormented past and a tortuous present situation. Her occasional erratic behavior caused problems with some of the employees too, but Martha was quick to rectify the damage.

Martha understood Ian completely. Ian's emotions had been cheated and bounced so cruelly in the past that any odd behavior from her was understandable.

Meanwhile, Ian's speeches gained popularity each day. In almost every state, people waited for her new audios. In some places, there were long queues for booking her next release. Ian spoke on different genres – from domestic abuse, to motivating youngsters. Her discourses encouraged and motivated people. There were numerous blogs written in her praise and many confessed that Ian saved their lives. Her talks were regular in substance-abuse clinics. Ian's audios worked as a prescription for the depressed.

Ian showed what could be accomplished with one's life, but she was stretched between her work and home. At one place, she was used and insulted as Devki and at another, she was respected and adored as Ian.

*****

No one in this world can defy love and Ian was no exception. She could not take the separation from Mike for a long time.

Mike's company had been a great relief from what she was going through at home. She longed for his closeness. And when Mike said "Sorry!" with his puppy-like face, Ian couldn't help laughing. With Mike's heart-felt apology and humor, the strain in their relationship vanished and they once again became one.

Many times, he insisted Ian for an evening date to which she persistently declined. He raised questions about their future, about her marriage but failed to receive any satisfying answer.

Workload increased day by day. They were all busy. When Devki got her driver's license, Martha was elated, "Thank goodness. I hated this chauffeur job."

*****

"I need to go out of town!" declared Martha.

"Why? And Where?"

"I need to take care of an important contract."

"We will miss you terribly!" Mike intervened. He overheard Martha talking to Ian as he walked into her room. Ian looked at Mike and saw mischief in his eyes. Martha noticed some intimacy between them, although they kept it under cover, away from her. She did not pester them. *They will tell me when they feel the need to do so.*

It was a beautiful sunny afternoon, and as Ian walked along with Mike, he said dramatically, "Will your highness grace the apartment of this slave, for some humble home cooked lunch?"

Ian laughed, "Ha! Just lunch? I know what this slave is capable of."

Mike winked and smiled.

The previous night's usual episode with Gagan, dampened Ian's mood but she did not wish to disappoint Mike. On multiple occasions, when Martha was away, Ian visited Mike's apartment for lunch.

They purchased some snacks and walked to his apartment.

Once inside, Mike locked the door behind him and pulled the blinds of the windows. He played Ian's favorite jazz on the music player.

Ian half sat on the bed resting on her elbow. Mike bowed in front of her, "Will My lady care for a dance with this commoner?" Ian acted amused and gave her hand. They danced holding each other. Mike was in a playful mood. He knew her love for him. He kissed Ian passionately on her cheeks and neck, Ian nudged him politely with a "No."

"Hey, I am just making my lady happy," winked Mike.

He pulled Ian closer to him, she pushed him back.

Mike caught her wrist and twisted her arm slightly behind her back and whispered lustily, "Enough of this my highness, now submit to your slave." He started kissing her on the lips.

Ian squirmed "Mike, Mike, please stop!"

Mike mildly pushed her into the bed. He pulled out his shirt and climbed over her slender figure. Ian resisted, as she turned her back toward him, "Come-on Mike, stop it!"

Mike whispered, nibbling her ears, "Wrap your hands around me and make love to me. Let this slave serve you." Mike knew his words would generate fire in Ian.

He desired to see her face, to see her response to his actions. He tried to turn her around, but she resisted, holding tightly the bedsheet underneath her. Mike caught her by the shoulders and forcefully flipped her around.

With his left hand, Mike bonded both her hands behind her head and kissed her intensely.

"Today your slave will see all the treasures. Bear all for your slave!" Mike's voice was smoky.

He started unbuttoning Ian's blouse. His curiosity took over him; in his subconscious mind, he was still unable to accept the fact that he had not seen Ian naked, there was something hidden, some secret. He unhooked the first button and then the second…

Ian's squeezed her eyes shut. All the veins in her forehead popped. Before Mike could guess anything…Ian screamed with full strength, "Stop! Stop raping me! Stop It!" her voice shook the entire room.

Mike was startled. His love and passion evaporated in a flash. He jerked out of the bed and started getting dressed. Ian was still moaning, "Stop raping me…please, please leave me alone."

Mike stared at her, aghast at her behavior. *Who is she? Do I even know her?*

Soon it dawned on Ian that no one was holding her. She opened her eyes and saw Mike moving away from her.

"Mike, Mike please don't go, I can explain," pleaded Ian. "Mike please listen to me!"

Mike was in no mood to stop or listen. He stormed out.

*****

After a couple of days, Martha returned from her trip and called Ian at her house. "What the hell happened to Mike? Why does he sound so hurt?"

Ian wiped her swollen eyes and spoke in a wobbly voice, "Thank God Martha you're back. Can you please ask Mike to meet me in the office at nine tomorrow and you be there too"?

"But what happened?"

"I cannot explain everything to you right now!"

"Are you sure you want to meet Mike at work? If you have something personal to discuss, you can meet him outside, and you sure want me to be present?"

"Yes, please, at the office!"

Ian was already at her desk when Mike arrived. Martha thought of leaving the two alone, but Ian signaled her to stay. Mike still appeared hurt, yet on seeing Ian, a faint smile came on his lips and his anger subsided. There was some awkwardness, but it soon faded away.

He approached Ian, saw Martha in the room, hesitated for a moment, then decided there was nothing to hide, "Hey, there must be some misunderstanding. You wanted to tell me something. I am here to listen." He tried to ruffle Ian's hair, she moved away.

Ian turned her back on him and looked outside the window. Numerous faceless buildings, some small, some tall, were each competing for survival in the small space. Big buildings proud and towering, the smaller ones trying to beat them. On the far end, on some building, Ian saw a large billboard bearing her name – 'Ian speaks'.

Ian avoided Mike's face. She turned toward Martha and looked through her. She spoke, choosing each word cautiously, "Mike, you should resign today."

"What!"

"Yes, this will be the best in a situation like this."

Martha raised both her palms up, stunned, "Situation like what?"

Mike protested, "Whatever happened… has happened…don't punish me, don't punish yourself for it. I understand, there should be some reason! I am here for you Ian – I will protect you."

Ian turned toward him and screamed. "I don't need your protection. I don't need any help from any man. I am not dependent on anyone. I don't want to…"

Martha gulped the air, puzzled. *What the heck?*

"I love you Ian," cried Mike.

Without acknowledging Mike, Ian continued, "I don't want to be hurt, won or hunted again. I know you are not like others but the men I knew, were not like that either. They swore their love for me too. They were supposed to protect me too."

Mike was perplexed *Who are the men she's referring to?*

Ian breathed heavily. "If it's in our destiny, we shall meet again someday, but for now, you'll leave."

"Are you crazy? Do you know what you're saying?" Martha interjected.

"If you speak in between, you are fired too!" yelled Ian.

"Oh! So, now I'm fired," said Mike.

Ian looked outside, stone faced. "Not today!"

"If Mike leaves, then I leave too." Martha's threat fell on deaf ears.

Ian did not look at anyone. She turned around, picked up a file from her desk and pretended to read it. The conversation was over.

There was a deafening silence in the room. Mike stood lost, unsure of his next move.

Martha pursed her lips and broke the silence, "I cannot leave her," her words coming out in bits and pieces, "You… understand Mike… someone needs to take care of this crazy lady and now that you are gone, I need to stay back and take care of her."

Mike gave a lasting look to Ian – the woman he lost even before winning over.

He left.

Ian kept reading the document. Her eyes couldn't hold all her tears, a tear slipped through her cheeks and fell on the paper she was holding.

Chapter 32

As soon as they arrived at the parking lot of the bus station, Neel parked his bike and ran toward Neeta, still anxious about her response.

He jumped in front of her, "So, what's your answer?"

Neeta stuffed her scarf into her bag. "Come on, Dubeyji! Can we focus on Saira for now?" Neel heaved a sigh and threw his hands into the air.

The bus station was small. The buses starting from there travelled in only one direction.

The bus to Shivpuri was running late, they strolled for a while and had dinner at a nearby restaurant. Neel called Martha and updated her on the developments. Martha was skeptical about their venture, but Neel assured her – they had to follow all the leads. With all doors closed, they need to be imaginative and deductive.

In case they did locate Saira, Neel asked Martha to give them the clue which would gain Saira's confidence. Martha agreed to send him some texts but cautioned that under no circumstance, they should read them, unless until they are in front of Saira.

Neel wrapped the call and checked back on the bus – it was still behind schedule. Neeta, meanwhile, massaged her neck and moved her head from side-to-side.

Neel took a seat in front of her. "So, how's this going to work and what do we do once we reach Shivpuri?"

"That's where I'm stuck too!" Neeta stretched her legs.

"Your instinct says Saira should be a teacher," asked Neel. Neeta nodded.

"What grades does she teach?"

"Probably smaller kids."

Neel crossed his legs under the chair, "This will narrow down our search a bit. At least we don't have to wander around aimlessly in an unknown place."

Neeta took out a notepad and a pen from her handbag. Neel looked at the full-size notepad, amused. *How much stuff can a woman's bag hold?*

Neeta's pen moved rapidly on her notebook, "We need to search all the schools in the town. It's a daunting task, but we need to start somewhere."

"True."

Neeta bit the tip of her pen, "Suppose, we do go to a school, how do we track down Saira? She will not be standing with a placard bearing her name."

Neel sipped water from a cup. "We'll have to look for the Teacher's register or attendance and look for her name."

"Teacher's register? And who will let you see the teacher's records?"

It was getting more arduous than she had imagined. Neel circled the tip of the glass with his fingers and blew air bubbles into the water. Water splashed on the table with droplets falling on Neeta's arms. She glared. *What a kid!*

"I have an idea," Neel smiled. "We will narrow down on a few schools randomly and visit them – acting as School inspectors."

"You are exceptionally smart Dubeyji," Neeta smirked. "And how do you think we will prove ourselves as School Inspectors?"

Neel winked. "We have to do it, no other way. This trick isn't new to us!"

Neeta recalled how they had gone inside Saira's house earlier, by using fake badges.

She chuckled.

"There's still a problem," Neeta clasped her hands.

"What?"

"What if Saira has changed her name?" Neeta's last word trailed off and faded in the sound of the approaching bus.

Neel gauged the crowd inside the bus. "We have to take our chances...now let's go."

The bus arrived way behind schedule – they were still confident of reaching Shivpuri by the early hours as it was a short journey.

Neeta took the window seat and Neel sat next to her. As the bus gained momentum, Neel dozed off within minutes, open-mouthed, with his head resting on Neeta's shoulders.

Neeta looked at him with a soft eye – *How cute!*

As the bus paced smoothly, Neeta rested her head on the glass window and closed her eyes to catch some sleep. It had been a long day; yet, she could not distance Saira from her thoughts. The bus jolted and Neeta opened her eyes. She looked at Neel, he was still half slumped on his seat and in deep sleep. Neeta took a quick sip from the bottle.

She looked outside and noticed a few candescent lights on the sides of the road. Some town was approaching. The bus slowed down and then came to a halt. Neeta peeked outside – it was a small bus station. It was still dark outside, she squinted her eyes to see the name on the board, it read 'Karera'.

The name sounded familiar to Neeta. She pondered on the name for a while and then realized, she had been there to attend a wedding. She was in middle school then. She massaged her memories further for some time and glimpses of her childhood zoomed before her eyes. She checked her watch, it was a little past 1.30am, the bus was moving faster. *We should be reaching Shivpuri soon.*

As the bus started again, Neeta drifted in and out of sleep. The thoughts of Saira filled her mind. *Will we be able to find her in the new town? What if my intuition is all wrong and Saira never reached Shivpuri? There would be numerous schools in this town, how on earth will we find Saira?* Neeta's mind was confused, and before she could apprehend more on it, she cuddled with Neel and slept.

They woke-up startled, when someone banged on the side of the bus and announced 'Shivpuri!' It was still dark outside. "Dubeyji- quick- get down!" Neeta hurried toward the door pushing through Neel's leg. Neel was wide awake, by the time he jumped behind Neeta.

There were still a few hours left before dawn. Neel looked at his watch, the time was a little past three.

"We need to look for a hotel. We have to get ready in the morning." said Neel. Neeta did not speak but kept walking beside Neel. With no hotels near the Bus station, they walked a little further and came to the main road. Neel spotted a decent looking hotel and guided Neeta.

Neel frowned. *Should I book one room or two? She didn't respond clearly to my marriage proposal.*

Once at the hotel, Neel proceeded to the reception desk and Neeta walked toward the couch in the lobby. It was a small area with a few couches, and a dining section to its left. A sign with 'No Credit' hung behind the duty clerk's desk. A map of Shivpuri, highlighting the 'places to visit', adorned the wall.

"Need a room," said Neel. "I mean rooms, for tonight."

The middle-aged clerk raised his eyebrows in suspicion, "Where's your luggage?"

"We don't have any luggage."

The Duty clerk stared coldly at Neel, "This is not that kind of a place. We are a decent family-run hotel!"

"What do you mean?" said Neel, "We are school inspectors on an official visit." Neel flashed his badge right onto the clerk's face.

The clerk expressed apology and picked a thick register, How many rooms?"

Neel paused for a second, "Two."

The clerk first looked at Neel and next at Neeta, and signaled Neel in the direction of the couch. Neel turned back; Neeta lay slumped on the couch, her legs raised against the armrest, fast asleep.

Neel half smiled at her condition and turned to the hotel clerk, "Give us one room. I will also crash here for now. We will use the room in the morning to freshen up."

Neel checked his cell phone but there was no text from Martha. The battery of the phone was dying, he kept his phone on charge and fell on the couch adjacent to Neeta's.

*****

Neel woke up with the sound of vehicles from the nearby street. The brilliant sunrise escaped through the windows and fell on his eyes. Neel reached out to check his phone. There were two messages from Martha. The first one was a text, "Don't open the next message with the image till you find Saira."

Neel admired Martha's smartness. She had embedded the message in an image, he cannot read the message without clicking on it. He respected Martha's decision and did not click on the image.

Neel looked around for Neeta who was nowhere. The duty clerk spotted his confusion, "Madam went to the room. She woke up a few minutes after you fell asleep. I gave her the keys."

Neel used his fingers to straighten his messy hair and

rubbed his face with his palms. At that moment, he saw Neeta coming from the other end of the lobby. Her hair was wet, although she wore the same clothes. She looked as fresh as the morning. Neel forgot all his tiredness on seeing her.

Neeta handed over the keys to Neel, "Dubeyji get ready. We have to visit many schools today." He rushed to the room and was ready within minutes.

By the time he returned to the lobby, a new female clerk was on duty. Neel explained their objective to her; they were there to inspect some schools and needed a list of the schools in the area, with a focus on primary schools or junior high schools.

"That's strange! Don't you have the school list already with you? This is a hotel, how are we supposed to have information on schools?"

"Oh, in a hurry I forgot the list right on the table at my desk, and it would be too late by the time I call my department to get the addresses," said Neeta quickly. "Will appreciate your help."

The clerk acknowledged and requested them to wait. After a brief search in her cabinets, all that she could find was information on the best places to visit or eat in Shivpuri. She made some quick calls to her contacts and scribbled the information on a piece of paper.

At the end of some four to five calls, she handed over a list of schools to Neel. They again discussed the direction and distance of various schools with the clerk. They restricted themselves on five likely schools. They hoped their mission to be accomplished within these schools.

Chapter 33

It was still morning when they reached the first school. The school had a modern architecture with a security guard stationed outside the school premises. Everything appeared polished and synchronized. *Saira can never be in such a school* thought Neeta. Yet, on Neel's insistence, they soon found themselves sitting at the Principal's office.

"I haven't received any notice for an inspection!" The Principal scrutinized the detectives.

"Sorry sir," said Neel in a passive voice. "This is a surprise inspection and we're not allowed to send notices for this kind of visit."

The Principal eyed both Neel and Neeta, found them to be decent enough for their description, and failed to notice any vibe of mischief from them. "What kind of inspection?"

"We would like to look at the Teachers attendance record," said Neeta, "and if needed will talk to some of them randomly …same usual stuff."

"You know how these formalities are," added Neel.

"Okay!" The Principal looked at some files on his laptop, and soon handed them a printout.

They went through the list of teachers and found nothing noticeable. Unable to recognize or relate to any name, they made some casual queries and after a few minutes, Neeta turned toward the Principal, "That's it. We're done. See, as we told you, this is just a formality. We are mainly checking the maintenance of teachers' records. Everything seems to be perfect."

They came out of the school in ten minutes.

The next school was old but their search was in vain at that school too. None of the teachers' names interested them. There was no point in talking to them, they had no time to waste. When the search at the third school turned out to be futile, Neeta became nervous. "Looks like I was wrong all along. Sorry for dragging you here."

"We still have two more schools to go. Let's be positive." Neel's encouragement did little to uplift her spirits.

The fourth school was in the outskirts of the town. It was run by a charity organization. The school seemed smaller from outside but was spacious inside. It was a three-storied building with an open ground in the middle and classrooms, labs and library surrounding it. As the two approached the principal's office, they heard someone yelling from inside.

"Our Principal screams a lot, but he has a soft heart," said the school attendant who was guiding them.

The Principal was a heavy-set man with a round abdomen matching his much-rounded cheeks. Beads of sweat formed on his bald head with all the admonition he was giving to a staff member. As Neel and Neeta entered the room, he growled, "What do you want? Who gave you permission to enter my office?"

"We have come from the board of education for inspection."

The Principal's temper subsided by their statement. "Inspection?" He seemed upset but used a polite tone. "We haven't received any intimation regarding the visit."

Neeta shook her head, "Believe me, many of the schools we visited said the same, but this is a surprise inspection, we are not allowed to inform anyone."

The Principal peered suspiciously at them, "How can I be assured that you are school inspectors?"

Neeta pretended to be annoyed, peeped into her purse as if looking for her official badge. She raised her voice, "You will be assured, when we report on the cleanliness around your school!"

Neel waved his hand as if calming her down, "That's okay, he has got the full right to know who we are." He turned toward the Principal, "I understand your concern. This is a primary school and, you don't want any intruders in your premise."

The Principal softened a bit, "Which class do you want to visit?"

"Today we are not here to talk to the kids. We will only look at your teacher's register and see their attendance," said Neel. "The department has become strict in maintaining the records of the schools and their staff."

The Principal shifted uncomfortably in his chair.

"Hmm. We have forty-three teachers and we maintain their records manually." He opened a drawer next to his chair and pulled out a register.

Neel crossed his fingers. *Please God, let Saira's name*

appear in this book.

The register was placed in front of them. It had a list of each teacher's name, address, and subjects they taught. Neel and Neeta looked at it greedily.

Neel examined all the names on the first page, he tried to turn it but Neeta held the edge, taking her own time to read. As she finished, Neel turned the page over.

They leafed through the pages one after the other, but there was no familiar name. They started reading again from the first page and reached the last page without any success.

All the while, the Principal's eyes stayed glued to their faces. He noticed their disappointment. "Are you looking for someone in particular?" asked the Principal.

"No, nothing specific, we are just making sure." Neel took a deep breath. Their search was coming to an end.

He was about to conclude the meeting, when Neeta's voice echoed in the room, "Well, now we would like to meet a few teachers."

Neel looked at Neeta and saw a gleam of hope on her face. His eyes followed Neeta's fingers on the register. She was on the second page, 17th row, and it read, "Saina Siddhique."

Neel scanned the row of Saina Siddhique in the register. Every teacher had a subject assigned but Saina had none. "What subject does Saina teach?"

"You see, Saina is a special case," said the Principal. "She works with everyone. She is not assigned any particular subject; she helps wherever needed. She talks to the parents, she helps weaker kids in studies, and she decorates the school during annual functions. She acts as a mentor. She is wonderful and one of a kind."

Neel and Neeta looked at each other. The profile matched Saira's. "Okay. We would like to meet some of your teachers and finish our formalities."

The Principal crossed his arms across his chest, "I understand about this unnotified inspection, but why talk to teachers? You can inspect our classrooms, see how we teach, what we do."

Neeta nodded in approval, "Yes you are right, but this inspection is newly introduced to check any kind of irregularity concerning the teaching staff."

The Principal agreed with reluctance. "Okay, tell me which teachers you want to meet."

Neeta selected four teachers randomly and included Saina in the list.

The Principal nodded at his attendant, "Okay. I'll call them in a minute."

*****

Neel ran through his thoughts, *there is a chance that Saina Siddhique is Saira. They need to be prepared just in case. If she is Saira, they need to discreetly communicate to her.*

Neel clicked on the image texted by Martha earlier, it read 'Devki waits for you Saira.' He nudged Neeta to draw her attention on his phone. She read and repeated the message without producing any sound.

Neel took a business card from his pocket but then decided against and put it back. He quickly tore two small pieces of paper from the notepad and wrote his contact information with the correct one on one paper and a fake on the other. Next, he wrote 'Devki' in big letters on the top of the one having his correct phone number.

They waited patiently for the teachers to arrive.

The first one to arrive was the social studies teacher, Mrs. Sushila Gupta, she wore a red sari, her face highlighted with a purple lipstick. With the Principal in the room, she was extra respectful and had made up her mind to praise the school. The Principal, though pretending to continue his work, had his eyes and ears on the conversation.

The fake inspectors asked some random questions to Sushila about her qualification, experience, etc. Sushila happened to be talkative, she rambled about her wonderful experience in the school. Neeta yawned twice in between; they were least interested in such details. Their minds were focused on Saina Siddhique. *Hope she turns out to be Saira*, both wished.

When the second teacher arrived, the drill was the same, they asked some irrelevant questions and listened uninterestingly. They waited patiently for Saina. And when Saina's turn came, Neel and Neeta became alert.

A woman in her late 30's opened the door. She gingerly

closed the door behind her, without making any sound. She was thin, with a fair complexion, rather pale from poor nourishment. Her walk was slow yet confident. Her presence made the room naturally serene. She had a spartan look – her hair tied neatly at the back, no makeup, no jewelry. Neeta noticed the trace of grey color in her suit, which had faded with multiple washing.

Her expressionless face and gloomy eyes revealed her detachment from life. Her presence, however, generated such respect that Neel fumbled and rose from his chair to greet her. The woman tried to smile but failed.

Neeta's heart pounded hard. They waited for months for this moment, perhaps their wait was over now. She asked Saina to take a seat on the chair directly opposite to them. Saina politely lifted the chair and placed it farther away, as if she needed extra space in between.

Their eyes were fixed on the lady in front of them; amidst his excitement, Neel forgot what to say or ask. Neeta crossed her one leg over the other and tapped on her notepad. She broke the silence by pretending to read from a document,

"So Saira," Neeta took the chance, "Is that the right name. Did I pronounce it correctly?"

Neel noticed a twitch in the lady. She clutched the armrest of her chair tightly and crossed her heels under the chair.

"My name is Saina."

The Principal looked from under his glasses, "Her name is Saina Siddhique."

"I apologize for the mistake," Neeta smiled embarrassingly. "For no reason, I wrote the name wrong as Saira Ja…" she let her voice trail and paused to inspect the woman in front of her.

Neel appeared embarrassed too, "She always does this. I tell you – the people of Jhansi make blunders with names." He looked at Neeta, their eyes smiled. They were enjoying their teamwork.

Saina's face flushed. She glared at Neel and Neeta.

"So Saina, is Shivpuri your hometown? Where did you study?" Neel framed the question – saving Neeta from more scrutiny.

Saina paused for a second and spoke in a dispassionate voice, "I come from Mumbai."

Neel looked at his notepad, "And how many kids do you handle a day?"

"It depends on the day and the work I am doing. I manage around 20 students or more a day."

Neeta smiled, "Do you like the school environment?"

"Yes."

"I am sure the management takes good care of the staff." Neel twitched his lips and nodded at the Principal, receiving a smile in return.

Neeta continued, "This is a routine inspection, there is not much to it. We will take a look around the premises and finish our work."

Neel rose from his chair, "And oh yes, I forget to give my contact information to other teachers, in case of any questions, you can reach us anytime." He handed over the piece of paper to Saina – the one on which he had written his contact number and the words 'Devki'.

He turned toward the principal and extended the other piece of paper, "And here is one for you Sir. We are government employees, we don't carry business cards, that's my number, you can call me anytime."

The Principal took the paper and carelessly threw it in his drawer.

Saira looked at the information on the paper and her eyes sparkled. She stole a glance at Neel and Neeta, they both smiled back warmly in acknowledgement.

She folded the paper inside her palm. Neel was unable to interpret her expressions – whether she was scared, confused or happy.

The pair took leave of the Principal and promised to send their report by postal mail.

*****

Siana came out of the Principal's office and checked the paper again. It read 'Neel Kanth Dubey', with a phone number. The word written on the top caught her attention. The name which she recalled many times in the past few years – 'Devki' – the words sparked her memories.

The last image of Devki was still plastered in her mind – a bedsheet tied to each shoulder with babies inside. A handbag around her shoulders. Weak but fierce, ready to die for her daughters.

Devki and Saira were never friends like other regular ones. They never went to movies together or hung-out at shopping malls. They were not college buddies, nor did they share any recipes. They hardly spoke to each other, yet they were connected by the bond of humanity. They were bounded with an unspoken understanding. They were not blood sisters but sisters by circumstances – awful circumstances.

The mission that night was to help Devki escape.

Saira still remembered when Devki moved into her neighborhood as a newlywed. Their houses were next to each other, the higher floors were connected by a small strip of concrete. The houses were so close that they could speak to each other over the walls.

A couple of weeks after Devki's marriage, Saira visited to introduce herself and to welcome Devki to the neighborhood. Devki was alone in the room upstairs and seemed lost. She half smiled seeing Saira and showed no excitement. Saira was disappointed – she had been excited and hoped to befriend Devki since they were of the same age. Devki failed to speak much and answered in a word or two.

Saira decided to leave when Devki caught her arm. She spoke nothing but lifted the long sleeve of her top, to show a scar on the wrist and one above on the forearm. The scar on the forearm was fresh. Saira felt sorry for Devki and searched the room for an ointment or a band-aid. Just then Devki's mother-in-law entered. Devki quickly pulled her sleeves down and spoke in a loud voice for the first time that evening,

"Thank you Saira for visiting us, we'll talk soon."

After that visit, Saira did not see Devki for a couple of months. She tried to visit her, but Devki was unavailable. Saira was told that Devki was either sleeping, busy or was out to meet her parents.

Once Saira spotted Devki outside her room, drying clothes on the clothesline. Saira shouted, "Hey, got too busy with your husband that you have no time for me?"

Devki turned toward her, she looked weak, her eyes

dropped. She placed her index finger on the lips forcing Saira to stay quiet. Devki showed a fist and an open palm but Saira couldn't understand the meaning of it. It was their first muted chat. Devki vanished inside her room in a flash.

She was not seen again for months.

Later Saira did see Devki outside her room many times but they hardly spoke. The meetings were always short, and gradually reduced over time. They always conversed with each other across their respective houses – with most of their conversations being muted using signals and gestures. Sometimes Devki needed some supplies or sometimes just wanted to convey how much she was thankful over Saira's help. On one such evening Devki appeared happy, which was a rare moment. She kept her hand on her belly and smiled. Saira smiled back broadly and showed a hug.

After many years, this was the first time Saira heard or read Devki's name – and from complete strangers. *Who are these people?*

Saina darted in all directions but the visitors were gone. She ran across the school; they were not in sight. She came out of the school building and spotted the duo, who were pretending to scrutinize the building.

Siana was behind them, when she whispered loudly, "Hey you. So, the people in the school are right, you are some frauds."

Neeta turned and saw Saira standing right next to them… She nudged Neel – there was no point in hiding anymore.

"We are here for you Saira Jamal!"

Hearing her real name, Saira was stunned. She minced every word and spoke in a low voice, "Who…who are you? Did my husband hire you to find me or kill me?"

"No, Saira we are your friends. Believe us we are here to help you. Someone is looking for you for a long time." Neeta spoke in one breath.

"Who is looking for me?" Saira retorted, moving away from them.

"A friend of yours is looking for you," pleaded Neeta.

"Friend? I have no friend!"

"Dubeyji, show her the message sent by Martha."

"Martha? Now, who is this?" Saira turned toward the school.

"Wait, wait Saira," begged Neeta. "Give us a minute and we will convince you that we are telling the truth."

Neel turned his phone towards Saira and showed the image sent by Martha – the image contained the text message. Saira read the message, "Devki waits for you Saira."

As if the time froze, Saira's hands trembled. She slowly repeated, "Devki waits for you Saira?" Saira gulped some air, "Are you Devki's friends?"

Neeta, choked with tears, having no idea who Devki was, nodded frantically.

Saira spoke again, "Devki…Devki managed to survive?" and laughed and jumped a little. It was puzzling to see this expression from a woman who was ferocious a few minutes ago. Neel and Neeta were unsure of what she meant but nodded profusely.

There was a big transformation in Saira. A smile came on her face and showed signs of happiness and hope. She jumped once again like a little girl and repeated, "Devki survived …she lived!" She felt a sudden flare of joy. "How are her daughters?"

Daughters! Ahh! Neeta recalled the same question from Martha when she posed as Saira. Neel grabbed Neeta's hand and addressed Saira, "We don't have much time now, meet us in the evening …call me."

"Yes, you guys must run from this place. There are murmurs in the school that you are imposters. They might come after you."

Chapter 34

Neel and Neeta sprinted, cutting across the open grass fields. They had left the school far behind but continued running to ensure their safety.

Neel was ahead of Neeta by a few meters. He looked back now and then to see how she was doing. Neeta was out of breath and panting hard but still ran frantically.

Neel turned back again, failed to see the small swamp in front of him and ran straight into it. His ankle and shoes got laden with the sticky wet mud. Soon Neeta approached the swamp. She came to a sudden halt, perplexed, seeing no way around it.

"Dubeyji," cried Neeta. "Do something! How do I cross this?"

"The way I did," laughed Neel. "Just go through it."

"No, I cannot. Help me!"

"Why can't you? If I can, so can you. Remember the 'equality' of women."

"Dubeyji, do you want your 'wife' to get dirty in this mud?" Neeta said sheepishly.

"Wife!" screamed Neel in delight. "Did you say, wife?" Neeta had not responded to his marriage proposal until then. Neeta did not speak, her face blushed red.

Neel jumped and punched in the air. "Wife!" He raised his eyebrows and repeated with mischief.

"Don't over dream now…would-be wife." Neeta giggled.

Neel placed a small a rock between the wet-mud and threw his coat at Neeta. She placed her one leg over the stone and caught one sleeve of the coat, with another end held by Neel, she consciously crossed the swamp.

As she walked past Neel, he caught her arms. "How about celebrating our engagement with a kiss Mrs. Dubey?" winked Neel.

"First clean yourself," Neeta pushed him on the chest. "Did you see your condition?" Neeta ran in the direction of the city giggling. Neel followed her behind.

Later, Saira called and they fixed a time to meet her.

They were early at the restaurant, to meet Saira. They were discussing the activities of the day, when Neel sensed someone standing right behind him. He looked behind and gasped for a moment. "Saira! for God's sake, make some sound when you move!" Neel laughed.

As Saira joined them, she shot an array of questions about Devki, "So, you are friends of Devki. Tell me, how is she, where is she?"

"We don't know who Devki is, have never met her," said Neeta.

Neel added, "Today was the first time we heard her name. We've been speaking to only Martha."

Neel relayed everything to Saira – how Martha had contacted him months ago, their efforts to search for Saira, the trip to Saira's husband's house, interaction with the auto driver and all. Saira sobbed in between and at the same time lauded their tireless efforts. She could not believe that someone would care for her to this extent.

Neeta moved closer to Saira, "We ourselves didn't know much, but now everything is getting clear. I think Devki is in the USA and Martha is her friend."

Neel handed over his phone to Saira, "In a few minutes, Martha will call on my mobile to talk to you. She has been waiting patiently for this day. We will take a walk in the town to give you some privacy."

Saira sighed – *Devki. Life has made a full circle.* She least expected to hear from Devki ever again.

That night was an arduous one and still gave her chills. Shakeel had thrashed her badly and threw her out of the house. Whenever he got mad, he threw her out and allowed her inside only after a few hours. She had nowhere to go, she always pleaded for his mercy from outside the house. He had done the same on that night too. Saira did not cry, her tears had already dried. She was worried about Devki too, she had not seen her for a long time. She was aware of Devki's pregnancy and distress and threw food packets toward her room to feed her starving young friend. She came to know later that Devki had given birth to twins.

She was anxious over Devki's welfare and tiptoed near her house. She peeped in through the window near the ground floor and overheard Devki's husband Sudhir and his parents. They were framing a plan to kill Devki and her infants.

Saira panicked on hearing the conspiracy and decided to save Devki against all odds. Saira was outside her house and there was no easy way to notify Devki. Saira scaled her house wall from outside. It was difficult but not impossible, the design of the house was such that the wall was lower on her side. Her hands and knees were grazed but she was successful. After climbing the wall, she threw a stone toward Devki's room and ...

Neel's phone buzzed, breaking Saira's chain of thoughts. She answered the phone instantly, "Hello."

Martha, on the other end, sounded warm and loving. Listening to Saira speak, she had no doubts about her identity.

Saira had a series of questions, "How is Devki? Is she okay? How are the kids?"

"Devki is fine. She has grown big, not in size but in stature," laughed Martha. She updated about Devki's daughters, Saira broke down on hearing that Devki had named one of her twin daughters after her.

"When can I meet her, or talk to her?" Saira held the phone tightly.

"Devki is onto great things, I have disappointed her on earlier occasions, so this time I want to surprise her." It was their first conversation, yet they spoke like old friends. Martha continued, "You should come here to the USA. She will be too excited to see you."

"USA! I've never travelled alone so far."

"No worries, you will not come alone."

"I don't even have a passport."

"It will all be arranged."

After the soulful session, they bid goodbye to each other.

Saira sat in the restaurant, reflecting on her time spent with Devki, how they had survived the cruelty of the people who were supposed to love them and care for them. She recollected their last meeting, the night when they both attained freedom. Neither of them had imagined that each other would survive. And now, Devki has reached such great heights. Saira's eyes turned misty, as she walked down memory lane.

The duo soon returned from their stroll in the market, Saira updated them on her chat with Martha and her invitation to the

USA.

"USA! Dubeyji can't we go to the USA?"

"We would have gone to America, if you would have acted a little better like Saira."

They all laughed.

It was time for Neel and Neeta to return to Jhansi. They invited Saira to join them. Neeta insisted that Saira could stay with her and promised to help her in getting a job, but Saira refused. She would love to meet Devki but will never return to Jhansi again.

Neeta and Saira hugged, "Devki must be a great soul to have a friend like you." asked Neeta.

"Yes, she is, I am so grateful to her, to remember me and to look for me after all these years."

"What did you do for Devki, were you such thick friends? Why does she remember you this much?"

"I did nothing compared to what she is doing for me. I only helped in saving her life and the life of her two daughters."

Neeta embraced Saira tightly once again.

*****

The bus station was deserted when they arrived, and the bus to Jhansi awaited its passengers. Neel and Neeta were overjoyed with their success. Months of running and stress reaped a fulfilling result. They had found Saira and they had found each other.

Neeta wrapped her arms around Neel's, "Dubeyji thank you for everything. Thank you for supporting me and believing in me!"

Neel looked at her with soft eyes, "You are amazing Neeta, all this has happened only because of you. This is our success. You are the most deserving partner in my company."

Neeta looked at Neel – *He loves me, and I have tortured him terribly. I am nothing without him.* She moved forward and placed her lips on Neel's. He had waited patiently for this moment. They were hungry for each other for a long time. They kissed till eternity. Neeta's hands were on Neel's neck and his hands explored her body.

Suddenly Neeta's trance was broken, she moved away from Neel and spoke in fake anger, "Dubeyji, taking advantage of a poor girl!"

Neel was startled, "Who me? No! Never! Why would I?"

"I was just kidding Dubeyji." Neeta bubbled.

Neel cuddled her, "I will always be with you, my love. We will marry and have a small house. We will have small detectives of our own."

After some time, the bus started. They were exhausted and slept in each other's arms. It was the beginning of their new journey.

Chapter 35

Gagan looked at the morning sun through his office window; he rubbed his forehead. Stress and age had drawn streaks on his face. The ups and downs in his life had hardened him.

There must be a solution.

He closed the magazine in front of him and looked at the cover page again. Every month, the magazine published an article about a celebrity, with their picture on the cover. This time there was no face – only the name, 'Ian Scovich'.

The article elaborated about a speaker called Ian but there were no pictures of her. According to the writer, there was a new sensation, a new guiding light by the name of Ian Scovich. Her series of talks were transforming people globally. *This is my chance… a business opportunity* thought Gagan.

Gagan had worked hard for years to gain his current position as the partner of a publishing company. Gagan adjusted his name plate that sat in front of his desk – 'Gagan Mishra – Director, Sales, and Distribution'. *If I can get into partnership with Ian to sell her audios, it will be a profitable deal for the company.*

Gagan pressed a button on his phone and called his assistant. Vick soon showed up with a coffee mug in his hand. "I have an interesting assignment for you," announced Gagan as Vick walked in.

"Ever since I started here, you've been assigning interesting and challenging tasks to me."

"This is different and big."

"Shoot!"

"You know our company is trying to compete in this new market of online books and information. The way to improve our sales is to look for new opportunities."

Vick took a seat in front of Gagan and leaned forward.

Gagan tossed the magazine in front of Vick. "Have you heard about this lady named Ian Scovich?"

"Of course!" Vick replied promptly.

"I thought so. Who hasn't heard about Ian, but how do you know her?"

"I listen to her audios regularly. I found purpose in life through her talks."

"Hmmm, interesting. Ian's reach is farther than I imagined."

Gagan leaned back on his chair. "Listen, get in touch with this Ian and express our interest in doing business with her. It would be a lucrative deal if you can convince her to give us the distribution rights of her work," said Gagan. "I understand Ian's identity is unknown, but still, with a little effort and persistence, I'm sure you'd be able to trace her."

Vick chuckled, "No way! There's no way to contact Ian."

"What do you mean?"

Vick looked deeply into his coffee mug as if it was bottomless. "I mean, there's no information, no pictures, no profile, no contact number, no email. Nothing!"

"There must be a call back number, customer service, business address...there has to be something."

"There is none," said Vick. "No one has ever seen her or met her. No one knows who Ian is. People desire to meet her, but she is nowhere to be found."

"Hmm, mysterious! These Russians can be deceptive in everything."

"Russian! Ha-ha! No one knows Ian's origin. It is as if Ian doesn't exist – which could be true because she is too good to be true! Ian is a unique name for sure."

"Aww! Come-on! She must be an old bitch sitting in some corner, minting money," said Gagan without thinking.

"Gagan!"

Gagan sat straight in his chair. Vick's tone startled him.

"Sorry, we don't speak of Ian in such a manner," said Vick.

"We?" Gagan's eyes locked on Vick.

"We – I mean fans and listeners of Ian. She's enlightening millions – she's shaping lives."

Gagan was nonplussed by the change in Vick's tone. He recalled his conversation with a colleague a few months earlier and had noticed a similar dedication toward Ian. Gagan's lips skewed, "What did you learn from Ian? How did she shape your life?"

"Ian transformed me. A few years ago, I was not the kind of a person you see now. I was heading in a wrong direction when I was introduced to Ian's audios. And believe me, she changed me for good." Gagan could see the emotions bubbling in Vick.

Vick continued, "And now I have sworn to change the life of others too. I work with a charity organization that supports abused women and kids... anyone in need."

"I am impressed!"

"Yes, I follow the path shown by Ian. It's the responsibility of each human being to help others in need."

"Okay, if you're this passionate about Ian, find everything about her. I am not interested in knowing who she is and what she does but want to get the distribution deal for our company. It could mean a good bonus for you too." He seemed passionless about anything else.

Vick's eyes flickered as if remembering something, "It doesn't matter who Ian is and what she does, as long as you can understand what she says."

He walked out, leaving Gagan speechless.

*****

Vick himself wanted to meet Ian, for his own reasons. It seemed like yesterday, when he heard Ian's name for the first time.

His mother had raised him alone. His father had left them when he was still young. Growing up alone, Vick was shy and soft-spoken, but things changed with time. He became angry and violent, and the Chicago suburbs fueled his anger.

There were incessant brawls and fights. He was fighting a war he did not know against whom. His mother could only yell and cry. It continued till his adulthood and he was lucky to have survived. He barely managed to complete a diploma but was unable to settle in a job.

One night, he returned home late, when his mother stopped him as he climbed the stairs to his room, "Vick, you have your own reasons for living your life this way."

Ahh! Another drama! thought Vick.

"Today is your birthday, can you not give your mother a gift on this day? It's a special day for me too!"

"Okay! What do you want?" He wanted to cut the conversation. His mother reached out and took a CD from her bag. "Please listen to this my son. It'll take only a few minutes but promise me you'd listen to it twice."

That's it? This will shut down all the fuss! Vick agreed.

Once settled in his room, he played the CD. The title of the

CD itself was peculiar. It read 'Learn how to kill successfully.' *Holy shit! they made audio on this subject too and see who's gifted it to me. Looks like mom has accepted my ways,* smirked Vick.

The speaker's voice in the audio sounded strange, "Dear friends, this is Ian and today we will learn how to kill!"

As the speaker spoke, the words gained on Vick. He listened attentively. As the talk came to an end, "Friends, you owe this to yourself! You owe it to Ian!" Vick touched his moist eyes, *What the hell! When did this happen?*

He turned the CD cover – 'Learn how to kill successfully By Ian Scovich'

Vick looked for more information on the speaker, there was none. He played the audio again.

After a while, he walked down the stairs. His mother was still in the kitchen, and hearing his footsteps, she whined, "I know, you did not listen to the audio. You cannot give your mother anything. This old woman cannot get anything. I will die seeing you like this."

"Mama," Vick's voice was heavy. The tone of his voice told the old lady that something had already changed. Vick had a question, "Who is Ian?"

Mother's voice trembled, "No one knows, dear. No one knows. But it doesn't matter who she is, as long as you can understand what she says."

Vick came down the remaining flight of steps and walked toward the main door.

"Where are you going now?"

"To tell my friends about Ian!"

Over the months, Vick was called by all sorts of names, 'little sister', 'coward', 'little girl', 'sissy'. He paid no heed to them. He kept listening to Ian.

Ian helped him kill all the violence…all the negativity in him. To get away from all his past, he moved to Atlanta and joined the publishing company as an intern. He flourished in his job this time and was soon offered a fulltime position. Since then, he devoted the rest of his time to serve others in need.

Vick wanted to personally meet Ian Scovich – to thank her for rebuilding his life, for saving him, for giving him another chance in this world.

Chapter 36

Months had passed since Mike left and the days were hell for Ian. Although there were twelve employees in the office, Ian felt lonely and desperate. Multiple times, Martha tried to inquire the reason for Ian's strange behavior against Mike and what transpired between them, but Ian was always tight-lipped about it.

She got less patient – sometimes she behaved like a strong woman and sometimes cried like an insecure little girl. She was on the edge always; as if ready to break some shackles.

Ian loved only her fans, her listeners, who were increasing in numbers day by day. She was tormented whenever she heard about someone being abused. Ian had long discussions with Martha on how she wished that no woman should ever be abused or trafficked. She wanted to provide a sense of hope and direction to victimized women; what she was unable to do for herself, she wanted to provide for others.

She distanced herself from Gagan day by day. Gagan noticed a few times, her absence from home during the day, but every time, she returned with shopping bags in hand, and on time before the kids arrived.

*****

"Interesting," muttered Ian and continued to read the article that elaborated on 'Helping Sisters', a charitable organization which supported destitute women and children. There was a mention of one Vick Smith who was working diligently with the organization. The article ended with a reference about Ian Scovich, that the members of the organization gained inspiration from her speeches.

Martha was engrossed in correcting some endless list and crunching some numbers when Ian placed the newspaper in front of her. "Did you read this?"

Martha squinted on the newspaper, the title of the article caught her eye, 'Helping Sisters, a new ray of hope!' "What about it?"

"They're are doing some extraordinary work and appreciate our speeches."

"Not 'our' but 'your' speeches," corrected Martha. Ian did not acknowledge her praise. It was a team effort. She was not doing anything by herself.

Ian thought for a moment, "They seem to offer great service to the needy and run their operations with the donations they receive."

"Hmm, what's your point?"

"We should do our part. The article mentions our speeches, they buy all our audios. Let's give them for free."

"Free!"

"Yes, they need our audios, after all, we create our stuff for people like them. Moreover, this center is doing what we are unable to do!"

Martha's eyes gleamed, "Now that's an idea!"

"By the way, how much money do we have?"

"A fortune!" Martha's eyebrows danced.

"Then we should donate the money too, support them in their needs, join hands with them in uplifting the downtrodden."

"That may jeopardize your secrecy."

"No, it should not. We need to be cautious!" Ian continued, "You should visit them, check how they are doing and inform them about our offer."

Martha agreed happily.

"Try to meet Vick, I read he is doing some incredible service for them."

Later in the afternoon, Martha made a few phone calls. She contacted Jayesh, who had a big network. Once convinced about the authenticity of the 'Helping Sisters' organization, she made an appointment.

*****

Martha arrived at the 'Helping Sisters' location where Jenny, the manager, greeted her at the entrance.

Jenny was in her late fifties and dressed in an ankle-high skirt and a peach top. She herself was a domestic abuse survivor and the job meant an escape from her past and an opportunity to save others.

She was all smiles seeing Martha, "It's a pleasure meeting you." Once they were seated in her office, "How can I help you?" asked Jenny.

"We saw an article about this place in the local newspaper and got interested in knowing more about it."

"Certainly, I will show you around our center."

Both ladies stepped outside, with Jenny leading the way for Martha. The path opened into a lawn. There were big verandahs with rooms on either sides.

It was evening and kids of all ages were playing in the yard, under adult supervision. Some senior members were taking a stroll around the lawn, while a few were reading books. Some elders were sitting outside and watching the activities around them.

Jenny took Martha from one room to another introducing her to the inmates. Many rooms were empty as the occupants were outside in the lawn.

The place also had a small hospital and a library. Jenny explained how they lived and operated. They had a strict routine from morning to evening. Kids were sent to schools in the morning and adults were assigned different jobs.

Looking around, Martha admired, "This place gives the feeling of a hostel."

Jenny nodded, "Yes. We keep it that way, because, the people who live here including myself, have gone through a tough life that it is important to keep them in a schedule."

There were girls and boys who were rescued from traffickers. There were women who were abused and beaten and had no place to go. There were sick inmates who needed constant medical care. Many local doctors visited them as part of their voluntary work. There were old people abandoned by their kids and the society. Martha was surprised that all this happened even in the USA.

Martha praised the lady, "You guys are doing an excellent job, you have sheltered all these distressed people!"

Jenny smiled, "We are doing our duty for our fellow human beings. All this has been made possible mostly by individual donations coming from people from all walks of life."

Martha was impressed by their dedication and effort. As they entered the lobby of the library, Martha saw a huge poster of Ian's audio cover adorning the wall. A couple of Ian's quotes were painted on the wall too. The poster in the library said, 'Ian Speaks'. It was blown to a large size and had hundreds of signatures on it. Martha looked at Jenny who was looking at the poster with a proud smile. Martha played ignorant.

"What's that?" She was curious to know how much they were connected with Ian.

Jenny turned and looked at Martha astonished, she looked again at the poster. "This is Ian!" as if introducing a physically present Ian to Martha. Jenny bowed slightly in front of Ian's poster. Martha was pleased with her gesture.

"A few years ago, when we were unable to guide our girls and kids, to show them hope, to tell them that there is light at the end of the tunnel, someone introduced Ian to us. Her talks inspire and motivate people in distress."

Martha was thrilled, "Ian has impacted you this much! Have you seen her?"

Jenny continued to look at the poster with respect, "We've never met Ian, never seen her picture either. We have only listened to her voice."

Jenny took a slight left and walked across the library hall, "No one knows who Ian is. She is an angel or a spirit, who gives us hope. Ian's voice echoes in this hall every evening. We all listen to Ian's talks repeatedly and wait for the new ones."

"Didn't you try to find her, to meet her?" Martha was moved on seeing Ian's impact at such a worthy place.

"We tried! We tried hard, and eventually resigned since there was no clue about Ian," Jenny sighed. "And later we settled to what Vick says, 'It isn't important to find out who Ian is, as long as we can understand and follow what she says!'

Oh yikes, Vick! Martha forgot about him.

"Talking about Vick, I read that he contributes much to your organization. Where is he, will I get a chance to meet him?"

"Vick is a gem, an asset to our establishment. Without him, all these are impossible. He works during the day at his job and comes here every evening. He should be here any minute."

It took an hour to visit the whole place. When they returned to Jenny's office, she offered Martha a drink.

"So, tell me something about yourself. On the phone, you had expressed your desire to help us."

Martha took a sip from her drink and caught her breath. It was a long walk. "We are a small, local business. We learnt about your organization recently. I am sorry I acted ignorant of Ian earlier, I wanted to see to what extent you utilize her audios."

Jenny was amused but smiled as Martha continued, "We are also a huge fan of Ian. Her talks inspire us too. Since our interests are similar, we would like to take the responsibility of providing you with Ian's audios. If required, you can also order any older copies and we'd be glad to provide you them as well. Anything bearing Ian's name will be our gift to you."

Jenny's eyes showed delight; it was a worthy offer. "And you want to do this because …?"

"We want to assist you. You guys are doing a great work and we want to support you."

Jenny smiled in gratitude. She had received a lot of donations in the past, yet this was a unique offer – someone presenting Ian's audios.

Martha continued, "And these audios will be made available to all your other centers too." Jenny moved forward from her chair, leaned and clutched Martha's hands.

"Thanks, Thank you!"

Martha smiled, "Oh, please don't thank me, thank Ian. Her speeches motivate us too, we are the largest retailer of her speeches."

Martha took a pause and spoke again "And…"

"Is there more?" asked Jenny. What she just received already ran into hundreds of dollars. Martha smiled at Jenny's response and took another sip of her drink,

"And we would also like to help you with any other need you may have."

Jenny looked at her curiously.

"I mean financially," added Martha.

"Wow!" Jenny clasped her hands and closed her eyes. *This is a lucky day.*

"Are you the owner of your company? I missed its name, what was it?"

"That doesn't matter. Believe me, we are legitimate, but all donations will be made as anonymous, we don't want any name or advertisement."

There was a sound of the office door opening. Jenny looked in the direction and rose from her seat, "Vick, meet our generous donor!"

Martha looked around, a young man, half of her age was standing behind her.

"Nice to meet you," Vick, extended his hand toward Martha.

Chapter 37

As Vick took seat beside Jenny, Martha studied him. He was slender, tall and young – dressed in a brown suit. He was younger than she had expected. He looked like someone who had just stepped out of his teenage, but his demeanor seemed mature.

Jenny introduced Vick formally to Martha, "This is Vick, one of our key members. We need young blood like Mr. Vick to keep things moving here." She turned her revolving chair and opened her palm toward Martha with a smile, "And this is Martha, our much-needed friend."

Martha expected some excitement in Vick, but he remained unruffled.

"My apologies, I overheard you talking as I walked in," Vick said. "Thanks for your consideration."

"Jenny told me how much you all love Ian. We will be gifting Ian's audio books to your organization,"

"We already bought a lot of them ourselves," said Vick.

"We will be donating funds too. Anything we can do to support the cause."

"Ah, money," Vick raised his eyebrows, "What else?"

"What else?" repeated Martha. "You have dollars, what else will you need?" She was a bit annoyed by Vick's responses, but his expressions told her she made a mistake.

Vick folded his arms across his chest, "Yes, this world needs a lot of money," stressing on his words. "But that's not enough!"

Martha moved in her chair, while Vick continued, "Money is the easiest commodity to give. People give money to help the needy and think their work is over. Done!"

Where is this going?

Vick continued, "Don't get me wrong… rich people think they are doing a great deed by donating funds, but do they ever realize that the poor are doing a big favor to them? Because the poor…" Vick took a quick breath, "by accepting the charity, are relieving the rich of their guilt."

Martha's face flushed. *Is this guy crazy?*

"Easy, just give your dollars and sleep. All the world's problems are resolved!"

"Vick," whispered Jenny under her breath, trying to control Vick's tirade.

Vick pushed away his chair abruptly, "Can I show you something?"

Martha stared at him. *He has some nerve.*

He spoke again, "I'm sorry for my behavior but," Martha failed to notice any expression of apology on Vick's face, "It's not that I don't appreciate or respect you. You are one of the rare people who take time to visit our center, otherwise we get hundreds of checks, and no one ever cares to even visit us."

Martha's face remained fixed. "Okay, what do you want to show? Is there anything remaining to be seen or heard?"

"Give me a few minutes of your time," said Vick as he walked out. Jenny smiled apologetically at Martha and gestured her to follow Vick.

It was late in the evening. Lights were on in the rooms and the lawn was deserted. They walked toward the library without speaking a word. They came across the same lobby. Martha glanced at Vick; his face appeared expressionless as they passed by Ian's poster.

In the hallway, many women and young kids were seated on rows of chairs, each of them in their own world. As Martha passed through the hallway, a familiar voice came through the speakers, "Standup for yourself, standup for Ian. You owe this to yourself! You owe this to Ian!"

Vick, Martha and Jenny were soon inside a medium-sized theater. Vick asked Martha to take a seat. Martha was still upset with Vick, but played along, to see the end of it. The lights were switched off and a movie played on the screen.

Martha recognized the building in the picture, it was the 'Helping Sisters Center'. The video showed how the inhabitants of the center stayed and supported each other. It also had interviews of many women and kids; how and why they arrived.

Martha was soon lost in the movie, she realized how isolated these people were. They needed love and care. They helped one another, elders and young adults took care of the kids. Sick and older people were attended by volunteers, they fought every day for resources and love.

Vick flipped using the remote and a video of some other

city or country played…it showed how women were treated, how drugs played havoc in the society; how young girls were abducted, beaten and sold; how adolescents were used as drug mules; how innocent children as small as five-six years old, were sexually abused and assaulted. Vick played another video with similar woeful content from a different part of the world.

Martha was choked with emotions as the different scenes played on screen.

This was the life she had experienced, hustling her way through, in Mexico.

Martha was still recouping her feelings, when the lights came on. All eyes were moist.

There was complete silence in the theater except for the sound of a machine in the background.

Vick broke the silence, "Do you see? These people don't need your dollars alone. They need you!" Martha wiped her eyes.

Vick continued, "They need compassion, they need love, they need hope, they need human touch – they need Ian!"

"Ian!" repeated Martha in a muffled voice stunned by the utterance of Ian's name.

"Yes, Ian – people like Ian," repeated Vick. "Ian has to take more responsibility here."

Martha composed herself. *He's talking about Ian.* "Why Ian? Why do you think Ian needs to take more responsibility? Responsibility for what?" Martha's voice pitched higher.

"Have you heard any of Ian's talks?"

Martha paused for a second, "Yes, a few."

"Then listen to them all. You will notice a pattern there. Ian's speeches show her agenda. Her talks reveal her fight to give people hope and happiness!"

Vick became more excited, he spoke rapidly, "Her speeches clearly show the direction she is taking. She takes genuine responsibility to reach out to abused and troubled people …to give hope. She works as a counselor, she works as a healer to a bruised soul, she works as a teacher."

Martha listened attentively.

Vick continued, "When Ian's heart is with the people and when she takes it so personal, why doesn't she come out and help? Why doesn't she appear in front of these desolate souls?"

Martha noticed passion and urgency in Vick's voice. He was still speaking, "When her speeches can help to this extent, just think how much she will inspire, if she is in front of the world."

"But why do you assume I will know Ian?" Martha blurted out.

Vick stared at her and smiled, "I presume you don't know her, but this is the first time…"

"First time what?" Martha cut him out.

"We have received money and other donations in the past, but this is the first time anyone has offered Ian's audio recordings."

"That doesn't mean anything. We distribute Ian's audios and since the newspaper article wrote about Ian, we thought it would be useful if we donate her works."

"Perhaps YOU don't know Ian, but someone should be familiar with her. May be Ian herself doesn't know the enormity of her impact on her fans. We should convey the message to her through some means. Once she knows that her followers keenly await her, she will come out to meet them."

Martha stared at Vick, dumbfounded.

"Hope you don't mind, but we cannot accept your money!"

"Do you understand what you are…" gasped Jenny.

Vick waved his hand to cut her off, "We don't need money, we need people, and we need their time. We have opened more centers, not because we have money but because we are needed there."

Martha felt poor in a long time.

"We will be thankful, if you can donate us some time and help us in spreading our word for Ian." Without waiting for any response, Vick walked out of the theater. Jenny looked on helplessly.

Martha walked out of the building teary. Once inside her car, she slammed the door, unable to control herself, she clutched the steering wheel tight. She remembered Sofi, remembered her family, her sisters and her aunts back home.

She wept.

Chapter 38

Ian sipped her coffee slowly as Martha narrated her visit to the 'Helping Sisters' center. Martha gave her a vivid picture of her experience at the center.

"I had no idea that I am making such an impact on people. Vick is right, I do feel we need to provide help and hope to those in need." Tears welled up in Ian's eyes. She continued, "My life hasn't changed much." Seeing the amused look on Martha's face, she added, "Okay, I agree, my life has changed a little, but I am still living where I lived earlier. I still live with the same people; I still have the same insecurities as before." She took a deep breath, "I am surprised and elated that my talks are inspiring the outside world to this extent!"

"That's nothing! I've often witnessed at many places, people talking about you, looking for you. Recently, I came across a social media page dedicated to you!"

"Yes, I saw some banners around the city asking me to come out from my hideout. Why? Why me?" Ian said in a painful voice and caught her head in her palms.

"You've changed their lives. They feel you – they love you, and they adore you. They just have not seen you."

Ian sat on her chair, leaning against the head rest with her eyes closed. She remained in a meditative state for a while and moved her head left-to-right and murmured, "This is not right, it should not be this way."

"What should not be this way?"

Ian opened her eyes and lurched forward on her chair, "Hope you didn't tell Vick that you know me."

"No way! I didn't tell Vick that I work for you."

"Work with me."

Martha looked at Ian in appreciation. Over the months, she had understood her position. Ian was no longer the timid girl she first saw. She had become big – bigger than Martha, bigger than anyone. Martha felt honored that Ian considered her as a friend, but in reality, Martha was working for her. Ian was everything.

Ian was livid, "I am not doing justice to my fans. I shouldn't be living this double life… I should be true at least for the sake of their unconditional love for me. I must not preach what

I cannot practice."

Martha edged slightly on her chair. *This is leading to something*. Perhaps the time has come for Ian to separate herself from Devki. "I've told you many times earlier to break out of that Devki character. You are independent now. You need not take any crap from anyone!"

Ian rubbed her face with her palms, "I don't know, maybe I have a split personality, at home I'm Devki and once I'm here, I become Ian."

Martha nodded, "Remember I told you the other day, when we were coming out of Jayesh's house. Stop being Devki and become Ian, Devki must die for Ian to grow."

"It's easy for you to say," Ian looked at Martha. "What about my kids? I am still dependent on Gagan for my visa. If he comes to know about this, my dreams will be shattered, and I may have to leave this country with my daughters and…and their future will be in jeopardy. Do you understand?" Ian slumped into her chair again.

A few minutes of silence prevailed, before Ian spoke again, "So, Vick refused to accept money although their organization is in dire need of it!"

"That's what he said. They're opening new branches to serve more people, to reach out to the masses. Vick does a full-time job and he donates most of his salary to the organization."

"He…. refused the money," repeated Ian as if talking to herself, "That means he thinks that I can be more useful than dollars."

A ring on Martha's phone interrupted them. "Think of the devil…" Martha let her phrase trail as she answered her phone, "Hi, Vick."

Ian signaled Martha to put the phone on speaker. Martha raised her left hand, gesturing Ian to show patience. As Martha spoke with Vick, Ian could sense some urgency. All she heard from Martha were short phrases of, "Yes, aha…" She noticed Martha's face changing as the call proceeded. Finally, Martha concluded, "I will try Vick, cannot promise how much, but you did surprise me."

Martha disconnected the phone and answered Ian's gaze. "He changed his mind."

"What do you mean changed his mind… about what?" asked Ian.

"He will accept money now." Martha grinned.

"Accept money, which means that I am no longer important to him and …"

"You are always important, but he said that there are these African girls who were rescued from some terrorist group in Africa."

"And?"

"Some of these girls are taking refuge in the United States and Vick wants to rehabilitate them."

Ian rubbed her temples and shrugged. *This guy is something.*

"So now he needs money from wherever possible!"

Ian was furious, not at Martha or Vick, but at herself. She clutched her bag. "This guy is giving whatever he has, risking everything and here I am creating these fake speeches and making money!"

"Your talks are not fake. You feel them and that's why your listeners are connected with you." Martha spoke in a softer voice, "And money is only an outcome of it. You didn't create your speeches for money!"

"I am tired of this dual life," said Ian. "My daughters hate me; my husband hates me and now I hate myself – for not being a role model for my children, for not being a role model for the society." Ian was emotionally exhausted.

"Then take a position, bear your responsibility. Attain the freedom which you helped others achieve".

Ian stared at Martha.

As Ian walked away, Martha dialed Vick.

Chapter 39

Devki walked out of the office. Her legs trembled as she hurried to her car. Gagan had bought her a car after she insisted for one – for picking up and dropping off the kids, and for shopping. The car was old, but in excellent condition.

Devki gunned the engine, uncertain about her destination. The last thing she wanted was to go home. There was no home. She felt ashamed and betrayed by herself. *Am I cheating myself and my people?* She drove aimlessly for a long time.

Her talks reflected her feelings from within. She spoke from her heart, whatever she thought was important. She wanted to eradicate abuse and helplessness from the world. She preached – *'Your fear, your insecurities are all within you. If one can search inside himself, all these problems can be resolved. Your body can be enslaved, but your soul is free. One should not make relationships with the body but only with his soul.'*

Her speeches elaborated often about freedom of soul, freedom of expression. *Why then, I myself, am unable to follow my own teachings?*

I have been foolish to think that Devki and Ian are the same. What a grave mistake! Should Devki listen to Ian's speeches too? Giving lectures and following them are both entirely different! Perhaps I need to listen to my own speeches for some motivation and inspiration.

Why am I hiding? Why am I scared of revealing my identity? People are giving everything to save this world. Am I really being blackmailed by my own insecurities or does Devki like the life she lives now?

After wandering for a long time, Devki wanted to walk and inhale some fresh air but there was no place to walk. There were heartless, concrete highways 75North, 285 East. *Where do these roads lead anyway?*

Devki desperately wanted to get off the car. She took the next exit and came on to the riverside drive. She knew there was a public park, where kids and adults spent their evenings. Once she entered the area, she parked her car and yanked open the door as if the car was holding her hostage. She breathed fresh air. The cool breeze of the fall season touched her face. She leaned on the car bonnet and tried to relax; her thoughts were still racing.

Suddenly her eyes lit up. She reached for her phone and dialed the number,

"Hi Bhabi," answered Renu in her usual voice.

"How is your brother?"

Renu was startled with Devki's tone and the question she threw at her, "Is this a joke? He lives with you." Before Renu could gather herself from the weird question posed to her, Devki shot another, "Why haven't you ever visited us?"

"Oh, it's too far, difficult to come."

"Atlanta is not that far from California, that you cannot visit your disgusting brother!"

"Bhabi!" yelled Renu, "Mind your language. I know my brother well. I talk to him every day! Where is he?"

Devki breathed heavily. "Do you know your brother is mentally sick? He is an animal. You already know this; you know him better than anyone else…don't you?"

"He's short-tempered, but is good at heart. Things that happened in the past have hurt him, you can change him with your love, won't you?" Renu tried to sound affectionate.

"You should be ashamed of your brother. You know he beats me; he rapes me every night!"

"Devki!" Renu shouted on the top of her voice, "You don't have to discuss your personal life with me, and sometimes a husband's love can be misunderstood!"

"Huh! Personal life… love!" sneered Devki.

"Listen Devki…"

"Don't call me Devki anymore. Devki is dead! Devki doesn't live here anymore!" Her voice resonated in the emptiness of the park.

Ian was relieved after disconnecting the call. A burden seemed to have been removed from her mind.

It was getting late, and darkness encompassed the park.

*****

Ian jittered seeing the darkness and lights of the cars on the road. She had momentarily forgotten her fear of moving lights in the dark. She clutched the car steering tight and drove cautiously.

The lights of the cars crisscrossing startled her every time. Anxiety engulfed her and she drove slowly. She looked in the rear-view mirror, she had created a long line of cars behind her. People honked and jeered at her. Ian panicked and hit the pedal of her car. Her car lurched forward and was about to hit the car in front, when she slammed the brakes, and the car came to a screeching halt.

To avoid the traffic, she changed the lane and came to an internal street. The headlights of the incoming cars jolted her. She breathed hard and became scared of the unknown. She fidgeted with her car's interiors and accidentally switched off the lights. She drove in the maze of lights and honks feeling helpless.

A sudden sound of a blaring siren and flashing lights struck horror in her heart. She looked behind – a cop car was following her. Ian stopped her car on the shoulder of the road and waited for the Police car behind her. Ian's heart raced and tears seeped on her cheeks.

A female police officer approached her car and knocked on the driver side of the window. As Ian lowered her window, the officer witnessed a horror-stricken tearful woman.

"Are you okay ma'am?" asked the officer. Ian shook her head up and down in 'yes', tears filled her eyes and her body trembled.

"This is a routine stop – I saw you driving without the lights on. You are driving too slow and stopping the traffic. Is everything alright with you and the car?"

Ian's lips quivered. "I ...I laal aa lights I am scaa scaaa." She stopped.

The officer gave a cursory look inside her car. "License and registration please."

With trembling hands Ian handed over her documents to the officer. Everything was in order.

The officer returned the documents, "Looks like there's some problem with your car, let me take you home. Follow my car slowly and make sure to get your car checked first thing in the morning." Ian nodded and followed the officer's car.

The lights of the other cars still scared her. Sometimes she squeezed her eyes shut for a moment and then focused on the car in front of her.

She prayed for the time to pass soon – the way it passed in Jhansi many years ago.

Saira's voice echoed in her ears, 'Devki, Run! Run!'

Devki's aversion to moving lights had roots in her past.

Chapter 40

It was the night when Saira helped her escape from Jhansi. They were on the deserted road in Jhansi with no signs of any transportation…

Saira had said, "Now run Devki, run as fast as you can and as far as you can. Once your daughters grow up, tell them about me. If you survive, tell people about me, about us."

Devki was all by herself, she looked around and became aware of the surroundings. There was no traffic, nothing moved on that night. Devki checked the knot of the bedsheets in which she carried the babies. The babies were fed and possibly will sleep for some time.

She had to make a quick decision.

If she took the direct road to the railway station, despite being a longer route, she might be confronted by a police patrol. Devki remembered a short-cut by the side of the water-tank. It led straight to the railway station, but it was unsafe. There was no road, just the railway tracks, where the trains passed at the scheduled times. Walking on that path was suicidal, but with little options, she decided to take it.

Devki had learnt to walk on the railway tracks from her father during her childhood. She was ready to break the most important rule her father taught – 'Never cross a railway track during the night.'

But Devki had no other option…to save her life, she had to risk her life first.

Devki ran toward the water-tank and slid by the side of it. There was a small stone trail leading to the railway tracks. The tracks were laid like an unending mesh of wires running in all the directions. They were not new to Devki, she grew up by the side of them.

A layer of sweat covered the nape of her neck and ran through her spine. Devki tried hard to keep her breath steady and stepped on the tracks. It was dark except for the faint lights of the signals. The iron tracks made spooky sounds in the dark as they shifted for the incoming trains.

The side of the tracks was filled with gravel, which made it harder for Devki to walk. She opened her eyes wide to see better in the flickering light of the lamp posts and train signals. She took a great risk – trains could come from any direction and it was tough to identify on which track the trains were approaching.

Devki walked between the tracks – taking one step at a time. Her eyes darted in all directions. One small mistake can cost their lives. She could see the faint light of the platform in the distance. She stepped across each line, mindful of an accidental fall. It was a short distance but with two babies and a bag, walking on the gravel exhausted her.

She stopped to catch her breath when she suddenly noticed train lights advancing from opposite directions. She was in the middle. It was difficult to judge on which tracks the trains were advancing.

From the approaching lights, Devki guessed at least one train to be coming on the track on which she stood. Unable to decide her next move, she squeezed her eyes shut and waited for the inevitable. She held the babies close to her chest and waited for the train to run over her. As the sound of the train approached her, she screamed "Aaaaaah!" her voice died in the noise of the trains.

The strong wind from the trains hit her from the front and back as the trains passed on both sides. Soon, all Devki heard was the fading noise of the trains. She opened her eyes and found herself alive. She looked in both the directions, the trains were moving away from her – they had passed on different tracks. She was drenched in her own sweat. The babies murmured a bit and slept again.

*****

Devki's knees ached – weak from malnourishment and exhaustion. Soon she saw the welcoming platform. The train at the platform appeared bigger. To avoid any suspicion, she controlled her breath and wiped the sweat from her face. By the time she reached the platform, the train was ready to leave. There was no time to buy a ticket, and she was not even sure if she had enough money to buy one.

Devki boarded the first unreserved compartment she came across. It was crowded. It was way past midnight; some passengers were awake, but most were dozing off. There was no place for anyone to sleep. Looking at a mother with two babies, a kind soul offered Devki a seat. The train started within minutes. Devki smiled at the co-passengers and calmed her nerves.

Soon she felt a tap on her shoulder – Devki turned back and saw two dark round eyes staring at her. "Ticket! Ticket!" A Ticket inspector nodded at Devki to show her ticket.

Devki's face flushed but she quickly recomposed, "Ttttt tickets with th my hhh husband."

"And where is the husband?" Ticket Inspector raised his eyebrows suspiciously.

"Wawa we were late so my hhh husband boarded a different caca compartment."

"Where is your luggage?"

"Thth that is aaa also with my hhh husband."

The other passengers suppressed their laughter at the way Devki spoke. The inspector regretted for putting a poor lady with two infants, in such a position and walked away.

The sound of the moving train sounded like music to Devki's ears. It was like a band of trumpets blown to celebrate her freedom.

A poor laborer woman sat on the ground, next to Devki. The infant on her lap was wailing in hunger. The mother tried to pacify her but in vain.

Devki checked on her babies who were fast asleep. A faint smile played on Devki's lips. She unzipped her bag and took a milk bottle. She extended the bottle to the woman.

The woman was surprised. "You have two babies, why give me your milk? My child has to get used to hunger."

Devki held her hand, "I cannot see a baby crying."

The woman took the bottle and fed her baby, who finished the whole bottle in a minute.

Soon, Devki's babies woke up with hunger and wailed. The woman looked at Devki apologetically.

"Don't worry! My kids are used to hunger," said Devki.

Chapter 41

Devki followed the cop's car to her house. She turned into her driveway and waved off the cop. The events of the evening had drained her.

She noticed Gagan's car in the driveway. *The kids must have gone somewhere.* She checked the time – 7.00pm. She had never been this late. Ever.

Devki parked her car and entered the house. There was no one in the living room. Her shoes echoed across the house as she placed her handbag on the table.

Gagan emerged from a room, "Where were you?" his voice icy. Devki ignored as she put her keys in the bag. "Did you check the time? Where were you?!" Gagan snarled. Devki chose not to respond. "I am asking you, dumb lady!"

Devki returned his gaze, "I was with friends, or maybe doing shopping or might as well be dead…why do you care?"

"Oh, with friends! And who are these friends that made you forget your family?" He continued, "And what is that attitude?"

Devki gave a cold shoulder and turned toward her bag. She wanted to avoid any confrontation, at least for now.

"I am seeing that you have got some wings," Gagan tossed a pillow at her. "Perhaps I got too busy with my work and you started messing here."

"Please leave me alone, I don't want any argument with you." Intending to walk out of the room, she snatched her handbag from the table, when it yanked open, spilling the contents all over the floor.

There were all sorts of stuff on the ground but Gagan's eyes were caught by the CDs.

Damn! She was always careful not to bring things from work but had no clue how those CDs showed in her bag. Perhaps they were on Martha's desk and she picked them by mistake. It was too late to do anything. *It's better if he knows this way.*

Gagan's eyes narrowed on the CDs. He had seen those somewhere earlier too. To get a better view, he moved one of the discs closer to him, using his foot.

"Hmm 'Ian Speaks'. So, this is where all this fire comes from!" reflected Gagan.

Devki froze, staring at her stuff, not knowing what to do.

"You cannot become Ian by just listening to her," said Gagan. "You are worthless, and you will remain worthless."

Devki gasped in relief. *What a fool!*

Gagan continued, "Do you know how much Ian earns with her audios, how many people are impacted with her talks and look at yourself! You are penniless, munching on my money with no gratitude!"

"Yes, Ian's speeches are valuable. They help everyone, you should listen to them too!" Devki mocked.

"Ha! Her speeches are for bitches like you, not for a man like me."

Sounds of laughter came from outside and the girls entered the house pushing each other but sensing the tension in the room, fell silent.

Esha looked at Devki and Gagan. Her eyes scanned the assorted items on the floor. The CDs on the floor caught her attention. She knelt and cautiously picked the CD from the floor, as if her touch would spoil the cover. She wiped the cover with her shirt and pressed the it against her heart. She closed her eyes for a moment.

"Who bought these CDs? Are these yours Dad?"

"Huh...mine!"

"A friend gave me these," Devki quickly interjected. "She talks highly about Ian. This is the first time I got them."

"I don't want Ian's CDs in my house," said Gagan. "They give wrong notion to people."

"No Dad, Ian never teaches wrong. She shows direction to lost people. She gives hope."

"Do you even know her?" asked Gagan.

"No one knows Ian, but everyone wants to see her, meet her and touch her. It doesn't matter even if you can never meet Ian, because she stays in your heart forever."

"You never know dear – she could be a fake or a machine-generated voice. Don't get emotional over this Ian!" said Gagan, annoyed at her attachment toward Ian.

"Ian is real, I know her. She knows my heart. She speaks for me; she speaks to me!"

Esha continued, "Remember Dad, you were surprised when

my grades started improving. It was because of Ian's speeches. In fact, you were the one who gifted me her CDs, the first time."

Gagan recalled, *Indeed I did!* after one of his colleagues suggested him.

"You can keep these. Take them as a gift," said Devki.

"You don't want to listen to these?" Esha raised her eyebrows.

"Don't know sweetheart, if I will ever get time from my house-hold work, but they are important to you, so you keep them."

"You better make time to listen to them. Ian is for all."

Devki felt weak in her knees. It was late-night and by then, everyone had retired to their rooms. Devki tossed and turned on the couch in the living room.

Chapter 42

The signal turned green, Vick pressed the gas pedal, turning his gaze away from the SunTrust plaza building on the left. As he drove through the downtown to reach to the other end of the city, he passed through several high-rise buildings and beautiful architecture. It was late in the evening, the traffic was heavier in the opposite direction. Martha had invited him to discuss regarding the charity.

Vick had researched Martha's company 'IMS LLC' and found it to be an online retail company. He had heard about them earlier too, but Ian's audios were sold by many companies world-wide. They were listed as one of the largest sellers of Ian Scovich's audio books. *No wonder they are donating CDs to the center.*

Vick parked his car in the garage and walked to the elevator. Martha was waiting at the lobby near the elevator to receive him. As they walked in, Vick noticed a large banner of 'Ian Speaks' and quotes from Ian's speeches on smaller wooden wall-hangings.

"You guys take your business quite seriously. What about your other clients, do they complain about you giving more importance to Ian?"

Martha smiled. "We sell only Ian."

"Only one client, great business model!" Vick gave two thumbs-up.

He swept his gaze over the surroundings – it was a large space. Several cubicles were lined on both sides, with a walkway in the middle leading to a room with a door. Vick caught a glimpse of large rooms in the far side, which looked like store rooms.

"This place works as a distribution, labeling, shipment center and storage. We do everything here," explained Martha as they walked toward her room.

Vick understood it was Martha's room, and noticed a pair of similar tables and leather chairs. *Probably Martha's colleague.*

As soon as they sat, Martha handed over a document, titled 'Non-Disclosure document'. Vick scanned the document as Martha spoke, "This is a formality. Our company gets this Non-disclosure signed by anyone visiting us. It says that whatever you see or discuss here cannot be disclosed to anyone without our prior permission."

Vick signed the paper. "That's reasonable, you are handling such sensitive copyrighted material. You cannot risk Ian Scovich's speeches being copied!"

Once all the formalities were done, "I called you to discuss about our telephone conversation we had the other day," said Martha.

"Regarding my need for money?"

"I discussed with the management. They had offered you the money earlier, but you refused."

"Yes, the need for money is greater now, though that doesn't nullify the importance of Ian or her human time."

"We understand. So, we have decided..."

"What about Ian?" Vick interrupted, "You are the biggest seller of Ian's audios, you have to know about Ian! What if something goes wrong with the audio, what do you do in case of any questions? Someone in your office must be knowing her."

Martha looked at Vick for a while contemplating an answer and spoke, "Usually there are no problems, but in case we come across any issue, we contact their agent."

"Which city, what's her company name?"

"I don't know, please don't ask me such questions, let's focus on the things in hand," Martha was strained.

"I... I'm sorry. I have no intention to intrude," said Vick showing regret. *She knows something.*

Martha ignored his apology and continued. "So, as I was saying, we have decided to contribute for your charity, but we don't want any name or advertisement. You guys are doing an awesome job and we want to support it."

She handed over a check for a generous amount, bearing her signature. Martha looked at Vick's face, expecting some happiness, some satisfaction, but there were none. *There is no way of impressing this guy.*

Vick took a deep breath and blew it out by circling his lips and looked back at the check.

"Not enough?" asked Martha.

"Don't get me wrong, this check is big, bigger than any we received in the recent times."

"Then?"

"You see, our needs are big, our demands are bigger, people's expectations from us are huge. This is certainly useful. A drop of water, can save someone from dying!"

"Drop of water! Is this a drop of water?" Martha clenched her fingers.

"I did not mean any negative but hope you discern what we are doing, how much we are doing, and how many people in this world need help."

Martha took a deep breath, "This is the first installment; there will be a second one too. I'm sure you have other donors besides us."

"Absolutely," said Vick. "This money will for sure fulfill our short-term needs."

Martha stared at him; she was sure he was not done yet. Vick continued, "This, or any other donation, can buy things but cannot buy happiness. This money can buy appliances, build houses but cannot build hope. The only way to ensure the long-lasting solution is through…"

"Ian!"

"Yes!" grinned Vick.

Martha got up, "This meeting is over Vick, and remember if you insist on things which don't make sense to me, you will not be able to buy things or build houses, at least not from this money!"

Vick folded the check and pocketed it. He bowed and beamed as he walked out of Martha's room.

What a clever fellow. Convinced me for a second installment! thought Martha.

Chapter 43

Gagan did not fail to observe a shift in Devki's behavior over time. She avoided him, although she was loving and affectionate to the kids as always.

Her defiant behavior disturbed him; *this foolish woman has got some wrong notions about herself. She needs to be tightened. I've been so considerate to her, and she's taking advantage of me.*

Devki was lost in her own world. She was physically present, but her mind had already checked out. She was never late after the last incident. She took care of things at home, looked after the kids, but slept on the couch every night. Gagan tried to intimidate her, he found fault in whatever she did, but this was not new to her, he had been like this for long. Sometimes she found her car tires flat.

All these obstructions failed to inhibit her. She was in a different realm, trying to find herself. Although Devki visited office less often, she did not stay at home too. She wandered around – sometimes shopping, sometimes to the library, wherever she pleased.

It was a special Sunday for Devki, being her twins' birthday. The kids had gone to the swimming pool in the community center. Devki tried her best to avoid such situations, where she had to be alone with Gagan, but today she had no choice. She wanted to prepare the kids' favorite dishes.

"Devki, Devki!" called Gagan.

Devki came out of the kitchen, "What do you want?"

Gagan looked at her from top to bottom, "I'm having a headache, can you massage my head?"

Devki dreaded this moment, "If the headache is unbearable, please take some medicine."

Gagan's voice became soft, "Come on dear, why need a medicine when you are here to heal all my pains?" He winked at her.

"I need to cook and have less time. Please take a pill," said Devki impassively and turned to the kitchen.

Gagan caught her by her elbow, "Come on sweetheart, why are you occupied all the time? Give some time for your husband too." Gagan spoke while drawing her closer to him, nuzzling her neck.

"No Gagan, please stop!"

Gagan's hands were all over her body. "Why do you wear these big dresses nowadays? Why are you fully covered like this?" He moved his hands over Devki's hips.

Devki struggled in his arms, "Stop Gagan ...please stop!"

But he dragged her toward the bedroom.

With all her strength Devki pushed him back, "I said stop it!"

Gagan was not ready for such an attack, he lost his balance and fell on the floor. Devki glared at him. Before she could defend herself, Gagan leapt to his feet and slapped her face.

Slap! brought back images of the past in front of Devki.

As she gasped for air, another slap came flying across her cheeks. Devki's face shuddered and blood oozed out of her lips. Her knotted hair fell loose and flung tousling over her face. She returned Gagan's glare with the same vehemence.

He was not done yet and was getting ready for another blow, "This is what you get for not taking care of your family and disobeying your husband!"

Devki was undeterred, "Are you done, or do you have some more?"

Gagan shook with temper. His face strained, nostrils flared.

Some more blood oozed from Ian's lips and dripped on the ground, "It feels good hitting a weak woman, doesn't it?"

"I'll kill you!" Gagan displayed animalistic rage.

"You did a good job Gagan, you managed to kill Devki today. I know you were trying for years and today you succeeded!"

Gagan stared at her. He wanted to smash her face again but controlled himself. His breath labored and felt warm under his nostrils. Sweat covered his whole body; unsure of his next action, he stormed out.

Devki heard a car cranking and speeding away from the driveway.

Chapter 44

Devki went to the bathroom and splashed cold water several times to soothe her open wounds. She checked in the mirror – there was no big cut, only minor bruises.

She picked a couple of towels and cleaned the blood stains from the floor.

Later she visited her closet. There were plenty of assorted clothes; she touched each one of them. There were some which she brought on her first trip from India to USA. There were several other short dresses and skirts hanging in the cabinets. There were some she had purchased from her own money.

After she was done with her closet, she walked to her daughters' room. There were clothes and stuff thrown haphazardly on the floor, on the bed and in the bathroom. Ian always kept their room neat, although it faced a storm everyday with the invasion by the little ones. Ian slowly picked the stuff lying around – skirts, pants, shirts, shoes, skates. As she folded and arranged them, she realized how much her kids have grown up.

She felt a massive lump growing in her throat and tears flowed down her cheeks. She worked in the closet for an hour and later waited in the living room for the kids to arrive.

Saira came running inside followed by Mini and Kajal; Esha walked in last. All the kids came to a halt at the door as they watched Devki sitting in the middle of the room with two suitcases next to her.

There was a dismal silence in the room.

"Mom?" Esha broke the silence.

Devki took a deep breath, "Esha and Kajal, take care of each other. We…we are leaving."

"We?" all four voices echoed instantly.

"I mean I am leaving with Saira and Mini." Ian avoided their eyes.

Esha was confused, "But where? Are you going on a vacation? Why aren't we all going?" The rest of the kids had similar looks on their faces too.

"We are leaving this house. We…we… will be close by but where, I don't know right now!"

"Why are we not going?" asked Kajal. Understanding the gravity of the situation, Esha hushed her.

Devki was solemn, "I want to take you girls, but your father needs you here."

Kajal was still confused, "But what about you?"

"He doesn't need us here, he never needed us anytime." Devki's voice was drained but firm.

"In that case..." Esha wanted to ask something. She recalled a similar conversation with Devki months back.

"Please don't make this hard for me. I know I owe you guys an explanation, but I cannot tell you everything at present."

A car engine roared and died in the driveway and soon Gagan entered the house. He joined the kids standing near the door. He huddled them in and saw Devki standing in the middle of the room with the baggage.

He looked around, "What's going on?" He did not like the looks on the kids' faces.

The room stayed still for a moment but soon Devki's voice shattered the silence, "I am leaving this house with my daughters."

"Leaving as in," Gagan's eyebrows strained and mouth twitched.

"Leaving as in never coming back."

Esha and Kajal closed their mouths tight and sobbed.

"Have you gone crazy – to create a drama like this in front of the kids?"

"They have to know it one day, better today."

"We can talk this through, have some sense!" said Gagan, though not pleading.

"There is nothing to talk. I should have done this long back. Thanks for making it easy for me today," said Ian.

Esha plummeted on the chair and wept loudly.

"Okay! If you have to go, then go, but never come back again begging me to take you back."

Ian pushed the bags with one hand and held Saira's hand with the other.

Gagan spoke coldly again, "My daughters will not go with you!"

"Your daughters!"

"Yes, my daughters. I love them, I take care of them. I will never desert them the way you're doing."

"They are not your daughters Gagan, I am their biological mom, and I can take care of them!"

The girls cried. Mini ran towards Gagan and hugged him.

Ian hated herself to put the kids in such a situation but she was determined.

"My daughter's will not stir out of this house! You go wherever you want!" yelled Gagan.

"Are you trying to keep my kids' hostage because they are not your kids? You have not adopted them legally yet!" She continued in a higher pitch, "Do you want me to call the cops?"

Gagan was taken aback. "You will regret this. You have no money, no job, no prospects. You will come back crawling on your feet in a couple of days."

Devki ignored Gagan's comments. She dragged the heavy luggage under her weight. The faster she tried to get out of the house, the heavier the bags felt. "Come on girls, help your mama and don't worry, we will not be far. You can visit your sisters anytime."

Esha rested her head over the chair's arm and wept. On the way to the door, Devki stopped near Esha and kept her hand on Esha's shoulders, "I love you dear, I always did."

Esha shoved her hand away, "You never loved me. No one loves me. Everyone leaves me."

Ian struggled to control her tears, "I …I wanted to be your mom…sweetheart…always," words fumbled under her shaky voice.

Devki stopped near the door and turned back. For the last time she wanted to see the house which provided shelter to her body but battered her soul.

Her eyes turned glassy, "Gagan Thank…"

"Get out!" Gagan growled.

Devki walked out with Saira, Mini and a heavy heart.

*****

Once in the car, Ian felt relieved and liberated, she rolled down the car windows and drove away. She picked the phone and dialed Martha but later decided against it. *Will stay in a hotel tonight and take care of the rest tomorrow.*

They checked into a hotel. The kids were quiet – in shock

with the sudden turn of events. They could not fully understand the circumstances. Once in the room, Ian ordered pizza for dinner.

"Everything is going to be okay," Ian assured the kids.

Saira asked, "Mom are you going to divorce Dad?"

Ian took a deep breath and tied her hair up, "I am undecided at this moment, but I think that would be the best for us."

"Don't worry mommy, it's okay and you have to look at the positive side," said Saira.

"Really?!"

"Yes mommy, many kids in the school have divorced parents. They tell me it's great, because, they receive gifts from both the parents. Every birthday, every Christmas, two gifts," chirped Saira showing two fingers.

Ian laughed her head off. She pulled them close to her heart.

After dinner, Ian put the kids to bed. They had so many questions, all of which she couldn't answer. *Lots to be done tomorrow; I must have a peaceful sleep tonight.*
*****

The next morning, Ian walked into the office with the kids. Everyone cheered and waved at them.

Martha was surprised to see them, "No school today?"

"They'll be going to school tomorrow. Today is fun day!"

The kids were surprised. "Do you work here mommy?"

"I help Aunt Martha sometimes."

When Martha and Ian were alone, Ian narrated the turn of events the previous evening. Martha was glad – Ian was free at last.

"You should've called me. You guys could've stayed with me," said Martha with a motherly affection.

"I wanted to be alone with my daughters. Now please look for an apartment for us."

"Yes, but till then, you will stay with me. I'd love to have you all. I will spoil the kids with my pampering."

"I don't know, it's going to be diff…"

The kids came running inside the room. Martha cuddled the little ones, "You guys want to stay with Aunt Martha for a few days? You'll get hot chocolate, lots of candy and unlimited movies."

"Oh yeah, yeah!" the kids danced.

"See? All said and done!" said Martha and Ian reluctantly agreed.

"You must be feeling free and relieved now!"

Ian played with the tip of the pen, "Oh yes, now I can devote my whole time to the cause. As Vick said, I can come out from my hiding and meet my fans; work with them closer and contribute."

Martha nodded with great enthusiasm.

Ian continued, "I may take some time in adjusting with this new life. The kids have to adjust too."

Martha updated Ian on her last meeting with Vick. "Vick is doing a wonderful job. We can ask him for suggestions on how you can contribute."

"Arrange for a meeting with Vick," said Ian.

Chapter 45

Vick was considered by many as money minded. He was constantly contemplating new ways to earn more. He devised different schemes to raise funds.

Although 'Helping Sisters' was a charitable organization, Vick managed it like a business. He often quoted, 'Money is the oil that keeps the society running.' He wanted others to understand the hardships in running such a center, where funds were constantly in demand.

Ever since Vick moved to Atlanta, he worked with a mission. He retained a full-time job only because it paid him good. He hardly had any needs of his own, it was all for his people, they were his family. His mother, proud of her son, moved with him to support his cause.

Men of his age were busy chasing money and girls, while he deliberated on how he can be of service to the next in need. He attributed his entire thought process to Ian.

Vick was thrilled to receive a phone call from Martha for his second check. More money meant more service. Although Martha could have mailed the check, she insisted, "Meeting face-to-face is invariably better, and we can catchup on the work as well."

Vick was eager to visit Martha again, he hoped to gather more information about Ian. As Vick stepped out of the elevator, Martha greeted him.

"You don't have to receive me like this every time, I can meet you at your office."

"Special people require special treatment," Martha winked.

It was evening again, and as usual, no one was present except Martha. They walked across the hallway; Vick stopped and opened his file to show Martha some of the pictures of his work. Just then, he heard someone walking from behind – the sound of shoe heels hitting the hardwood floor. He looked at Martha, whose eyes were already fixed in that direction. *Must be her colleague* thought Vick.

Soon someone appeared at the entrance. Vick was unable to recall any introduction to this person but felt a strange familiarity. The lady walked toward Vick without any expression. As she walked, the length of her gown wiped the floor. The top she wore covered till her chin. Her hair fell carelessly on her shoulders and swayed along slightly. Her gaze was steady and intense.

Martha broke the silence, "Vick this is …" but he was not listening. His gaze was frozen. Vick's body shook and lips parted in disbelief – his hands and knees weakened. The file he was holding slipped out of his hand, papers and pictures scattered on the floor. No introduction was necessary. His teacher was in-front of him.

Vick fell on his knees. Martha couldn't understand anything from his inaudible murmurs. His body trembled – the wait was finally over.

With his head bowed, Vick raised his hands, upon which Ian placed hers. Vick softly touched them over his eyes and kissed each hand. Martha witnessed an event - it seemed like a meeting between a great saint and her biggest disciple.

Ian kept her right hand on Vick's shoulder. "You are doing an exceptional job."

The voice was different, but it mattered the least to him. Ian had surpassed all the boundaries of gender, language and region.

"It's all you Ian. It's all you. I have done nothing but followed you," Vick was still on his knees.

Ian moved away from him and walked toward the window, "A follower is as big as his leader. The air is important only because we breathe it." Ian turned and looked at Vick, who was now standing. "People like you make me worthy – you give meaning to my teachings."

Vick trembled, "You're God's own messenger to us!"

"But I learn from you. I learn from my people. I learn from the millions who fight their battles day and night and don't resign their hopes."

"And you are that hope Ian." Vick folded his hands in reverence.

"I am nothing. I have not struggled like you did. I have not suffered like my other sisters."

"What's your wish for me?" Vick looked directly at Ian for the first time. She was not tall but appeared taller. She was medium height and slender. She looked younger than he had thought. Her thick hair swayed as she spoke and moved. She looked like a queen from some epic – fierce and powerful. Yet, she reflected humbleness and politeness. She was the physical persona of her speeches.

Vick couldn't believe his luck – the whole world was waiting to catch a glimpse of Ian and here she was standing right in front of him. Vick's heart was filled once again with awe and respect. "What's your wish for me?" He asked again like a soldier asking his commander.

"I want you to first quit your job."

Vick nodded obediently.

Ian spoke again, "With such arduous work at hand, you cannot be held in a nine-to-five job. We'll take care of all your expenses."

"And?"

"I want you to tell me how I can help you. I want to aid you in your efforts!"

Vick's eyes gleamed with happiness.

*****

Later, Ian, Vick and Martha sat together, discussing their next move. It was a long day. Ian took a sip from her coffee mug and looked at Vick and Martha. *No more hurry to go home. No more hide and seek.* Thanks to Martha, Ian found a spacious apartment. A nanny was arranged for the kids.

The trio brain-stormed on how and where Ian could start. "You need more hands. I can also come to the center and share your work."

"And what about this office?" objected Martha.

"You already take care of things around here. I won't be needed much." Ian was amused at Martha's possessiveness.

Vick circled his pen on a notebook, his eyebrows skewed as he thought hard, "You are right, we need loads of service at our different centers located here and other cities."

"I cannot travel right now; I need to take care of the kids."

Martha looked from her glasses and spoke, "Let us know in which areas Ian or I can help."

Vick thought for a moment, "We have to make better use of Ian's time. I know my inmates will be thrilled to meet Ian. They are her biggest fans!"

"I can come to your place and spend some time with the

residents," Ian suggested.

"Yea but still," Vick was not convinced if that will be the best gift from Ian.

"What troubles you the most? What's that one thing which bothers more than anything?" asked Martha. "Anything you need in your office, human resources...whatever!"

Vick cleared the wrinkles on his forehead and counted things – new appliances, day-to-day operations, apartments for the new girls, medical facility, employees, "Things I need and want to do, are impossible to accomplish, so it's better if we start with whatever we can do."

Martha threw her hands in the air.

Ian smiled.

"Okay, okay," Vick raised his hands, "I need money... lots of money. There are many expenses, new commitments." He took a deep breath, "There are loads of expectations. We can open more branches, reach out to more people."

"So, you're saying our donation won't help?"

"It would, unquestionably, I have many other donors too, but all this wouldn't suffice."

"Won't the second installment be enough?" asked Martha.

"These contributions are indeed useful, but we need more. The requirements are endless. We need money, huge amounts for today, tomorrow and much more in future. As long as a single soul on this planet is suffering, our mission remains unaccomplished."

Ian smiled warmly. Vick resonated her feelings.

"Yes, if our aim is to uplift as many individuals as we can, we need a lot of resources, not only in terms of money, but in terms of commitment too," said Ian.

She ruffled her hair and came out of her office while Vick and Martha followed her. She paced around the hallway with her chin drooped and hands behind her back.

Ian spoke as if to herself, "That means one, two or ten contributions will not suffice. We need more people to contribute. We need people to get involved and stay united for the cause."

Vick and Martha couldn't agree more.

"Have you tried any fund raising?" inquired Ian.

Vick nodded, "Yes, we did try some fund-raising events in the past, but got mediocre results."

Ian looked at the ceiling for a moment, "Tell me, how anxious were you to see me?"

"I was quite desperate in search of my guru! I tried all the ways I could but was never able to find you. For a long time…"

"Do you think there are others in this world who would like to meet me or see me?"

Martha appeared puzzled.

"Of course! You are an international star. Your audios are selling world-wide in millions. People like me, charity organizations, companies, corporate houses, individuals – they're all keen on meeting Ian." Vick continued, "I know people in my center who want to meet you, I have seen many discussions online, social media pages dedicated to you. Ian's diehard followers are searching for their Ian."

"Why do you ask?" inquired Martha, who was a silent listener until then.

Ian glanced at both Martha and Vick. They looked at each other. "In that case, I think I should not come out in the public for some more time!" stated Ian.

"What?!"

"Yes. Listen to this," Ian bit her lips and her eyes gleamed, "Though I want to meet my fans, let's create a charity event out of it."

"Means?"

"Means we could conduct a charity event in which I will speak. That will be the first time the world will get a glimpse of Ian."

"Brilliant!" Martha threw a fist in the air.

"We will sell tickets for the event. We will take sponsorships. We will charge the corporate houses for the events. Advertisements will be allowed. Entry will be free for the socially backward, but others will have to pay."

"This a wonderful idea!" Vick's eyes sparkled. "We can even sell the telecasting rights to cable companies."

Ian gave him a sideways glance, "Now don't get carried away!"

"It's true Ian, you don't know how big you are. We can have a packed event like rock stars. People will die to see and hear you live."

"The money which we will receive from this event will meet most of our requirements. We will get people committed for the cause. We will all get united."

"Marvelous!" said Martha. "This is the finest idea I've heard in a long time!"

"And that's how Ian motivates people," clapped Vick.

Ian's eyes drooped "But there is one problem."

"What?"

"I have never spoken in front of a huge gathering!"

"Ian, you are so natural, you speak from your heart, you touch souls. I am confident you'll be able to do it!"

Chapter 46

Gagan read the email again, "Resignation!" Vick had emailed his resignation in the morning, and now in the afternoon, he was at Gagan's office. "But why now, why so sudden?" asked Gagan.

"Honestly, it took a while to decide. It's hard to manage both my job and my mission."

Gagan took notes of their meeting, "Is it something related to the charity? Because, that would need a lot of money and this job grants you that."

"Yes, we do need resources, but my presence at the center is more important, besides, we've been receiving plenty of donations, so it should be okay."

Gagan had hoped for some news about Ian from Vick, "What about the assignment I had given you?" He seemed annoyed at Vick's decision.

"Which one?"

"The one to get a deal with Ian. Did you track Ian?"

"Oh yeah, though not completely! In the search for Ian, I discovered that she does meet people but selectively. If you're keen, I can try to arrange a meeting between you and Ian."

Gagan leaned forward. "So, you did sniff out Ian!"

"I recently received a large donation from a company which sells her audios. They are dedicated followers of Ian, and perhaps, can introduce us to her."

"Will Ian work with us?"

"That's between you and her. It's up to you to convince her."

Gagan closed his notes, "And will you do this for me?"

"Come-on! You've been my boss and a constant support in my growth, I'll try my best."

Gagan rested his elbows on the table. "So, what's the strategy?"

"Okay, it goes like this," Vick continued, "I'm organizing a fund raiser for my charity and will invite Ian to speak in it."

"That's cool, but in the past, many charity events had failed to get their invitation accepted by Ian."

"This time it's different," Vick whispered, "As I said

earlier, I am connected with this company and they've promised to get me in touch with Ian."

"Interesting!"

"There's one thing I must tell you."

"What?"

"This is a charity event, and if Ian did come out to meet people, how many can she meet? A whole lot would like to meet her."

"Yes, that's true", Gagan squinted his eyes and stressed on his words, "What should we do?"

Vick smiled, "I have an idea for that too."

"You seem to be having a lot of ideas today, why don't you spill them all at once?"

"Since this is a huge event, there will be a vast crowd, Ian cannot meet everyone in private, but she has to meet the sponsors of the event, said Vick. "I'd suggest you become one of the main sponsors."

"Hmm," Gagan started to think. "What if, after all this arrangement, Ian doesn't come with us for the deal?"

"Well, I sincerely hope she does, but even otherwise, it shouldn't matter, you will be the main sponsor, your name will still be with the event. You will get a big exposure."

Gagan nodded, leaving Vick unsure of his approval. "Okay, when is this event?" asked Gagan.

"Dates are yet to be finalized."

"Did Ian confirm her presence?"

"Not yet, but trusted people are in touch though."

Gagan rubbed his chin, "I can talk to the other partners and ask their opinions about sponsoring the event." He was persistent, "So when can I meet Ian? I will hand over our donation check personally to her."

"I don't think meeting before hand is possible." Gagan's face went blank. Vick continued, "Although I haven't received any assurance on Ian's presence, there are talks in the close circles that she will meet and greet only on the day of the event, and not any earlier."

Gagan felt dodged. "Are you kidding me? You don't know the date of the event; you don't know if Ian has agreed to come to the event; I cannot even meet her in advance!" Gagan paused and then continued, "How can I donate the money without knowing who Ian is, whether she will attend the event or not?"

Vick crossed his legs under the chair, "You are not giving money to Ian, you are giving the money to charity. You are donating to a cause and not to an individual. It doesn't matter whether Ian is present or not as long as your money is put to a worthy cause."

"But everything is business!"

"You should be concerned about our work, whether we are doing the job well with your money; if Ian makes an appearance, she is only supporting us."

Gagan crossed his arms against his chest.

"So, are you going to be our sponsor?"

Gagan rose from his chair, "Give me more details and I will talk to my management."

*****

Martha, Vick and Jayesh got busy in preparation for the event. Considering the size of the event, they decided to hold it three to four months later.

Jayesh suggested to hire an event management company, bearing in mind the extensive work and professional handling required for such a huge event. Moreover, they wanted to make Ian's entry into the social world as grand as possible, the success of the event depended on Ian and her talent as a great orator. Their prime responsibility was to maintain Ian's secrecy till the last minute. Their basic premise depended on the fact that everyone will pay to see and hear Ian. If she was exposed beforehand, all the euphoria will be gone.

Martha and Vick visited many companies. Many big organizations showed interest yet none of them signed up, their concern being – 'When Ian failed to show herself in the past, what is the assurance that she will appear now?'

Ian had never been acquainted with anyone in the outside world, and now she was not ready to meet anyone before the event. Martha and Vick had high hopes, but nothing seemed to work.

Martha kept Ian away from all these discussions and day-to-day planning. She knew about Ian's troubled mind and left her undisturbed. She involved Ian only if there was some issue or if Ian herself walked into their meeting.

Martha was engrossed in some paperwork, when Ian's voice interrupted her, "What's your estimate? How many people will attend?"

Martha kept scribbling on the paper, "If everything goes as planned, there should be around twenty to thirty thousand people."

"Twenty thousand!"

"Probably more if we get the TV viewership too."

"What!" exclaimed Ian, her palms turned sweaty. She trembled hearing the number. "I have never addressed such a massive crowd before."

"Don't worry! You'll be fine." Martha folded the papers lying in front of her and stapled them.

"How can I not worry? Do you know how much is at stake?" Ian continued, "If I fail before such an audience, not only will Ian be vanquished, but all these spirits will dampen forever."

"But why do you think you'd fail?

Ian looked up silently and closed her eyes.

"It will go fine!" Martha convinced her. "I know you can do it. Don't underestimate yourself!"

"When I delivered my speech for the first time, you were there. It wasn't me, but it was you. I was able to speak so far only because of you."

Martha smiled, "I'm honored, but I'll be with you for this event too."

Ian smiled, "Thanks for being with me in this journey."

"This is the only way to achieve what we want, and what Vick is striving to achieve. This event should inspire enough people to donate so that we can reach many more in need."

"So how many sponsors have we got so far?" asked Ian.

"None!" came the reply instantly.

"None?! Why on earth?"

"I'm sure this event will be a big success, and it will gain momentum gradually," said Martha. "As of now, many have shown interest but none of them have confirmed."

Ian's eyebrows strained, "What's deterring them?"

"They don't believe that Ian would ever come out of her hideout."

"They don't trust me?"

"They do, but they don't trust us, they aren't sure if we're telling the truth. According to them, in the past, Ian has been invited to many such events, but she never turned up. What's the guarantee that she will come out now, for us, for 'Helping Sisters'?"

"Hmm," Ian acknowledged. This was a practical problem – how and why would anyone trust them.

"The question is – how can we or how can you make people believe without even seeing them or meeting them?" said Martha.

Instantly, they both looked at each other. "Bingo!" cried Martha punching in the air.

Within a week, Ian's new audio was released in the market and it resonated everywhere. Ian's usual voice echoed, "Dear friends, this is Ian and I am coming to meet you. Do you want to meet me?"

Chapter 47

"Hello," Esha answered the phone in a low voice.

"Hey it's me sweetheart!"

"Mom!" Esha sobbed hearing Devki's voice after many weeks.

"Come on Esha, don't cry ...you're a big girl, aren't you?" said Devki, touched on hearing 'mom' from Esha.

"I want to see you mom!"

"Me too. Why don't you and Kajal visit us? We are not far from you."

"Shall I inform dad?"

"Of course! I am still your mom." Devki gave her address to Esha and explained the directions.

*****

Esha drove to Devki's place with Kajal. It was an apartment community. It had a tennis court, a swimming pool and a walking trail. Devki's apartment was on the 3rd floor. They had least expected to meet Devki this way. When Devki was with them, they failed to recognize her value, but once she left, they missed her terribly. Esha pressed the call-bell and waited.

Devki opened the door and extended her arms. Esha was unsure how and when she started respecting Devki, but she did feel a high regard for her, more so from the way she left the house. Esha knew how difficult it must be for her and the kids.

She leaned and hugged Devki. Kajal hesitated for a minute and then gave in to Devki's open arms.

The apartment looked small and cramped compared to their house. "Where are Saira and Mini?" asked Esha.

"They are still at school having some after-school program. I haven't told them you guys are coming, else they would've never gone to school." The girls took the couch while Devki sat on the chair before them. "So how are you guys? Hope you are managing well and not missing me."

Esha gave a half smile. They chatted for an hour or so; Devki inquired about their school and other activities.

In between their talks, Esha said "Oh gosh, I forgot, I brought something for you." She unzipped her bag and pulled out a CD.

Devki instantly recognized it but pretended ignorant. "What is it?"

"This is a new audio from Ian. Now you have enough time, so please listen to it."

"Of course." Devki took the CD. The title of the audio was familiar to her – 'Everyone gets a chance in life!'

"Ian is magical mom, as if she knows you, this talk looks like specifically for you."

Devki smiled, "Ian doesn't know me…but she must be knowing you, since you listen to her every speech, perhaps she made this one for you."

There was a bang on the door. "The kids are back!"

Saira and Mini walked in and were surprised seeing the guests. "Oh, my gang sisters!" said Saira as they ran into the arms of Esha and Kajal.

Saira started her chatter on her new school, teacher and friends. "You guys should show your room to your sisters and in the meantime, I'll serve your favorite pasta on the table." said Devki.

Saira and Mini showed Esha their rooms, new gadgets and books. Later everyone ate at the table, enjoying the time together.

After the snacks, Esha turned toward Kajal, "Why don't you spend some time with the kids while I help mom with the dishes."

Once Devki and Esha were alone, "Mom, can I ask you something?"

"Don't make it too difficult dear."

Esha smiled. "Mom, what happened between you and dad? What was the reason that you…"

"There are certain things which I cannot explain, but sometimes you…," Devki paused and then continued, "you have to fight for your respect. Some decisions are tough to make, but you should never compromise over your self-respect."

"So…"

"Dear please, you need to grow a little more to understand all this. Don't burden yourself with all the complexities of life, but remember he is your dad and I'll always be your mom."

It was time to leave. They bid goodbye and promised to visit often.

Chapter 48

Ian's voice had such resonating power, such connection and honesty that it had glued the world to her. When Ian declared in her speech that she was coming to meet her fans, the environment buzzed with euphoria. Newspapers, magazines and television were flooded with the news – 'Curtains up! Ian to make an appearance!'

Soon 'Helping Sisters' popped up as the organization that was instrumental in bringing Ian to light. Vick, Martha and Jayesh were the forerunners of the event. They decided to hold a press conference as a curtain raiser. The reporters were anxious to get all details about Ian and bombarded the trio with their questions.

"Who is Ian?"

"What's her real name?"

"Where does she live?"

"How old is she?"

"Tell us about her family!"

"How does she look?"

Martha was overwhelmed by the barrage of questions, but she was quick to respond, "Unfortunately, we ourselves have not met Ian in person, although we've received endorsement from her. She will meet all of us on the day of the event."

A female reporter remarked, "It must've been very tough to convince Ian. How did you accomplish this?"

Jayesh responded this time, "We have done nothing – it's all Ian, in fact, she initiated the contact as she wished to be with her fans, she cannot be away from them any longer."

One middle-age reporter persisted, "She is supporting your organization, and that's fantastic, but she might be having some motive. What do you think is her objective?"

"It's an honor to have Ian with us," said Vick. "Her motive is always to support and guide people in need. She wants all of us to work together with her in her mission."

Another reporter with thick glasses asked, "When Ian comes to town, can you get us her interview? We are all dying to see Ian for a long time."

Martha closed the session, "It's on Ian, she decides whom to meet and when, we just follow her instructions."

Martha, Vick and Jayesh's phones rang incessantly and kept them busy in taking the sponsorship enrollments.

The event was turning out to be massive and soon, an event management company was hired. Banners and posters of Ian coming to town, plastered the walls of the city and the internet. Companies grew competitive in their contribution, to grab more advertising. Additional staff were hired to take care of the phone calls, mails, invitations and contacts, the whole environment was electrifying.

When the date of the event was decided to be Jan 14th, workload grew manifold. Atlanta did not have cold winters, making January the perfect month. The venue was decided, arrangements were made at the Centennial park. It was the only place that could hold a large gathering. The event management group worked efficiently; tickets were sold at every possible outlet.

Martha was impressed by the event team – they were dynamic and creative. Talks were on for worldwide telecast. Ultimately, Ian's dream of helping people, reaching out to more people, was coming true.

Ian was left unperturbed from all the commotion going around. Her identity was kept strictly confidential and she was contacted sparingly. Everyone involved knew the importance of her secrecy. The whole build-up depended on the need for her fans to see Ian.

Ian was tensed – stakes and hopes were high. Whenever she recorded her speeches, Martha, Mike and Jayesh or any one of them were present. She needed an audience to speak, but she had never addressed a large crowd.

With live telecast, the audience would rise to millions. There were so many things that could go wrong – the speech, stage, acoustics, everything had to be perfect. Thinking of the audio setup brought back memories of Mike. Ian missed Mike terribly but remained strong headed – *I don't need anyone*.

Chapter 49

Ian was in her office alone, when an email popped on her laptop. She stared at the sender's name, sweat shimmered on her forehead – it was from Gagan.

The subject read, 'Devki you are finished'.

It had been months since she had any contact with Gagan. She had thought of filing for a divorce, but it eventually slipped out of her mind. She hardly gave any importance to it anyway. He had never existed for her, and she had never asked him for anything.

With trembling hands, she clicked on the email. It read, "Do you think it was right to leave me and my daughters like this in the middle? This is how you show your gratitude to what I have done for you and your daughters. Perhaps you've forgotten, but you are still dependent on me. You are in America because of my support and now I am taking it away. You wanted to be separated and now I will separate you, I will cancel your visa; you will be illegal in the USA, and you can go back to wherever you came from."

Ian could hear her own heart pound, her eyes widened and dazed, the color drained from her face. In her foolhardiness, she had forgotten that Gagan still had her in his clutches. She remembered the things that happened in India. Her past came glaring at her again. She got visions of returning to India, life in a prison and the situation of her kids.

And now, here, thousands of tickets have been sold for my upcoming event, which is supposed to happen in two months. If I must return to India at this juncture, I will be held responsible for all this mess here. That will be forgery; Martha and her team would be in big trouble.

Ian moved away from her desk, trembling. Her knees gave in and she held the table for support. *How did I let this happen?*

Terrified by the thoughts, Ian dialed Martha, who was on the other side of the city, in an important meeting with the sponsors. She excused herself on seeing Ian's number. Ian was always important.

"Mmm Mart," Ian struggled.

"What is it?"

"Mmm Marth," Ian couldn't complete her sentence.

Oh my God! Devki is back! cringed Martha.

"Stop that, don't let Devki surface. Tell me calmly what happened," said Martha in a stern voice.

"I am ddd done for. I am ddd destroyed."

"Can you tell me what the hell happened?" Martha became anxious.

"Cacaca om come here please!" begged Ian.

"It will take me 45 mins to reach you, can you hold that long?"

"Ye Yes."

Martha left the meeting with apologies. Vick stared, surprised at her strange behavior. *Cannot believe she is leaving such a meeting!* But Martha had no choice, Ian's call sounded urgent.

It took Martha a little more than an hour to reach the office. Ian was pacing around anxiously. "What happened?" asked Martha loudly.

Ian opened her mouth to speak but couldn't find words. She caught Martha's hand and dragged her to the computer, pointing at the email on the screen.

Martha read the content of the email – her face went white. She read it again and looked at Ian.

"Doesn't matter… Doesn't matter," Martha repeated, "Don't forget you are Ian!"

Ian shook her head up and down like a child.

Martha pressed Ian on the shoulder, "No one can stop Ian!"

Ian repeated like a small girl, "No one stops Ian."

"Ian is bigger than anyone!"

"Yes, Ian is bigger than anyone. Ian revives distressed people," Ian slowly moved her numb limbs.

"People wait for Ian and Ian doesn't disappoint them!" Martha said loudly.

Ian managed to take control of herself, but still shaking, she blinked nervously and rose from her chair speaking in trance, "Everyone loves Ian. Millions listen to Ian. Ian creates history!"

"That's my girl."

Dreading the consequence, Ian's forehead furrowed, "We need to find a solution to this problem."

"We will, we will," said Martha undeterred. *Her insecurities will put herself in trouble one day!*

They both sat beside each other. Ian slowly recovered from her initial shock. Martha asked, "What does he want from you? Why will he do such a thing?"

"He wants to destroy me, that's all, he has big ego!"

"Ok tell me everything about him."

"He is an executive in some publishing company," said Ian.

Martha typed Gagan's full name on the internet and it returned several links on him. The screen was visible, yet, she leaned closer. Martha looked at his profile and recognized the company.

"Goodness gracious! This company is one of our event's sponsors, and Vick is handling the account. Gagan is one of the partners." Martha laughed at the irony – *Gagan's company sponsoring Ian's event and here he is threatening to revoke her visa.* Martha scrolled down to read more about him, "Vick mentioned that this company is interested in doing business with Ian. We can offer him the business provided he sits quiet!"

Ian gave it a thought, "No, we cannot do that. First, if he knows I am Ian, he will not care for Ian either, and furthermore, we cannot give away our sales to someone else, we cannot let greed run this, we have a purpose and he doesn't, he will only eye the money."

She talks sense thought Martha.

Ian and Martha discussed the option of filing for Ian's own visa or permanent residency as a celebrity, but it would expose her identity to the public and would take a long time as well. In any case, it was not feasible before the event. The only workaround was by convincing Gagan to retain Ian's visa at least for now.

"Okay, tell me more about this Gagan and his family," asked Martha.

Ian started with his daughters and told everything she knew about Gagan's family.

"There should be someone who can convince this idiot!" said Martha. "How about this lady Renu, his sister? How is she?"

"She is nice to my twins and close to him." Ian rubbed her temples with her fingers.

"Maybe we can convince her to talk to Gagan."

"I don't know how to approach her. I was harsh to her the last time we spoke."

"What about his elder daughter Esha? You said she's is a regular listener of Ian."

"Yes, she is."

"See, there's hope! You ask these two wonderful ladies to convince Gagan."

Ian's eyes gleamed with hope.

"Remember to talk to them as Devki. And let Devki live for that purpose only. Don't bring her back for anything else!" Martha still had some doubts, "But tell me, why are you so scared to return to India?"

"Don't you remember? I told you what occurred there – a criminal case is pending on my name!"

"Hmmm, I'm not sure about that, we discussed about this earlier too, let me inquire with my contacts about the case and whereabouts of that former family of yours."

"Be discreet and make sure it doesn't open any can of worms," said Ian. "By the way, did you find Saira?"

"We are close on her trail," said Martha without revealing much.

*****

Later in the afternoon, Ian dialed Renu's number. She repented over her last interaction with her. Renu picked the phone after several rings, although with the least interest.

"What do you want?" Renu's tone was icy.

"This is…"

"I know. I can see the number," said Renu. "Why call me? What do you want now?" Renu was abreast of what had occurred between Devki and Gagan.

"It is unfortunate what happened between me and your brother, but I had no choice."

Devki heard only Renu's passive breathing. Devki spoke again, "I need your help Renu!"

"I cannot do anything – you have closed all the doors."

"If two people cannot get along, they should live separate. Isn't that the case? Can't we take it that way Renu? Your brother and I never got along, then why stay together?"

"You should have thought of it when you married him.

Instead, you deserted the family; did you even think about the kids?"

"I cannot argue with you on this, there are many things I cannot tell you."

"What do you need from me now?"

"Gagan is taking revenge on me. Couples should stay together on a mutual decision and you cannot force anyone to live with you."

"Revenge! What revenge?"

"He is revoking my visa, he knows that my living status in the USA depends on him and if he revokes it, I will have no option but to go back to India."

"Serves you right. You don't want to live with him anyways, so why bother?" mocked Renu.

"Don't say like this, please. I love India, but to my daughters, India is a foreign country. This country has been their home since early childhood. They will have a hard time adjusting there!"

There was a pause on the other side.

"You love my daughters, don't you? You are still their aunt. We never had any problems between us."

After a brief pause, Renu spoke, "You guys are separated now."

"But that doesn't change my relationship with you."

"Gagan will not listen to me."

"He will listen to you Renu, please try. I am not asking for much, he has to give me a few months of time, for my daughters to settle."

"What you did is unforgivable Devki, but I'll try for the sake of the kids!" said Renu and disconnected.

A few days later, Ian received a message from Renu. 'You are safe now but should make your arrangements soon.'

Chapter 50

With her visa problem resolved for the time being, Ian focused more on the upcoming event. Martha assured she would take care of everything and advised Ian to concentrate on her speech preparation and the kids. It was of paramount importance for Ian to relax and practice her speech delivery. With little over a month left for the event, nothing could be left to chance.

Martha worked for longer hours. Since she stayed alone, she was able to dedicate more time. More than anything else, she wanted Ian to succeed.

Martha was the key in the company on behalf of Ian; everyone came to her with their queries regarding the event. Their company still posed as the largest seller and distributor of Ian's audios.

Martha was in the conference room with Vick and Jayesh, when her phone buzzed. It was an international number.

"Can you please excuse me for a few minutes...I need to take this call," Martha hurried into her private room shutting the door. She took the chair and answered the phone.

It was Sofia – Martha was hearing her after several months. "Mama...I am dying!" Sofia's voice sounded tired and feeble.

"What!" Martha jerked out of her seat in shock. She did hear from the loyalists that Sofia was sick, but she least expected it to be this serious.

Sofia spoke with labored breath, "You cannot save your Sofi this time Mama. God is calling me. I have cancer!"

The room spun in front of Martha's eyes. She crumpled on the chair avoiding a fall on the ground. "Sofi!" she muttered.

"Yes Mama. I am dying. I...I don't have much time left. Doctor says I may be gone any moment." Sofia continued in her broken voice, "I want to see you Mama... for the last time."

Martha's voice cracked, "Yes...yes my baby, Mama will be there for you."

Martha disconnected the phone and sat in silence. She couldn't believe what she just heard. Glimpses of Sofi's childhood and the events that occurred in Mexico flashed in front of her eyes.

Time had passed too quickly – she had not seen her daughter for years. Since the time she came to the USA, they only had phone conversations and the frequency of calls too reduced over time. When she left Mexico, Sofia was young, and the thought of losing her forever gave shudders to Martha.

Now, how will I meet my Sofia?

The loyalists had warned her never to return. To make it worse, they were digging up the old cases. Besides, Ian was in dire need of Martha for the event, which still had much work undone. Ian often struggled to perform without Martha. *But Vick and Jayesh should be able to handle.* Sofia needed her; she was not there for her child all these years but now her baby may be gone soon, forever.

What if the loyalists' warnings are true? I may get arrested as soon as I land at the airport. Yet, I must do this for my Sofi. How long can I run and for what? Sofia's need is predominant at the moment.

Martha thought of informing the loyalists about her arrival into Tijuana but later decided against.

She contemplated her next course of action and returned to the conference room where Jayesh and Vick were still waiting for her.

"I am sorry, we need to adjourn this meeting right now," said Martha.

"What happened, is everything okay with Ian?"

"Yeah, she's fine. I need to talk to Jayesh in private for now and can I call you later Vick?"

With Vick leaving the building, Martha turned to Jayesh, "There is some change in plan, I need to visit Mexico urgently."

Jayesh tried to get the gravity of the situation without being intrusive. "Hope everything is okay with you…have you spoken to Ian about it?"

"Not yet but I'll talk to her soon and she'll understand my situation," said Martha. "Also, you know how things are here, and Ian doesn't take part in day-to-day business activities, so you need to take over my place for now."

"You're just going on a break, and you'd be back soon, won't you?"

Martha ran her hands over the crease of her pants, "Hopefully, yes. But it's better we do some knowledge transfer, we never know…we shouldn't take any chances, and under no circumstance things should stop here. This mission should never fail." Martha snatched a quick breath, "You already know most of the stuff, but we should go over it again."

Martha discussed various things about the business, accounts, etc. Jayesh took notes, bid her farewell and left.

Later Martha called Vick and informed him about her departure. He was upset initially but understood that Martha would not leave at this juncture, unless the reason being serious enough. They discussed about sponsors and other event-related things.

Now the toughest part – to apprise Ian about the situation.
*****

Ian was at home when Martha called. She requested Ian to come to the office to which she complied.

"Need to discuss something urgent with you," said Martha as she shuffled the papers on her desk.

"Everything okay?" Ian looked at Martha's puffed eyes. That was the first time she saw Martha in such a state.

"I need to visit Mexico."

"What! At this time! For how long?"

"I don't know, probably for a long time."

"We need you here Martha! You know I cannot manage without you. I just cannot do without you!"

"You have to learn Ian, you shouldn't be dependent on anyone, I cannot stop myself this time. I have to go," Martha's eyes watered as she cleaned her table.

"What happened?"

Martha briefed Ian about Sofia's call. "I don't know what to do, one side is my daughter and the other side you, this event!"

Ian moved from her chair. Her eyes turned glassy, but she suppressed her emotions. *Martha's departure will affect everything, the event will be in jeopardy.*

Ian forced a smile, "Don't worry about the event. It will go well. Sofi needs you, be with her, give all your love and attention to her."

"And you?"

"Remember I am Ian, if I cannot give strength to myself, how can I inspire others?" Tears crept up in the corner of her eyes.

"Don't fail me Ian, you need to do this for me, for people out there waiting for you. This world is yours…and you have to conquer it with your voice."

"I will, I will, now go and come back soon."

"Also," Martha looked into Ian's eyes.

"What?"

"You know my past…I may not be able to come back."

"Don't say that please," pleaded Ian. "Take the money, take everything, buy things, buy people, and do whatever it takes!"

"I don't know if money will help, things have changed in Mexico now!"

"Don't worry, everything is going to be alright. You focus on Sofia; God will take care of the rest."

Martha's voice quivered, "Once again …please let Ian win for me, people like me will live and perish but your voice is immortal. We need you Ian, you are the hope, don't let us down! You owe this to yourself! You owe this to Ian!"

"Yes, Yes! Now don't stress yourself now, forget about me, forget about the event! Now go and be with your beloved daughter and ggg give her mm my love too."

*****

Ian stood near the window. It was late in the evening. All the employees had left long back. Atlanta downtown was in slumber.

Ian was all alone once again. It was dark and there was no Martha or Saira to help. Ian was scared after a long time. Saira's voice echoed from the past, 'Devki… Run! Run!'

Run…yes… but from whom and from what? Running in the past and from the past had brought her this far and there was no turning back now.

Ian looked down through the window, the height from the ground didn't scare her. She fiddled with the window and tried to open it, but it didn't budge. She banged hard on the glass, but the thick glass was firm in its position. Ian hurriedly picked up the chair and walked up to the window but then she stopped. *What am I doing? Have I gone crazy? I am Ian.*

She turned on the laptop, a news reporter's image flickered, and his voice blared with excitement through the speakers, "Ian's event is getting closer! The countdown has begun! The savior who single handedly shaped and saved the lives of thousands is coming to your own town!"

Ian laughed hysterically and then cried.

"Mmm Ma tha …Ss sai saira" she muttered.

Oh! Saira! Martha was the only link to Saira.

Martha did mention earlier that she was close on the trail. Ian hastily dialed Martha's number, the phone rang once and played an auto voice message.

She had left.

Chapter 51

Martha boarded the plane to Tijuana. This time she did not want to hide from anyone. There was no point. She had been on the run for so many years but not anymore. *How would anyone even know that I'm coming into the city?*

When the jet touched the runway of General Abelardo L. Rodriguez airport, Martha's heart pounded. She looked out of the window and her town came into view.

Martha controlled her internal tremors when she showed her American passport to the immigration officer.

"So, what brings you to Tijuana?" asked the officer.

"Ah…family visit," Martha expected some secret phone calls or the officer pressing some hidden buzzer.

"Welcome to Tijuana!" said the officer with a smile and stamped the passport.

As Martha came out of the airport terminal, her eyes darted in all directions. She expected the worst – cops talking discreetly on their hidden microphones, police rushing at her with guns, cars with sirens, but to her relief, nothing of that sort happened.

People walked in and out of the airport as usual, each one in their own world. Some looked tired, some jubilant, while some were excited to see their loved ones. It was all normal activity – nothing out of the ordinary.

Martha controlled her anxiety and boarded a cab. "Dirección" asked the cab driver.

Martha provided him the address and the car sped away.
*****

Once at the hospital, Martha hurried to the nurse station. Her apprehension and the long journey had drained her, but there was no time for rest. The doctor was off duty; she spoke to the head-nurse and inquired about Sofia's health condition.

Another nurse was advising a handsome young man about his mother's nutrition plan. Hearing Martha inquire about Sofia, he looked inquisitively at Martha, "Abuela?"

Martha gazed at him for a moment. "Marco!" Grandmother and grandson hugged and kissed each other. Martha had left Mexico when Sofi was still expecting Marco.

Marco took her to Sofi's room.

Seeing Martha, Sofia went ecstatic. They were meeting after many years of separation. Martha found it difficult to see her child in such a condition. Her bed was hooked to multiple medical equipment & monitors. Her arms showed signs of syringe punctures all over. There was a needle on her left wrist injecting some medicine.

"Mama I'm sorry!" cried Sofia.

Martha held Sofia in her arms, "No my dear, you need not be sorry for anything. Mama is here now. You will feel better."

Sofia sobbed quietly with her head buried in Martha's arms.

"I want to go home, Mama," whimpered Sofia.

"Yes, we will go home."

Sofia wept for long in her mother's arms and later dozed off.

Once the doctor arrived, Martha inquired about Sofia's chances. There was nothing more a doctor could do. Martha took a deep breath, "Marco, it's time to go, arrange to take your mother home."

Sofia experienced peace at home. Martha took care of her, cooked for her and cleaned her. She spent all her time with Sofia, forgetting everything else. Time had stopped for her; she had missed Sofia all her life and she treasured every moment that was left with her precious daughter. She massaged Sofia's hair with oil, rubbed her feet, gave her sponge baths and fed her like a baby. Sofia looked happy but her condition deteriorated. She became weak during her last days. She behaved like a child – threw tantrums while eating and sleeping. Martha was always by her side.

After two weeks, Sofia passed away.

Martha became desolate and helpless. She mourned for days. She walked around the town all alone. The place she had grown up had changed much. The streets on which she once played as a child were full of automobiles. The trees on which she climbed as a child were long gone. The school where she taught had newer staff.

She visited her parents' graves and for the first time she shed tears for her father. No one heard her whisper, "Papa, I forgive you."

During her walk, she did get some distant smiles and nods. People who respected and loved her still existed but did not come out in the open.

While cleaning the house, she found a big stash of Ian's CDs in one of the closets. *Ian!* In her work and life, she had forgotten that Sofia would have needed Ian the most.

"Ian," murmured Martha. "What day and month is this?" Her life in the USA was out of her mind. She suddenly recalled Ian's event. Martha looked at the calendar and gasped, "Oh my God, I totally missed it!"

She hurried toward the phone.

Chapter 52

It was a cold morning. The temperature was low, although there was no sign of snow.

Ian looked at the person sitting in front of her and said, "I...I dddd do."

The event management director Sheela moved her legs restlessly under the chair. She was excited to meet someone of Ian's stature; however, she had lately observed that Ian spoke less and responded in only Yes or No's.

Sheela's world was filled with Ian's speeches. She had listened to numerous talks and proclaimed herself the biggest fan of Ian, though she was not alone.

She was excited to work for Ian's event but had lost hopes of meeting her before the show. She had many questions for Ian regarding the event but whenever she inquired about Ian to Vick or Jayesh, she was met with a cold stare.

Much to her surprise, she was invited by Vick one fine day.

"Interested in meeting Ian?" asked Vick.

Sheela blushed, "Aww! Who wouldn't be? I will be honored to meet her and also, I need to talk to her regarding a few arrangements for the event. Would that be possible?"

"It is, but do you love and respect Ian?"

"More than myself!"

"In that case you will meet her and assist her but remember what she is trying to accomplish. The success of this event depends on Ian's identity being hidden."

"You have my words Vick, I will do anything to support the cause," said Sheela. "A chance to meet Ian...what more I can ask in this life?"

Vick provided her Ian's address.

Sheela jumped up and down as she received an appointment with Ian. She closed her fists and paced across the hallway of her house like a teenager. She had so many questions for Ian, after all, she was her role model.

Finally, she was in front of Ian's house. She was surprised to see a modest apartment. She had expected Ian to be in a big mansion. With trembling hands, she knocked on the door. A lady answered the door.

Sheela was excited like a small kid, "I am here to meet..."

The lady stepped aside, and Sheela jumped right in. She was pointed to a couch while the lady sat on a chair.

Sheela waited for a few minutes, growing impatient with every second of wait. The lady looked lost and made no attempt to notify Ian of her presence.

Sheela clasped her hands on her lap, "Actually, I had called earlier, Vick directed me to come here to meet Ian. Can you please inform her?"

"Th...Th That's me," said the lady impassively.

Sheela looked at the lady sitting across her – hair disheveled, puffed eyes, frozen expressions and a weird dress.

"Excuse me!" Sheela blurted.

Sheela's dreams were shattered, she never expected Ian to look like this, it was nothing in comparison to the strong voice she had heard – 'You owe it to yourself! You owe it to Ian!' The affectionate and stern voice kept her fans clinging on to her, as a mountaineer on to his rope.

Ian's expressions didn't change on Sheela's reaction, she sat motionless.

"Are you feeling okay?" asked Sheela and she had asked the same question later on their every meeting.

Sheela had made several visits since then. She was proud to be among the chosen few to meet Ian. It was her job and she wanted to perform it diligently but every time she met Ian, she felt uneasy. *How on earth did this lady produce such master pieces?*

"Are you feeling okay?" asked Sheela.

Ian nodded, "Yeye yes, lil litt little tired."

Sheela continued, "That's surprising, being this eminent, you don't have any personal assistant!"

"It's ddd dd diffdiff different here," Ian stretched her breath, "Martha was responsible for all this bbb but unfortunately she's on vacation," Ian managed to complete the sentence, her heart pounded. It was long since Martha had gone. There was no call or text from her.

"What about our other requests?"

Ian muttered, "I don't ha ha have any papapa personal sound recordist either."

"We will take care of everything, but, since this is a big

event and due to the nature of your profession, it would be helpful if you had someone who knows you, your body language, your style, just in case of some last-minute glitch."

"I can tttt take care of it, I will be fine," Ian sounded irresolute.

"What about the dress consultant? She can assist you pick your wardrobe and get you dressed for the event."

Ian circled her lips, "I will nnnn not be comfortable with that either. I will ttt take care of my dress."

Sheela went through her list, time was always short in such meetings, "That's all I have. Please let me know if you need anything, I can understand an event of this scale can cause a lot of stress."

Ian fidgeted with her dress.

"Any instructions you have for me?" asked Sheela again.

"Esss Kaaa"

"Sorry, can you please repeat that?"

Ian picked up the writing pad next to her, she used it more often in the past few weeks. She scribbled on it and extended it to Sheela.

Sheela took the pad and read it, "Okay, this can be done. You want to extend our personal invitation to them. We can also send them a pickup on the day of the event."

"That will be bbb better."

Sheela made a note of the names and the address.

She looked at Ian and felt pity. She kneeled before Ian on the carpet and touched her on the knees, "Ian what happened to you? You have to speak at this event in a few weeks. Can I help you with something?" Sheela's voice cracked in the end.

Ian looked at her with dry eyes and pointed toward the door.

"I …I'm sorry," said Sheela and walked out of the apartment.

After Sheela left, Ian paced around in her room. The dream she saw for all these years was coming to reality now. Their charity had received millions of dollars from donations. There was a long list of sponsors whose contributions will enable them to open more centers. There were serious discussions on how the money could be used to uplift the downtrodden. Ian's company's revenue also soared beyond imagination.

Ian stayed away from all business-related discussions. She could not even comprehend the enormity. She seemed to be in her own world. When Jayesh had tried to explain her, she replied point-blank, "Don't tell me how much Ian earns, tell me how much Ian contributes!"

There were still requests coming in for the tickets which had all been already sold out. The media was buzzing with the news of the event. Most places in the town bore posters and cutouts of 'Ian Speaks' and 'Ian coming to meet you'.

A TV channel relayed how different groups were travelling from far off places to get a glimpse of Ian. Many were making their own placards and dresses for the occasion. They were excited to meet their loving long-awaited Guru.

It was all unbelievable. Who would have thought Ian would become this popular in a small span? It all came through like magic, like a whirl storm.

'There must be no more slavery, no more abuse in this world. You should be able to live with your free will and should achieve whatever you dreamed for. This is a promise to you from Ian, and with your help, we will eradicate misery from the world.

You owe this to yourself! You owe this to Ian!'
Ian's message echoed in the whole world.

Ian walked in her living room, her hands moist with sweat and knees trembling. It was long since she recorded any new speech. She had not seen Vick for weeks, since he was occupied in making arrangements. It had been a couple of months since she spoke to Jayesh. Martha had gone for almost a month. The kids were too small to understand anything. Ian was in solitude. There was no one to talk to; no shoulder to cry on; no one to face her tantrums – there was no audience.

Ian wished she could just vanish. *Where will I go? Perhaps I should kill myself! There will not be much impact on my friends if I'm gone. No one will blame them. At the most, people will curse me, for being fake. But, how can I? The hopes of millions are pinned on me. I am the role model of thousands. I am their way of life. How can I disappoint so many people? If I die or run away, I*

will destroy an entire generation. My listeners are my life. I live for
them and breathe through them every day.

Ian recalled Mike's advice – to visualize and speak from
her stomach. She walked in the middle of the room and tried to
stand as tall as possible. She closed her eyes and tried visualizing
her audience, but nothing appeared before her. She found it hard to
focus.

She opened her eyes and spoke, "Hi Thh thh isss Ia Ian."
Words failed her.

Ian tried again, "Ffff rrr ii ..friii eeeedddddds, thhh issss Ian
nnn." Her face flustered, veins popped on her forehead and neck,
but she could hardly speak.

She shrieked, "You owe thh this to yr yr yourself and u u u
you owe tthhh to Ian." Her heart thumped and voice stopped.

Ian slumped on the ground and cried. The emptiness scared
her. There were just mute wall-hangings, paintings, light bulbs and
lifeless furniture in the room. No one applauded for Ian today.

The sound of Ian's slow whimpering disturbed the silence
of the room. Many years ago, Ian had read that speaking in public
was the foremost fear of people; she had refused to accept it then,
but today she was experiencing and living the fear.

The table in the far corner still had the audio CD brought
by Esha on her previous visit. Ian read the title, 'Everyone gets a
chance in life!'

Ian's hands trembled as she picked up the audio.
*****

Sheela pressed the numbers on her phone, and was soon
connected, "May I talk to Esha?"

Gagan answered the phone and handed it over to Esha.
"Yes?"

"Hi, this is Sheela, Ian's assistant and…" All she heard was
screaming on the other side. Sheela smiled. She was used to such a
response from girls, when they heard Ian's name. "Okay listen,"
Sheela started again. "Ian wants to extend her personal invitation
to you at her event."

"Ian!" Sheela heard more jumping and screaming. "Ian
knows me?!" asked Esha, her face red with excitement.

"Yes dear. Ian appreciates that you are her regular listener
and wants to invite you and Kajal," said Sheela almost reading

from Ian's notes.

"Yahoo! I cannot believe this. Ian knows me and Kajal and inviting us specially." Esha jumped again and waved Kajal to come near her.

"So, this is how it will go," said Sheela interrupting the girls' celebration. "On the day of the event, I will send a pickup for you and Kajal. You will get special seats."

Esha recalled Gagan's mention earlier about the event tickets, "My dad's company is sponsoring the event, he has tickets for us too."

"It doesn't matter, you can use either."

Esha quickly thought about little Saira and Mini, "Can I bring my other family members too."

"Yes, certainly. You have got a personal invitation from Ian - you, your friends, all are welcome.

"Will I get to meet Ian?" asked Esha.

"That, I cannot promise. It all depends on her."

"Thanks. Please convey my thanks to Ian for remembering me among millions."

"Ian treasures fans like you." Sheela added by herself and disconnected the phone.

Chapter 53

Gagan stared at the object lying on his desk in dismay. His mind could not assimilate what he heard. He opened the entrance door of his house and stepped out. The cold air hit him like a spear, but it hardly affected him. He stared at the deserted street.

It all started a few days back.

The publishing business was soaring – the news that his company was one of the big sponsors of Ian's event brought huge exposure and business. Many times, Esha and Kajal requested him to listen to Ian's speeches, but his ego prevented him. He was too big to listen to some girly talks.

Gagan did not understand all the fuss around Ian's audios and paid no attention, but when one of the major partners in the firm asked him in a meeting about his favorite speech of Ian, he was dumbfounded. He was ridiculed for his ignorance. His personal interests were not in question, he should have at least listened to a few, for the sake of the business.

Taking a hit on his nonsensical pride, he borrowed an audio CD from Esha. On that morning, he played the audio with much reluctance. Within minutes, the speaker engulfed him. The voice, the content, everything ran close to his heart.

He looked at the cover of the CD again, it read 'Forgive yourself! by Ian Scovich'

Gagan played the CD for the fifth time that morning.

The speech ended with the note,

"If you think you have hurt someone, call them and ask for pardon. No matter how difficult it is, you have to make this call. It is not for them but for your inner peace. It will help you absolve yourself. You owe this to yourself! You owe this to Ian!"

All the past memories danced in front of Gagan like a movie, with him as an antagonist. In his anger, in his revenge, he had forgotten whom he really was against. His hatred toward women had grown beyond limits. His painful past had made him not only a chauvinist, but also a sadist. He failed to realize how much he had hurt the people around him. He looked at the mirror and could not recognize himself. It failed to show the true Gagan. He was never like that before.

The voice of the speaker echoed in his ears over and over

again, 'If you have hurt someone, call them and ask for pardon.'

"Devki," murmured Gagan.

He hesitated for a second, and then dialed Devki's number. He had dialed this number many times in the recent past to spew venom on her. He had verbally abused and threatened her multiple times, after which she had stopped answering. She failed to answer this time too. Gagan prayed in his heart, "Devki please, for God's sake, answer the phone!"

The phone rang and died. He regretted for having exploited Devki's innocence and helplessness.

Gagan dialed Ian's event team and begged them to let him meet Ian. Ian should tell him how to ask for forgiveness, when people he had hurt turned a deaf ear.

He was informed that he can meet Ian only during the event. Emotions and guilt drained Gagan.

Chapter 54

Jan 14th, the day.

Ian peeped outside the window – her eyes couldn't believe what she saw. To get a clear view, she pulled the blinds – what she saw struck horror in her heart. The backyard, deck, trees were all covered with ice. A thick layer of ice was all over the place, shimmering gold with the first rays of the sun.

Atlanta rarely had snow but received ice rain once or twice in winters. Nature had chosen the day to wreak havoc. Ice rain meant traffic problems, flight cancellations and accidents. People generally stayed at home in such weather conditions.

People were coming from all over to see her and if this ice rain continued, the event may get cancelled. For a moment, Ian felt relieved and happy, but quickly recouped her composure. It was still early morning, she dialed Sheela,

"Hello," came Sheela's excited voice. She was ready for the big day ahead.

"Do wawa we ha have to caca cancel the event?"

"No, but why do you ask this question?"

"Ice rain!" blurted Ian.

"Oh, this icy rain has been going on since mid-night, but not severe. Weather forecast says it will stop by eight in the morning and the temperature will rise after that. So, we are fine!"

"Oh!"

"I will be sending someone to fetch you in the afternoon. You can relax in your dressing room. The crowd will be pouring in earlier for the event." said Sheela. "And your voice, what happened to it? Please take care. You have to speak in the evening!"

Ian hung up.

She slumped on the bed and covered her head with a pillow. She tried visualizing her audience but failed again.

*****

By late morning, the weather had turned from gloomy to sunny and all the ice melted away. At the appointed time, the ride arrived and Ian was taken to the venue in an unmarked car.

As the car approached the spot, Ian noticed hundreds of people queued up. Although the start time was hours away, people were already taking their seats. The big screens were displaying interviews from various people.

Different snippets from Ian's speeches were blaring on the large speakers,

"Ian is coming to meet you…"

"Break your shackles and join the movement, help yourself and help your brethren…"

"You owe this to yourself! You owe this to Ian!"

Ian had visited the location earlier, but it looked different now with the crowd, decoration and lighting. The chauffeur had strict instructions not to stop anywhere and not to roll down the windows. He followed the orders and drove Ian straight to her dressing room.

The TV in Ian's room could display the whole stadium, but it was un-plugged on Sheela's instructions, as she did not want Ian to get distracted by the crowd. However, Ian was able to hear the crowd chanting her name outside "Ian!…Ian!"

She looked at the table in front of her, numerous gadgets and instructions overwhelmed her.

Sheela knocked on the door briefly and entered, "Your hairdresser, dressing consultant and makeup man are here."

"I tttt told you I don't need anyone."

"Sorry, I had ordered a dress for you, an evening gown. You will like it."

"I am fine Sheela, and thth this is how I dress."

Sheela scanned Ian from head to toe. A long light-blue skirt, covering her legs till the shoes. A dark-blue button-down top, which covered her to the neck, almost till the chin. Untied hair, carelessly thrown around. Sheela had high regard for Ian. People like her need not care for anything, but today was different.

Sheela tried again, "You wear this dress always; but you might need a more relaxed outfit today. With all this crowd and lighting, the temperature will rise too, you may not need that top. Perhaps you can try an off-shoulder…"

Ian's scornful look stopped Sheela on her tracks,

"Sorry," she said softly and walked away closing the door behind her.

The room was empty. There were thousands of people waiting for Ian, but she was all alone. Whenever the door opened for some service, she could hear the chant, "Ian!.. Ian!"

Ian missed all those who were close to her heart. She remembered Saira, Martha and Mike. Feeling uneasy, she paced around the room. *I don't need anyone. I survived this long, and I will survive today.* She recalled the incident in India, when she jumped from the wall and ran for her life. She succeeded then and she will succeed now. *Ian never fails. She empowers people.*

She opened the door of her dressing room, the chant from her fans gave her a sense of pride. *All these people waiting for Ian. Ian will help them. Ian will give her life for them. These are my children, my family, my fans.*

Ian had never experienced such an adulation in her life. She was always hidden, like the moon behind dark clouds. The experience was exhilarating despite her anxiety.

*****

He boarded the metro train after waiting in the long queue. The train was overcrowded for a normal day. He could not get the reason. *What on earth! Is there another Olympics happening in Atlanta? Why are people going crazy?*

He had been on a world tour. He was visiting places, or he was running away from himself. No matter how far he went, he was unable to forget the incidents which had occurred several months earlier.

He took the fourth seat from the door, the first thing caught his eyes was an advisement on the wall in front of him – it read, "Ian will speak to you today!"

"What!" he looked around the train and spotted more similar posters. He checked outside as the train passed through different stations, there were posters of Ian coming to town. *God! Which year is this? How long was I away?*

He looked around inside his compartment and observed a mixed crowd of teenagers, adults and elderly people. Everyone appeared excited. Two teenage girls were playing some game by hitting each other' palms and calling out "Ian... Ian" on every hit.

"Excuse me," he spoke to an old lady sitting next to him, "What's happening today? Why such a crowd and commotion?"

The lady snorted at him and many others who overheard him laughed too. "Ian is coming to Atlanta today. She will speak today live for the first time."

"You mean Ian coming out in the world today!"

"What do you mean coming out, she was always there with us, she is only meeting us face-to-face for the first time!"

Ian! His feeling of hatred vanished. *Oh my God! I was so selfish! Ian will need me today.* He gathered his stuff in a hurry and rushed toward the door, "Which station is this? I need to meet Ian immediately!"

Chapter 55

Ian had her eyes closed when she heard Sheela, "There is a man harassing our security. He insists on meeting you immediately. He says he can be of help to you!" Ian's eyes squinted on Sheela. Sheela continued, "We would have shoved him away, but he is relentless. He says if only he can speak to you once, you will understand."

"What's his name?" Ian closed her eyes again.

"He does not tell us his name, nor does he give us an ID. Did you invite someone?"

"No, I didn't. Probably some fan. I don't want to meet anyone right now, maybe after the event."

Sheela agreed but then chewed her lips and paused, "Maybe you can see him on one of our security cameras and decide."

Ian gave her a nod.

An assistant plugged the TV monitor and switched channels. Sheela watched Ian intently. An image flickered on the screen, a man with a backpack was surrounded by security personnel. Ian watched, though disinterested, and, soon a clear shot of the man's face appeared,

"Oh my God!" gasped Ian. She rushed to the door, but Sheela caught her in the last minute.

Ian stopped and turned to Sheela, "Get him, get him here now!"

Sheela spoke to someone on her earpiece and switched off the TV. Ian sat on her chair with hands clutched on the armrest and eyes glued to the door.

The ten-minute wait felt like centuries and when the door opened, Ian rocketed from her chair straight to the man's arms. Between her sobs, Sheela could only hear, "Mike...Mike I missed you!" The man held Ian tightly in his arms and closed his eyes.

Sheela excused herself out of the room.

Mike carried Ian to her chair, she wrapped her hands around his neck. Once settled, Mike inquired, "Where's everyone, where's Martha?"

"Marr marrtha is not here, no one is here with mmmm me!"

"What! Did you fire Martha too?"

"No", she said timidly. "It is a lo lonn gg story, but Martha is not here, and I don't know what to do!" Ian pointed at the gadgets on the table.

Mike sat next to Ian, "What happened to you? Good you made up your mind to come out but what happened to your voice?"

"I dddd…don't know, I lolo lost my voice, I shouldn't have agag agreed to do this event. Now I caca cannot speak. I am scared I will disappoint everyone; I will fail everyone."

Mike lifted Ian by her shoulders and gently cupped her face. He looked deep into her eyes. "Ian, I don't know much about you; you never gave me a chance, but I know – speaking is your thing and no one can take that away from you."

Mike continued "I have heard you speak, you are magical, and there is no one in this world who can speak like Ian. So, go out there and own this world. You have a heart of gold, you spoke because you wanted to make a change in the society, in this world. Today is your chance, go and tell your fans how much you love them!"

Ian's body shook, tears fell profusely.

"Ba…ba…but I can't. I al alll always spoke for a known audience…there is no familiar audience here…there are thou…thou …thousands of faceless people. I am scared that I will fff fail. If I fail, everyone will fail with me. We will all be destroyed!"

Mike pushed Ian back, "You don't worry about whether you fail or succeed. The people out there are your listeners, your fans. You have created all your work for them and now it's time to meet your loved ones. They love you, no matter what you say and how you say it."

Ian sobbed, "I caca can't!"

Mike spoke again in a stern voice, "Remember."

Ian looked at Mike, "wa what?"

"You owe this to yourself and you owe this to Ian!"

Ian nodded like a baby. She laughed and cried at the same time. "Ye, Yes!"

Sheela turned the knob at the door and announced, "You are on in 20 minutes."

Ian adjusted her dress while Sheela hesitantly combed her

hair. Mike went through all the electronic gadgets and fitted them on Ian's body. They looked at each other and smiled. Golden times were back.

"All the best!" Sheela shook Ian's hand.

"Go and conquer the world!" said Mike and hugged Ian tightly. She hugged him back and walked outside. Mike and Sheela followed her.

Chapter 56

There was a small aisle from the backstage to the main stage. The roaring chant of Ian's name escaped through the openings. The anchor of the evening, announced, "And now, ladies and gentlemen, a big applause for your loving Ian!"

The whole environment shook with thunderous applause and then everything went silent. The stage went dark, the entire stadium went dark. Ian took a deep breath and stepped on the stage. Her knees trembled and heart thumped. There were no faces as far as she could see, but endless small lights. Ian walked slowly to the center of the stage. She bathed in the white light focused on her. People went ecstatic seeing their mentor for the first time.

Gagan sat in the first row – his eyes widened in shock, he fell on the ground with disbelief and guilt. Esha, Kajal, Saira and Mini sat next to him. They looked at Ian and all screamed "Mommy!" but their sound died in the commotion. The crowd got emotional seeing Ian for the first time. People cried and hugged each other.

Ian's heart pounded. *These are my people.*

She took a deep breath and started, "Hi fffff friend ffresss." She paused – words did not come out. The sound engineers jumped onto their instruments, suspecting some defect in their devices. They turned the knobs on the equipment frantically, but everything was in order.

Ian pushed the microphone aside and cleared the lump in throat, "Dead dd dearrrr dea arr." Her voice failed her again.

Ian stood in silence.

The flashes of Jhansi appeared before her eyes. Saira's voice echoed in her ears, 'Devki... Run! Run! If you survive tell the world about me, about us.' *I cannot let Saira fail. Saira helped me survive not to fail but to flourish. This is the time to tell the world about Saira.*

I saved my daughters to give them a better future, now how can I take that away from them?

Ian recalled Martha's words – her exact words, while returning from Jayesh's, 'You need to speak for yourself Devki. You need to speak for women like you. Stop being Devki and become Ian.' And when Ian had asked her to clarify 'what kind of women' …Martha had said 'abused women.'

How can I disappoint Martha? The woman who loved me like her daughter, who always supported me, who desired to bring my dream to reality.

Ian recalled what Martha told her before leaving for Mexico, 'People like me will live and perish but your voice is immortal. We need you Ian, you are the hope, don't let Ian down!'. *Martha is risking everything for her daughter Sofia, how can I disappoint her? This speech should be dedicated to Martha and Sofia – for the fight they ensued in their whole life. How can I dampen the spirits of women around the world who get inspired by me?*

The crowd was getting restless with the silence of Ian. Sheela was backstage, unsure of her next action. She looked for Mike, but he wasn't seen. She first whispered and then yelled at Ian to continue but her voice couldn't be heard in the uproar. *What is she doing, is she hallucinating?*

Ian was oblivious of the crowd. She struggled with her thoughts…*My daughters – I need to show them by example, what dreams and passion can achieve.*

Also, my people all over the world, they live by my words. I am their hope; can I take that hope away from them? Can Ian fail them all?

Ian never fails, Ian lives for her people. I owe this speech to my followers.

Ian took a deep breath and sized her audience – an abused woman, a child sold by his poor parents, trafficked girls, drug addicts, abandoned old couples. There were many Ian couldn't recognize. She was seeing the faces she had never seen in her life.

The crowd was getting berserk. Ian closed her eyes momentarily and opened them again. The crowd went blurry for a second and came back crisp and clear. She could see the happy faces in front of her.

"Can you hear me now?"

The same strong voice; the same connection, the same honesty. The crowd knew her, her fans loved her.

"Yes!" The crowd cheered as one.

"Do you want to hear me now?" Ian screamed again.

There were thousands of 'Yes's.

Ian and Devki were one today. There was no need for her to hide anything anymore. She was with them – she was with her loved ones. She was fearless. The world was hers and she was with the world. The dream she saw years ago was now a reality. Her audience breathed with her.

As Ian moved across the stage, her long hair moved like a lion's mane. She appeared like the reincarnation of the Rani – who was ready to fight the mighty forces of the world.

The crowd was silent, nothing dared to move, the whole universe was glued with Ian.

The great Ian spoke, "Things happen because we let them happen to us. We are equally at fault as our tormentors, because we give our control to them. We should either live or perish but never accept anyone's dominance, as we are the masters of our present and future.

We have the strength to change our lives. Only we can decide and achieve our true destiny.

We will change this world. There will be no more bondage, no more abuse but only love. Let us unite, let us join hands. This world should not be divided by boundaries, language or race but should be unified with love."

Ian moved further toward the crowd and much to the shock of her fans, she caught the top-most button of her blue top and ripped it open. The top which imprisoned her for years was gone. The white buttons fell like diamonds on the stage.

Ian stood there with her bare shoulders – with her scars exposed in the light.

Sheela ran on the stage and wrapped Ian with a shawl.

The crowd was shocked and speechless. A dead silence engulfed the stadium for some time but soon erupted with, "Ian! Ian!"

"Let us forgive those who did injustice to us and give them an opportunity to change. Because, if there is a beast in each one of us, there should be a God within us too. Let us kill the beast and welcome the God."

Ian paused for a moment.

The audience were engulfed by her words and were eager for more. For a moment the crowd was still but then erupted.

Ian asked loudly, "Are you with me my friends?"

"Yes!" The whole stadium resonated with the crowd.

Ian smiled, "And... You owe this to yourself! You owe this to your Ian!"

The crowd rose on its feet and applauded for Ian. The thunderous roar continued for minutes.

Ian's gaze passed over the faces in the crowd. Ian noticed on her right, not too far from the stage, four people holding the mask of Queen LakshmiBai on their faces. As Ian looked at them, the first one brought the face mask down and waved, it was Martha. Ian was elated. *Martha is back! But how come she knows about the Queen?*

Next, the second and the third persons brought their masks down. They looked familiar but Ian couldn't place names on their faces. Though she was unacquainted with Neel and Neeta, they knew her well. And then she looked at the fourth one. The fourth person took the longest to remove the mask and when she brought it down, Ian gasped – *Oh Saira! My friend!* Saira extended her arms and signaled, 'You were always in my heart!' She showed her right fist and opened her thumb to run across her neck like a knife to warn Ian again, but this time, as a loving warning to continue her speech. Ian laughed and tears crept in her eyes. She nodded in gratitude at Martha.

Soon they were joined by Mike, Vick and Jayesh. They all waved Ian to continue.

The crowd was on its feet.

And then Ian continued...

The world swayed with her as an ocean wave hypnotized forever.

*****

Over the years, Ian produced 60 million audios. She took over 'Helping Sisters' and opened 250 charity centers across the globe. Her organization provided education, food and sheltered millions.

Vick, Jayesh, Mike and many others helped Ian. Martha was in charge of the USA and Mexico operations. Esha, after completing her college, moved to Columbus, Ohio and took in-charge of the USA North Eastern centers. She took directions from Martha and specialized in drug abuse while Kajal assisted her.

Little Saira took admission at a prestigious law college and

Mini opted for computer science. They both vouched to join the organization upon graduation.

Gagan's company stayed the loyal sponsor of Ian's events. Mike and Ian stayed friends though Ian's work schedule permitted her lesser time.

Many countries offered citizenship to Ian. Time magazine nominated her the most influential woman of the century. Ian became the peace ambassador of the world.

Saira always accompanied Ian on all her trips.

The municipal corporation of Jhansi offered to install a statue of Ian in the city, but she refused. There can be only one statue in the city, of the real warrior, the real inspiration – Queen LakshmiBai.

In a distant village near Jhansi, a daughter of a poor farmer, topped the prestigious civil services exam. A teacher from her college asked her, "Who is your inspiration, whom would you give credit for your success?"

The girl smiled, "I owe this to Ian."

The End.

Can I Ask A Favor?

If you enjoyed this book, I'd really appreciate it if you could post a short review on Amazon.

Thanks for your support!

www.ingramcontent.com/pod-product-compliance
Lightning Source LLC
Chambersburg PA
CBHW032211190626
46810CB00019B/2437